. . . "There she is," announced Dusty in a proud voice, taking Elly's hand gently in her own.

The curtain of snow turned rose-colored, off and on, from the diner's blinking neon sigh. As they sat, car idling, holding hands, the windshield fogged with their buoyant anxious breaths, and made the diner look, to Elly, like a rose-tinted dream. It was only about fifty feet long, but its shining chrome glowed so bright it seemed enormous. Red stripes ran like streaks of excitement the length of it. . . .

In her imagination, Elly dressed the diner. The shining building seemed, through its rose and white screen, taller than when they'd first driven up. She imagined it deeper, its booths secreted in corners, its restrooms perfumed, ornate, its kitchen and counters gleaming and covered with opulent foods that drew the workers, the commuters, the families of Morton River Valley. That drew, too, the factory owners, the politicians, even the bosses from Dusty's plant who threatened her livelihood for being gay. Dusty's Queen of Hearts Diner, she dreamed, on the Morton River, at the very center of the Valley, offering nourishment, warm welcome; a place known for its food and harmony; famous for the way it erased walls between people; where gays and straights, blacks and whites, poor and rich acted kindly toward one another. Dusty's Queen of Hearts Diner, a home for the tired world. The feeling of fullness grew in her.

WORKS BY LEE LYNCH

Toothpick House, 1983
Old Dyke Tales, 1984
The Swashbuckler, 1985
Home In Your Hands, 1986
Dusty's Queen of Hearts Diner, 1987

DUSTY'S QUEEN OF HEARTS DINER

a novel by *Lee Lynch*

the NAIAD PRESS inc.

1987

Printed in the United States of America
First Edition

Cover design by Tee A. Corinne
Typesetting by Sandi Stancil
Edited by Katherine V. Forrest

Library of Congress Cataloging-in-Publication Data

Lynch, Lee, 1945—
    Dusty's queen of hearts diner.

    I. Title.
PS562.Y426DB 1987 813'.54 87-11168
ISBN 0-941483-01-0

for

TEE CORINNE

my Southern femme

and inspiration

I want to thank Georgia Cole for her painstaking assistance.

I want to thank all the other people who, piece by piece, helped me write this book: Tangren Alexander, Kristen Aspen, Mary A., Norma Coleman, Maxi Faulkner, patient Katherine Forrest, B.G., Ann at Mother Kali's Bookstore, Lee Howard's *The Last Unmined Vein* (Anemone, 1980), at long last Sheila Jefferson, Susan Kenler, Edna M., Janna McAuslan, J.N., Katie Niles, Sandi Stancil, Carol Seajay, and Con Sellers.

Chapter Fifteen originally appeared in *On Our Backs,* in slightly different form, as "Dusty Eats Out."

FOREWORD

I set out to write this book with a growing desire to acknowledge lesbian literary tradition. A tradition at which I once scoffed, as I scoffed at myself, a mere lesbian in society's disapproving eyes.

Our literature is not new, not sparse, not despicable. It has simply been hidden in its own closets, stuffed there as surely as if every lesbian's family had come visiting for the century. Closets drain, weaken, pale. Coming out, claiming our own, and standing in the light, restores, strengthens, polishes.

For these reasons, I have drawn on two major literary sources throughout *Dusty's Queen of Hearts Diner*. Those readers familiar with Radclyffe Hall's *Well of Loneliness* will recognize frequent allusions to that powerful classic. "Dusty's Tales" are written after the device of "Moll's Tales" in Ellen Galford's *Moll Cutpurse* (Firebrand, 1985), a book which claims this seventeenth century rogue as one of our own.

Dusty would have recognized her ancestress in Moll or John Hall; Elly would have donned her femme finery and walked proudly beside either.

Lee Lynch
Southern Oregon
April, 1986

CHAPTER ONE

Elly smiled a slow smile of immense pleasure. Out the window of the braking train she could see, on the platform, her lover of six months. Dusty Reilly stood tall, her dark-framed glasses giving dignity, like the grey in her auburn hair, to her boyish face. Hands in the pockets of the aging peacoat she wore over a turtleneck and faded jeans, she'd propped one foot up behind her, against the wall of the old brick station next to the sign for Morton River, her hometown. So this was what it felt like, Elly thought, to come home to Dusty Reilly.

While the train still moved, Elly stood and lifted a shopping bag full of presents. She was almost holding her breath in anticipation. Coming home to Dusty, to this Connecticut town of Morton River Valley, even from Upton only an hour away, on a commuter train packed with business people, was as exciting as falling in love again. She stepped along the littered smoky aisles in her high heels, tense with the awareness that she didn't belong in this crowd. Though she'd just combed her cinnamon-tinted hair, she fluffed it again and fussed with the buttons of her jacket, a white imitation fur she'd stroked, dreaming of Dusty, all the way home.

She let the conductor help her down the steps and then she carefully balanced the heft of Dusty's Christmas present. She spotted Dusty again, pushing slowly away from the bricks, her own smile wide, her arms open, as if she hadn't seen her woman for a week. Most of the business people remained on the train, headed for the respectable suburbs north of Morton River. Daily, without a glance, they bypassed the hilly streets where close-set shabby homes surrounded a downtown of abandoned factories and struggling businesses.

The lovers hugged briefly, uneasily, afraid that all of Morton River was watching for just such misconduct on its threshold, watching and waiting for the first fools it could find to punish for the once-thriving town's recent miseries.

It was 1972—the northeastern industrial cities were foundering. George Wallace was considering a run for the presidency, Spiro Agnew was halfway there. The Valley was Klan country, a northern enclave made strong by the exodus of industry to less demanding labor markets. The unions had ultimately failed their workers; the desperate sought another group identity and solutions that did not always make sense. Morton River, in a valley populated by 28,000 primarily blue-collar workers, was not a good place to be queer.

Elly shivered. "It's so *cold!*" she said in her faint Tennessee drawl. She could taste these Yankee winters, smell them coming long before they did. It was the cold of a strange, suspicious place. She'd moved north for work, not for comfort, and though it wasn't any easier to be queen down home,

2

it seemed she'd been able to sense familiar dangers on the sultry winds. She took Dusty's arm in the dark shadows of the parking lot, looked up to warm herself with the thrill of the touch of their eyes. Dusty squeezed her arm tighter. Elly, caught in the flash of love, suspected they glowed bright as a streetlamp.

From the back side of Main Street, across from the parking lot, came a loud wolf-whistle. They moved hastily toward the car again.

"Dusty!" Elly warned in a whisper.

Dusty stopped short and turned to her own side of the car. "Can't even open the door for my girl around here any more," she muttered.

When they'd locked the green Dodge Swinger, Elly breathed deeply in relief. "Can you see who it was?" she asked.

"Kids," Dusty answered, almost spitting the word. "You can see them over there, under the streetlamp." Dusty didn't normally show her feelings so blatantly. She sounded angry enough to kill.

The group was a little Morton River-sized street gang. There were no jobs for kids, either.

"They probably thought we were a guy and girl about to smooch," Elly said, as much to reassure herself as Dusty. If Dusty got scared, who could she lean on?

"Animals," said Dusty, shaking her head. She grinned over at Elly. "Maybe you're right. Maybe they thought we were straight. You always see the sunny side of things, don't you, Lady?"

Elly felt her shoulders let go of their tension. Dusty might be the answer to her dreams, but her strong, confident exterior often needed bracing. Elly was an experienced brace.

Dusty eased the Swinger from its space. "Did you have a good time spending all your money on presents?" she asked, letting one hand steal to Elly's thigh.

Elly took her eyes from the gang. The hulking boy who seemed to lead them had not been a pretty sight. She hugged herself in the fur jacket. "I had a marvelous time, lover. On the train ride down, I kept remembering that first Christmas up North when I was so penniless I baked seventy-two dozen cookies and shipped them in shoe boxes down to Mama and everyone. I love to splurge on Christmas now, even the little bit I can. And you are such fun to shop for!"

"So are you," grinned Dusty. She took the Swinger gently over the railroad tracks. "Want some music?" There was one country-western station in the Valley and Dusty always played it, in gallant deference to Elly's tastes.

Dusty hadn't said she was going shopping, thought Elly. "Me? What'd you buy me?"

Dusty hadn't stopped smiling that sideways grin of hers. "Well, I thought of adding to your sexy nightgown collection. I thought of buying you jewelry and slinky sweaters and about six different books on the best-seller list. But I didn't." She looked across at Elly. "Why don't you scoot on over here, lady?"

Elly peered through the window one last time for a sign of hostile eyes. She snuggled against the bulky wool shoulder of the peacoat Dusty loved. She'd told Elly that the first thing she'd done when she left the Navy in 1953 was to find an Army-Navy store and buy herself this symbol of all the things she'd enlisted for—and hadn't got because she was a woman. Seventeen years later it was part of the Dusty—Korean vet, sailor's cocky stride, a uniformed past—that Elly loved.

They reached the stoplight at Main Street. Christmas decorations had been strung back and forth across the streets. Shoppers paused outside bright storefronts as if dreaming. Snow clouds lightened the sky. A church bell chimed six. Dusty looked over at Elly, smiling as if she were bursting with delight, glasses twinkling with Christmas lights, and said, "I bought you a diner."

4

The sound of the bells had warmed Elly's heart while the Swinger had heated her body. She felt as if she were moving in an oasis filled with tenderness. Dusty's sense of play was another thing she loved. "No, really," she said, rubbing against the peacoat, "can I have three guesses?"

They were traveling out of town. Gas stations and small shopping centers began to appear. Merle Haggard sang mournful words with lazy rhythm. Dusty glanced at her, one eyebrow raised, a slight smile on her lips.

"Dusty?" She was beginning to think she was serious.

"The one you said was so cute, next to the tracks. The one you figured out we could afford."

Elly pulled away a little. They crossed the Morton River itself, so different from her native Mississippi, narrow here, enclosed by concrete walls: a controlled power, dark and icy beneath them, still forcing life into a few factories. "A diner? You went and bought it? You *did* it?"

Out by the big shopping center, another traffic light stopped them. Elly tried to see Dusty's eyes through the darkness, but couldn't and felt a stab of terror that Dusty had been drinking again, had lost her security clearance out at the plant, lost her job, lost everything just as they'd been fearing. Dusty's ex worked at the plant too, and their breakup last June had been messy. Rita had made scenes at work since then, till the higher-ups couldn't ignore the situation and had threatened both her and Dusty.

The red reflections on Dusty's glasses turned to green. Elly pushed away her fears. She wasn't a little kid anymore, at home with folks who might be drunk any time of day, might start acting crazy. Dusty hadn't had a drink since they'd been together. Of course it would be okay. Joy replaced Elly's terror. Dusty was leaving just in time, she told herself, before her record could be marred by Rita. Dusty was being smart and brave. She was finally ready for her dream.

"How wonderful, lover!" she exclaimed, wanting to hug her, wanting to kiss her, wanting at the same time to be held and reassured as only Dusty could reassure her. She dreaded the risk of being poor again, of living without a shred of security when she, too, had finally begun to live her dreams of love and a home.

They passed the big dam, always thrilling to Elly, so much water coursing over the huge concrete spill, pounding into the River below, sending up a spray that misted the windshield. Its strength was invigorating.

"You bet I did it," said Dusty. "For better or worse. Let's hope it's not worse."

CHAPTER TWO

The house on Puddle Street had originally been one large room. The previous owner, then Dusty and Rita, had built squat little add-ons around the central core so that from the outside, in the dark, the white-painted structure looked like a mother house surrounded by baby rooms.

The inside was unique too. The main room was beamed and spacious, and would have been barn-like except for Dusty's novels and school texts lining the walls in homemade bookcases, and the big soft furniture she'd bought, used and mismatched, after Rita had taken her Early American set with her. Elly and Dusty each had a separate room for their clothing and privacy. They slept in a third room just big enough for the queen-sized bed Elly had brought with her. In her single days she'd called it her hope bed. "I don't," she'd explained to Dusty, "need a hope chest full of dish towels. What I do need is a bed full of woman!"

Into her own room Elly had fit a single bed and the refinished elegant and elaborate old vanity that had been her moving-in present from Dusty. She sat on its matching stool now in white slip and heels, watching herself think as she removed some of her makeup and freshened the rest. Cachet tonight? She sprayed some on, smiling at the way the fragrance filled the room, anticipating how it would hit Dusty in a wave. No, she decided, they hadn't finished celebrating.

She ran her hands down her silken slip, felt how she would feel to Dusty. Should she change to a negligee? She smiled into the mirror, blotted her lipstick once more. The slip would stay. Dusty, shy about her sexual feelings, went bananas over her when she wore nothing but it and high heels.

The woman in the mirror, twenty-eight, thin, had the delicate, almost frail-looking bones of her family. But she also had the stubbornly forward-set jaw and jauntily uptilted nose that told of their determination, generation after generation, to hold onto their little bits of land, or to strike out optimistically north or west—to do what needed to be done to get past the setbacks life held for the Hunnicutts and onto whatever joys they could find.

Dusty knocked and Elly turned from the mirror to greet her. But Dusty's shoulders sagged, her hands hung limp at her sides.

"What's wrong?" Elly was ready to hear that the plant *had* let her go.

"Angelica's limping."

Elly tried not to smile. "Oh, Dusty," she said with affection, chin raised toward her lover. "How in the world can you tell when a duck is limping?"

Dusty stopped and picked up Duchess, her white and black cat. "What do you mean? By looking at her, that's how you tell. Angelica's old, this could be the beginning of the end. And if the diner doesn't work out, I won't have any money to pay the vet bills and—"

"Stop it, Dusty," Elly said, stamping one foot firmly. "You sound just like my dad between drinkin' bouts. The littlest thing would set him off till you'd think the world was about to end." Despite her exasperation, she enjoyed watching Dusty lavish love on the cat. She sighed, knowing what she had to do to fix this crisis. "I'll take her down to the vet if she's not better tomorrow," she promised.

"Would you?" Dusty asked, the lines in her face disappearing.

As always, she wondered if Dusty really couldn't figure out how to solve her own problems, or if getting rescued was a way to feel loved. Elly's bare shoulders broke into goosebumps and she tried to rub away the chill, and a new wave of fear. "It's such a shame, in a way, givin' up your pension even if you do have your education to fall back on. I'm still getting unemployment. If only I could take your job out at the plant. Keep that money comin' in. Just in case."

"No way!" said Dusty, rising in her lithe way, nose buried in the soft belly fur of the cat she cradled. Now that Elly had solved the problem of Angelica, Dusty had brightened. "What do you think of that, Duchess? I buy her a diner, and she wants to give it up already." Duchess jumped to the bed, nestled again on Elly's pink comforter. Dusty picked up the robe Elly had laid out and gently draped it across Elly's shoulders. "It's your dream to waitress in your own diner," she reminded Elly, hands holding the robe in place.

"But yours to buy one and run it."

Dusty left Elly's side with an abrupt movement, her brightness seeming to fade. There it was again, thought Elly, that up and down, up and down moodiness since Dusty had stopped drinking. The slightest hint that someone disapproved of what she was thinking or doing transformed her from Amazon to mouse in a moment. Sometimes Elly felt just like her mama back in Tennessee who was always trying to fix things so Papa wouldn't start cursing or beating on the kids.

"Do you think it's too risky?" Dusty asked, pacing the limited floorspace, her face drawn.

Elly swallowed her anxiety. "I love you," she said, as if this alone would shore up Dusty. "And it's going to work."

Hands clasped behind her back, Dusty studied her face. "You really believe in me, don't you, lady?" she asked quietly. When Elly nodded she went on, "You're the best thing that ever happened to me, El. I mean it. And I'm going to name this diner for you."

Elly laughed, embarrassed. She drew a brush through her hair. "Hunnicutt's Hash House?" This time she couldn't pretend to be serious.

"Nope." Dusty dropped gracefully to one knee and drew Elly's free hand between her own, kissing it. "I want to call it *Elly's Diner*. Short, spiffy, proud. I want to light you up in bright red neon for the whole Valley to see."

Elly pulled her hand away, swung her stool toward the mirror, and began to rub cold cream into her hands, its perfumed scent familiar, always slightly exciting. How that woman could charm her.

But this felt wrong. Dusty had wanted a diner all her life, she should claim this one for her own. Dusty still grieved the loss of her first diner and her family—it hadn't been long after her father had left diner work for a job cooking on the railroad that he'd also left home for good. Her mother had worked all hours in that same diner, making it another home for Dusty.

With slippery fingers Elly screwed the cap on her cold cream. Dusty had dreamed for years of this day, had been too scared to make it happen until she'd earned her two-year degree. She'd never even mentioned it aloud until she'd left Rita.

Rita, Elly thought. She filed a hangnail without mercy. Rita had scooped Dusty up and tied her down, fed Dusty's fears with her own. Not deliberately, but . . . Elly made a face at her cuticles. That wasn't fair. They'd held each *other* back, Dusty and Rita. Had hidden from life in Dusty's house while the suburban developers had built streets and homes and yards around their quarter acre of land and the puddle-turned-duck pond that had given Puddle Street its name. Like her little piece of land, once considered on the other side of the tracks, Dusty was finally coming into her own and taking charge of her life.

No, Elly had to show her that it was important to take credit for the diner. To stand up in public and say *win or lose, I did this.* "I think you ought to name it after you," she said to Dusty's reflection in the mirror.

"Dusty's Diner? But it's ours." Dusty rose, swung Elly toward her, stood looking down into her eyes, one hand on her shoulder.

"It's your life savings. A second mortgage on your house," Elly said.

"I couldn't do it at all, though," Dusty countered, eyes cast down, a bashful, irresistible sideways smile on her face, "without my queen of hearts."

Slowly, provocatively, Elly twined her bare legs. The robe slid from her shoulders. The name, she thought, what a wonderful name. How to convince Dusty?

She realized that she was cold no more. Dusty's eyes had widened; Elly could tell she'd just become aware of the slip. "How about *Dusty's Queen of Hearts Diner,* sweetie?" she asked, fully facing Dusty. "You can have it both ways." To clinch it, she stood and walked Dusty backwards to the edge of the bed.

Dusty had nowhere to go; she sat on the bed with a thud and cleared her throat, as if to distract from the reddening of her face. "I like it," she said, recovered enough to reach under

Elly's slip, working her hand between her lover's knees, then between her thighs, moving up just far enough to find that Elly had removed her underwear. Elly closed her thighs on Dusty's hand, then squeezed against it, moved her hips a bit.

"I *meant* the name, lover."

"So did I," Dusty said, a low lusty laugh in her throat. "At least partly. I do like it. I should have asked you to name it in the first place. You're so good at that kind of thing." She paused, smiled, "This kind of thing too." Elly was opening Dusty's shirt, licking between her breasts. "The sign will cost a little more," Dusty said, "but it ought to pay for itself in customers who try us just to see what the name's all about."

Elly opened her thighs, felt Dusty's slightly rough hand rise further, trapped it, let it go, caught and squeezed it before she opened once more and lowered herself onto Dusty's fingers. She saw herself, lips parted, eyes nearly closed, doubled in Dusty's glasses.

"My smart, beautiful Queen of Hearts," whispered Dusty, pulling Elly on top of herself as she lay back on the bed. Duchess fled. Dusty's fingers never lost their mark.

CHAPTER THREE

As soon as Dusty got home from work the next evening, she took Elly back over the dark Morton River to see the diner. Heavy wet snow fell like a beaded curtain between them and the rest of the world. Elly nestled as close to Dusty's shoulder as she could get, trying to ease the quivery breathlessness that had taken her over at the start of the ride. The peculiarly northern wet woolen smell of Dusty's peacoat was not reassuring. It reeked of alien ways, of risk and uncertainty, but she rubbed her cheek against it anyway just to feel her lover's bulk. Her hand lay between Dusty's legs and she dreamed of the future, of the past, alternately.

This diner was just where she wanted to be right now, and to stay forever. There'd been another dream once. With

Butch, her first lover. She looked like Dusty, moved like Dusty, dreamed like Dusty, drank like Dusty used to. A softball player, her life had been organized around the team she played with, the summer tournaments, the traveling to play other amateur teams in the South. One day, Butch had predicted, there would be professional women's softball and she'd manage a team. She would live with Elly in Florida, travel summers while Elly stayed home in the trailer, watering the flowers they'd plant around it. Elly had seen herself lazing in wooden cushioned lawn chairs, talking with the other "softball widows," waiting for their butches to come on home between road trips.

In her dream Elly wore a yellow sundress, sun poured down on her. Butch, wearing the yellow and black team jacket, drove up in a tail-finned Chevy, and soon slipped the low-cut dress down her shoulders . . . . But Butch never did stop drinking the last Elly heard. And here was Dusty, driving the stolid Swinger with care through the slush on the most raffish side of Morton River. Elly pressed the inseam along Dusty's crotch. Dusty squirmed and smiled. They slowed in a dense snowy neighborhood, half of its buildings formerly lovely three-story homes gone to seed, the other half grimy brick factories. Here and there some of the old homes had been restored. Teachers and graduates of Valley University were beginning to settle here, where houses could be bought cheaply. She'd heard that the neighborhood was changing.

The Swinger stopped. "There she is," announced Dusty in a proud voice, taking Elly's hand gently in her own.

The curtain of snow turned rose-colored, off and on, from the diner's blinking neon sign. As they sat, car idling, holding hands, the windshield fogged with their buoyant anxious breaths, and made the diner look, to Elly, like a rose-tinted dream. It was only about fifty feet long, but its shining chrome glowed so bright it seemed enormous. Red stripes ran like streaks of excitement the length of it.

Elly wiggled in an almost sexual ferment on the seat and peeked over at Dusty's profile above the navy-blue turtleneck. Dusty's face was flushed deeper than mere reflection. "Dusty," she said, drawling to control the wild enthusiasm she felt welling up in her, "it looks just like you!" Her bracelets jangled as she clapped her hands together.

The worry lines were back on Dusty's face. "It's for sure not perfect, El. There's no parking lot. The factories shut out the light at both ends. With the tracks so close behind it, will the dishes rattle every time a train goes by? Will it be too noisy to hear the jukebox?" She rubbed the bridge of her nose, under her glasses.

Elly laughed, too thrilled to pay any attention to Dusty's worrying. "And will the River rise, swallow the tracks and then come after your Queen of Hearts?"

"El!" Dusty said, catching one of Elly's hands and stilling it, as if to contain her foolhardy ebullience.

Elly glanced around, pointed at the factories, smokestacks billowing their own white clouds to the sky. "Think of all the good things, Dusty! The workers will come for breakfast, for lunch, for coffee breaks. And that church across the street! Sundays we'll be mobbed."

"That's my sunny-side-up girl. You're right," Dusty conceded, her grip loosening. "Sam does a pretty good business in there now."

Elly was picturing herself contentedly directing a busy cordon of waitresses. She leaned against her door, feeling like a little kid before a Christmas tree. "We need a good crew, Dusty. The kind of girls who make hard work fun and make the customers feel part of things." She had grown quicker, friendlier, smoother over the years herself and was proud of her serving skills. She loved in particular the art of flirtation, which kept the men tipping generously even while she kept them at a safe distance. Tips, though, had long ago lost their appeal as the only tribute to her competence. In a business with Dusty she'd shine for the joy of it. That kind of attitude, she knew from experience, was catching.

She looked at Dusty and folded her arms. "Sweetie, it has class," she pronounced. She felt way too small to hold all her pride.

"You think so?" the sign blinked on and Elly saw a brightening in Dusty's eyes. "I think you're right," Dusty answered herself. She at up straight and slid an arm around Elly. Here in the shadows, under cover of the heavy snow, Elly knew that no one could see. "That's what I wanted, a classy little dive. Homey. I want people to feel comfortable. We'll need curtains in the windows."

Still feeling dreamy, Elly twirled a strand of hair around her index finger. "White ones, with red hearts," she fancied. The neon flashed off and on, off and on in Dusty's glasses as Elly watched her consider. She knew Dusty always took her time making decisions, pushing through all that self-doubt. But, like the diner purchase, when decisions were made they came like a raging river and changed everything.

In her imagination, Elly continued dressing the diner. The shining building seemed, through its rose and white screen, taller than when they'd first driven up. She imagined it deeper, its booths secreted in corners, its restrooms perfumed, ornate, its kitchen and counters gleaming and covered with opulent foods that drew the workers, the commuters, the families of Morton River Valley. That drew, too, the factory owners, the politicians, even the bosses from Dusty's plant who threatened her livelihood for being gay. Dusty's Queen of Hearts Diner, she dreamed, on the Morton River, at the very center of the Valley, offering nourishment, warm welcome; a place known for its food and harmony, famous for the way it erased walls between people; where gays and straights, blacks and whites, poor and rich acted kindly toward one another. Dusty's Queen of Hearts Diner, a home for the tired world. The feeling of fullness grew in her.

16

". . . everywhere," Dusty was saying. "Hearts and shining stainless steel everywhere. It'll look just like you, too."

"Steel?" Elly laughed. "Hey, lover, aren't you ever going to take your Queen of Hearts inside?"

Dusty came around to open the door. She held an umbrella over them as Elly stepped gingerly in her high-heeled boots through the snow. A low roaring sound and damp pervasive smell came from the River, across the tracks and down a steep cliff behind the diner. The dam wasn't far upriver. Elly felt reassured by the water's emphatic natural presence, soothing in its promise of yesterdays survived, tomorrows to come.

Dusty paused outside the diner door. She stood tall, shoulders squared, chest out, as if she was full of the moment too. She opened the door for Elly with all the panache of a Fifth Avenue doorman. Elly brushed against her as she passed. "I love you," she whispered.

The vestibule, though tiny, felt as large with promise as the River below. Dusty placed the umbrella in an old-fashioned wooden stand, then straightened, hands on hips, legs widespread, claiming her territory.

"This is one of my favorite parts," she said. "It feels safe, like once you're this far you've got it made." She unbuttoned her peacoat. "No matter what used to happen at school, when I got to my mom's diner I was warm and with people who didn't care how tall I was or how much I looked like a boy."

Elly shook the snow off her hair and laughed. "I wouldn't have you any other way," she said. She wiped her feet on a small red rubber welcome mat. "I surely appreciate this red carpet treatment, lover."

"Our mat will be heart-shaped." The flush on Dusty's face was not neon now, but her own high spirits. "I want to put a game out here."

Elly's heart fluttered at the sight of Dusty whipping one of the pennywhistles from a pocket. This Dusty was irrepressible. As the brief Irish ditty ended, Elly skipped onto an old penny scale. "Look at this, Dusty! I haven't seen one of these in years!"

Dusty fished in the pocket of her crisply pressed workpants and gallantly slipped a coin into the scale. Its clunk sounded some sweet long-ago memory inside Elly. She reached down to feel the white-fluted stand of the machine as she read, *You will begin a lucky venture.*

"Hey, I like that machine." Dusty stepped onto the scale. Elly stood on tiptoes to read over her shoulder. *A woman from your past will reappear.*

Rita, thought Elly, jealously flaring. That old Rita will try and get her back.

"You think this is a gay machine?" asked Dusty, eyes averted. "How did it know I'd have a *woman* in my past?" she joked. But her laugh was tight. Elly could tell she knew damn well Rita hovered in the vestibule with them like a disturbed ghost. Then Dusty opened the door with a courtly gesture as if to usher them both to safety.

There was the cheering smell of coffee and grilling hamburgers. Tiny Michael Jackson of the Jackson Five was piping out an enthusiastic love song on the jukebox. Half of a lemon meringue pie sat under glass on a stainless steel pedestal on the counter, chocolate layer cake occupied the next display. An older man gummed macaroni and cheese. Two teenaged boys eyed Dusty suspiciously, looked Elly up and down as if she were another layer cake. Two men in truckers' uniforms smoked and dreamed into the mirror. At booths a family calmed a crying baby; two older women intently feasted on fish and chips; a young straight couple held hands over a large order of french fries, the boy salting both the fries and his girlfriend's hand as he stared into her eyes. A cop came in, sank tiredly onto a stool. The place was two-thirds full.

The boys at the far end of the counter were still looking their way. Dusty's handsome butchiness always attracted stares, but these boys looked like part of the gang that had harassed them last night. A waitress hurried out of the kitchen. "It's Rosa!" cried Elly in relief and pleasure.

"Elly!" Rosa exclaimed.

The boys turned away. There is no protection, Elly thought, like a friend in enemy territory.

"Hi, Dusty! Hang on a minute. I'll be right back."

There was a certain smell to a diner, Elly mused, not just the food, but stainless steel and vinyl, heat and hurrying people, soap and wax, that was unmistakable. Nostalgia made her long to work again. "I love bein' a housewife," she whispered to Dusty, "but I'm going to love gettin' back to work even more."

They watched Rosa—short, pink-cheeked and freckled—do what Elly had done a hundred thousand times: cut pie, pour coffee, set creamers on the saucer. Rosa did it all humming. Elly had first met her when they'd waitressed together at a truck-stop diner after Elly moved north. Rosa had hummed her way through that job too. They'd met again when Rosa waitressed at The Pub, a gay bar and restaurant in Upton. She was an easy-going woman who'd come through a lot herself. Rosa's presence felt like a good omen.

"Come sit down," Rosa said, gesturing to the booth that is traditionally the help's break area. She looked over her shoulder as if to see what was needed. The other waitress waved her away. "It's time for a break."

"Does Sam give you breaks?"

"Are you kidding?" She talked quickly, with a Spanish inflection, and punctuated her sentences with a warm bubbly giggle. "This place always keeps me jumping. But we spell each other." She puffed hurriedly on a cigarette. "You enjoying your vacation?"

Elly smiled. "My first real vacation since high school. But it won't last much longer." She looked meaningfully at Dusty who stood waiting for Elly to sit.

"Rosa knows," Dusty said, with a wink toward Rosa. "Hell, Rosa practically twisted my arm to take over."

Elly threw a half-teasing, half-suspicious glance toward Rosa, but Dusty patted her hand and chided her, "You know Rosa's straight as an arrow. I'll tell you the story over pie." She turned back to Rosa. "I didn't get to ask you the other day, how are the kids?"

"Like a hornet's nest, I swear. Can't keep up with them. Thank goodness for Jake. Life's a lot calmer since he moved in." Her eyes strayed constantly to the counter, as if handling this hornets' nest was second nature.

"Jake?" asked Elly, surprised. "Blond hair? Blond beard? Short guy from The Pub with muscles on his muscles?"

"Don't worry, *mi amigita,* he didn't go straight. He's my roommate and live-in day care center. With his hours at the hospital dispensary, and mine here, it works out great. I save on sitters and he saves his rent money toward buying the pharmacy of his dreams." She watched two more booths fill up, sighed and rose. "No rest for the weary. You know how it is. I'll be back for your order."

They sat in the booth and studied the menu, criticizing more than selecting, eyes locking in excitement each time they shared an opinion. The clink of heavy cups against saucers, the murmur of conversation, a smoker's cough, drew Elly's attention. She leaned back to enjoy the colorful busyness.

"The floor tiles are worn," Dusty said, following Elly's gaze. "Some day soon we'll be able to replace them."

The tiles were red, with bold black patterns. Silver cylinders reached up from the floor to red vinyl stools. The counter was red too, the tiles beneath it cream-colored all the way down to a red-tiled footrest that ran the length of the counter.

"But they're perfect," Elly protested. "The wear and tear belong to the place. It's a fairyland diner. Look at all this brightness!"

Dusty watched her, hands clenched, forearms on the table. "I knew you wouldn't like a grimy looking place."

"Grimy! Look at all the stainless steel behind the counter! Sunbursts in stainless steel! Stainless steel coffee pots! Stainless milk machine! Even the clock is stainless!"

"Hot damn," said Dusty, opening her hands toward Elly, the sideways grin appearing again. "I think she likes it here! What I wouldn't do to take you out on the town to celebrate, with champagne. These days, I guess we *are* out on the town!"

Elly turned to flip through the jukebox titles. "Look, lover, my song!" Dusty supplied a quarter and Ray Charles began to sing *Sweet Georgia Brown.* "Now we're celebratin'!"

Rosa took their order and hummed off. Elly watched the life of the diner again. It was as if it had a personality all its own, part humming waitress, part many-armed cook, part shelter, mother, lover, cop on the corner—community. Kids bounced to the song, older people debated ball teams and brand names.

She looked toward the window. Reflected in it, people rushed about or sat in restful silence. Beyond it, snow fell wetly, thicker than ever, pink and white in turn as the sign blinked. Elly sipped her warm Coke, a southern preference, she claimed. It tasted rich and sharp. Dusty had turned to the window too. "Pretty," said Elly.

Dusty started, as if she'd traveled a long way down the road outside the window. "I was remembering yesterday afternoon, sitting in front of the diner trying to make a decision." She drew a long breath and folded her arms, leaning forward onto them, eyes on Elly's. "It was so grey. The factories, the sky, even the diner looked grey, not silver. And across the street—" She gestured with her chin, "—look at that old church: dingy stones, stubby like a prison, not something reaching for the sky. It's pretty likely they hate queers. And the houses around here, half of them look like they've been chopped into small flats. Maybe that's where all the guys in the gang live. Crowded, poor, bored. You know how dangerous that can make people."

Elly felt Dusty's fear in the pit of her stomach. Felt it and hid it. She knew fear bred fear; courage came from believing in what you were doing. "I wasn't sure you'd noticed them," she said.

"People like that make sure I notice them," Dusty answered quickly, harshly. "Yesterday a bunch kept walking by me, hanging around right outside the diner. Sam's retiring. He's been in the neighborhood forever, he knew their parents when they were kids." She paused, seemed to struggle for words. "I felt like I was surrounded. Everybody was shouting at me—the factories, the church, the people in the grey houses—*Outsider! Go home, queer!* The slightest wrong move and they could make life hell here." She slouched on her seat. "I was ready to forget it and go get plastered."

Elly breathed in sharply. "But you didn't, thank goodness," she said. "You *are* home here, lover."

Dusty shook her head slowly. "That's the trouble. I could buy a diner anywhere in the universe. Why Morton Valley? It's like whatever happens from now on has to happen right here. Whatever I do in this world, for some dumb reason I can't seem to want to do it somewhere else. Hell, the whole Valley's dingy and grey, the River always threatening to do us in."

Elly didn't say that the only thing wrong with Morton River as far as she was concerned was Rita's presence.

Rosa returned with their pie and drinks. Dusty shrugged and let a smile break onto her face. She helped Rosa set things down. "You're right," Dusty conceded. "At least I'm not hungover and sick. I'm not screwing up my life." She gestured to Rosa who sat down and lit another cigarette. "I can thank this one for that. She came by just in time, when I was at my lowest. You tipped the scales, lady, gave me faith!"

"Gave *you* faith!" Rosa cried. She lowered her voice, leaning toward Elly. "She brought *my* faith back!"

Dusty lit Elly's cigarette with the gold lighter Elly had given her for their one-month anniversary. Dusty didn't smoke and never remembered to carry matches for Elly. Their eyes met. Elly saw the lighter's flame in Dusty's glasses, the heat in Dusty's eyes.

Rosa briefly rested the back of her head against the seat to blow smoke toward the ceiling. "I was ready to quit, I swear." Her hands moved as quickly as her words. "Sam had just announced his retirement, said he'd gotten an offer from that crooked Rossi who's buying up half the town. I knew Rossi would put a manager in here who'd see nothing but bottom lines and waitresses' bottoms. I can get by on my alimony, I don't have to take anybody's shit. Unless," she added with that bubbly chuckle, "I want to give my kids a good Christmas, keep them in parochial school. Only the best for my little hornets. Then who do I see leaning against that old rattletrap of hers? *Mi cocinera.* And she tells me she's thinking of outbidding Rossi who won't buy it unless it's a bargain. But the neighborhood was scaring Dusty, this woman who could save my life. '*Mi cocinera,*' I say, 'the *world* is too damn scary to set foot in if you're going to worry about every move you make. All this neighborhood is, is one tiny bit of that scary world. I swear,' I said, 'I was just this minute planning to quit that diner the second Rossi took over. Much as I like the work and these funny cranky customers, I can't keep liking them unless the boss appreciates them too, like Sam does.' But I don't want to quit. This is how I get out, meet people, have a good time. I'll work till I'm dead on my feet if you give me a good boss. Together," she finished, rising, "if we all work on this thing together, we can take on Morton River Valley and the world! And you couldn't get yourself a better head waitress than this one," she finished, indicating Elly.

Elly met Dusty's eyes. Rosa hummed away. "So you've got your first employee," said Elly.

Dusty drained her teacup. "I feel like she hired me." She looked pointedly at Elly's lips, licked her own. "Want to come home with me, lady?"

"What put *you* in the mood?"

Dusty's eyes swept her breasts under the thin white sweater. "You," she mouthed. But Elly knew it was high hopes that had done it.

At the register, Dusty told Rosa, "I decided yesterday, that if your neighborhood's anything like you, we've got a fighting chance."

Elly stood in the vestibule while Dusty opened the car. She hurried, under the umbrella, through the snow to Dusty. As the Swinger warmed, they watched the diner hum, like Rosa, with life, its neon sign a pulsing red heart.

They didn't talk till they'd passed downtown. "Where will it all lead?" asked Dusty.

Elly watched big white flakes collide with the windshield and melt, watched shops vivid against the snow, watched the passing warm yellow lights in doorways and windows of homes and apartment houses. The night sky was luminous with snow, the road ahead full of dark ribbons of tire tracks left in the fallen white stuff. "It's scary," she answered, "but excitin'!"

Dusty seemed to swallow her uncertainty. "Don't be scared, lady. We'll tough it out. We'll just go in there and *do* it." She flashed her most confident smile at Elly. "It's a piece of cake," she assured Elly, snapping her fingers and reaching to turn up the radio.

Elly crossed her fingers inside her mittens.

CHAPTER FOUR
Dusty's Tales

Jesus, Rosa, I'm scared, scared half to death of this diner thing. I can't *do* it, I just can't pull it off, I know I can't. I'd back out if it wasn't for Elly. She's as excited as a kitten and she gives me hope. Yes, tea, lots of it, black as you can make it.

What I wish I had was a drink. A lot of drinks. Of all times to stop drinking, just when I need it most to keep my courage up. But you know it's funny, Rosa, when I stopped drinking I got this big surge of energy. I hoped I was wrong, that it was Elly, or the weather—anything but drinking. I liked drinking.

Loved it, as a matter of fact. How would I ever have gotten through the Navy, gone through all those women, without a bit of loosener-upper here and there and now and then? It's part of my style—or was. When I go to a dance now or, you know, make it with El, I'm all left feet and ten thumbs. I can't handle not being an old smoothie.

You really want to hear about my Casanova days? Okay, okay. I came over to cry on your shoulder, but it's your house, your cup of tea. I'll bend your ears any way you want them bent.

Women always want to know, "Did you have a girl in every port?" At a party they'd come over after I'd played a tune on my pennywhistle. Sometimes I'd answer, "Sure," and act Dusty the old salt. Now that I'm with Elly I pretty much tell the truth. The boring, grinding truth about living always on edge. And they think I'm covering up my wild adventures.

As a kid I wanted to be on a boat so bad I could taste the brine. Women still aren't allowed on shipboard and it's 1971! Half the men angled to get shore duty, but I wanted to feel detached from land. There's something about the lift and fall of water, something about balancing on top of an always moving mass that I dreamed would make an excitement, a difference from anything before in my life.

I loved the Navy; I hated the Navy. It got me away from home, but didn't do much more than that. I wanted to be a cook, like my dad had been when he served; but I was a woman, and the closest I could get was galley slave. Still, I was stationed at North Island off San Diego right out of boot camp. At least they couldn't keep me away from the Pacific on my days off. At first there'd be nothing to do with my free time but sit on the beach and read all the novels in the base library, under a western sun whose light was every bit as wide as the ocean I couldn't sail on. I'd watch the sun and sea play with each other. The sun threw rays down; the sea bounced them back up. The sea tossed vapors up; the sun burned them back

26

down. I used to watch those tennis games on the big smooth green-blue court day-in, day-out, like I was at some country club with the gods paying the bills.

I stuck with kitchen duty, and seaman grade. I liked it, and I enjoyed the perks. Now and then I'd trade off with the sweet-toothed base photographer—a party's worth of ice cream, say, for pictures of me and a girl I was after. Picnic goodies in exchange for scheduling me on watch at the same time as a new recruit I had a yen for. It's strange even now, making love in a place of my own, sober, not having to listen for an officer patrolling, not having to keep my clothes at hand for a quick heart-racing escape.

I had a good time. Despite the disappointments, I have some good memories, like a scrapbook full of formal portraits with my cruising buddy Les, or with girlfriends. I showed the pictures to Elly right away so I wouldn't have to hide them another seventeen years like I did with Rita. I wanted to start out honest for the first time in my life. Elly loved them. Sometimes I don't know about that woman of mine. Instead of getting jealous (and she does know how to do that!), she had her hand in my pants by page three, telling me what a hot number I'd been back then, and what she wouldn't have done to be born sooner. She's twenty-eight. I'm thirty-nine.

I enlisted for two years, reupped for another two. Why? The wonderful regularity of military life. Always awake at the same time in the morning, usually to bed on schedule at night—alone or not. Uniforms—never having to worry about dressing inappropriately, looking so different people stared and asked if you were a boy or a girl. The most variety we got in clothes depended on how much bleach we managed to work into our dungarees. The "saltier" they looked, the more handsome we thought we were, preening as if we were sailors back from long voyages where we'd grappled with white whales and pirates. I loved how the Naval regs were clear, reliable. The officers had to follow them with me just as I had to

27

with them. And after home, believe me, that was a relief. I took to military discipline like my ducks to water. Except my ducks *get* to water.

Probably I'd have stayed home if my dad hadn't switched to cooking on trains when I was real young. He was tall, dark-haired like me, a handsome Irishman, Ned Reilly. Played a hot pennywhistle. (Do you think *he* knew its effect on women?) He could outdrink anyone, except maybe me. He's the one who started calling me Dusty instead of that plain-jane Dorothy my mother named me. He met her at a diner—they were a cook and waitress combo like Elly and me. A couple of times he took me to work with him. Once he took me to the circus, just him and me. Another time we went to Radio City Music Hall. He thought the Rockettes were great, but I never got the feeling he wanted me to grow up to *be* a Rockette. He winked at me in the magic dark theater, like father to son.

But I guess all that travel, all that booze, were too much to share even with an eager kid like me. He came home less and less, and I could hear the lies in his voice when my mother asked him who he'd met, where he'd stayed on layovers between train trips. I knew she was trying to find out if he had a girlfriend. My biggest fear was that he'd marry the other woman—of *course* he had girlfriends!—and leave us for good. He simply wanted more romance than a diner, a family and Morton River Valley could provide. Finally he rode the rails off into the sunset when I was nine. I was left with a miniature chef's hat he'd brought me from one of his trips. Mom wouldn't let me wear it after he'd taken off, or play the pennywhistle he'd taught me to play, or even talk about him. When she couldn't keep me from growing up gangly and auburn-haired like him, what she did was ignore me.

I'd lost them both. Then I grew scared of really losing Mom, of losing the dog, the waitresses at the diner. I'd have elaborate fantasies of being left all alone and I'd cry and cry in my bed at night, my chef's hat hidden under the pillow. In the morning I'd be scared to go to school. What if I came home and everything was gone?

School was hell anyway. Besides all my worries I was tallest in my class, a reckless tomboy. I lived scared of kids and their constant taunt, "*Mis*-ter Dorothy Reilly." As soon as I was out of sight of school I'd start to run, full speed, and wouldn't stop till I got to Mom's diner.

I loved that old yellow and red place that looked more like a circus wagon than a restaurant. I loved the loafers smoking around the stoop who'd greet me with gap-toothed smiles on stubbled faces, maybe give me a friendly poke in the arm. "Ned Reilly's girl Dusty," they'd tell each other. I loved the lights that spelled *UPTOWN DINER,* unlit when I'd arrive, but full of an energy that would light up my little night when it was time to go through the wintry streets past the River toward home.

The Uptown's inside was done not so much in colors like the Queen of Hearts, as in wood and stainless steel. Mom worked through dinner, and I'd settle into the booth where the waitresses took their breaks. The smoke from their cigarettes sometimes got so thick it would mix with the late afternoon sunlight and screen me off from the rest of the diner, the world. After hugs, milk, pie from the waitresses, a wink from the cook who'd worked with my dad, I might dash to the library, dreading to meet my schoolmates, and return with a stack of books which I'd stash in my corner to devour, one by one, as I happily set out to places Ned might be, or I'd go some day.

For all the energy I expended on dreams I didn't get far. After a couple of years my mom married a man I *wished* would leave home. He was an optician whose office was the converted front and side porch of his house. I always felt squeezed into the background behind his important bustle up front. He was the guy who'd fitted me with glasses since my first pair at age six. I'd liked him all right then, but when he tried to be my father—how could a balding, round-eyed man who greased his strands of hair, who thought being dashing meant wearing white shoes and seersucker suits, even come close to a Ned Reilly who had elegance even in his walk? The best thing about old Round-Eyes was the money he made. He owned a house and Mom and I got the comforts for the first time. Then she had his three round-eyed sons. I stopped being scared of school and started being scared of going home.

The worst thing about him was the way he tried to force womanliness on me. Mom argued with him that she'd been a tomboy too, but she had less and less time for me and he was determined, before legally adopting me, to steer me away from the monster he thought I was becoming.

He called me Dorothy. I had to wear dresses at the dinner table. Jeeze, I was awkward. My long runner's legs must have looked like stilts under the flounces. Don't laugh, Rosa! You don't know what it's like to be stuffed into something so wrong for you and embarrassed into pretending it's right. I had to listen to lectures on womanly virtues like having children and sewing. My hands were awkward with sewing paraphernalia. He wanted me to think about boys, not bikes; about dolls, not trucks. I didn't want him for a father, mine was all I needed even if he wasn't around. I loved being a Reilly and different from this stepfather and my half-brothers. Something in me was determined to go out of his life as queer as I'd been when he came into mine.

You know, I never told anyone but Elly this next part, but it felt so good to get it out the first time—well, here goes.

At thirteen Old Round Eyes decided to hire me as his part-time secretary. It was how I would earn my allowance. But he was the one who took allowances, training me, big as I was, to perch on the boss's lap. He'd touch me. I'd squirm away. He'd tell me to get used to it or he'd send me away. I lived again with the fear of losing everything.

He'd tell my mom every little mistake I made in filing or making appointments and encourage the boys to laugh at my stupidity. I dreaded Mom's sigh and disappointed look, as if she was seeing my father's faults imbedded in my shamed eyes. I learned to stay still for his touches, though I'd be nauseated for hours afterwards. When he tried to get me to touch him, I went a little crazy. I thanked the heavens for the first time that my father's legacy to me was a fine strong body. I pulled away, but knew, this time, it wasn't enough. He grabbed for me and I pushed him over. He landed on top of his desk, twisted into an awkward position, groaning. He started to straighten and I took off, slamming out the screen door, leaping off the steps, sprinting, skirt and all, across the narrow lawn and down the hill. I didn't stop till I got to the River. Swift like me, it took every bit of anguish I brought it and floated it out to sea.

Old Round Eyes fired me that night at dinner. Told Mom I'd never learn and he wouldn't adopt me or put a penny toward my education. If I wanted college, I could pay for it myself with some rough factory job I could handle. I was so ashamed: first from the humiliation of his touches, second from my failure. The three little round-eyed boys watched me open-mouthed. I couldn't face my mother at all, sensing her survival depended on being able to stay with this man. I walked alongside the River for a long time that night, unable to decide between the two courses of action I could see: throwing myself into it or building a raft and travelling from river to river till I found the Mississippi where, of course, I'd read that an idyllic life could be made on the little islands.

Instead I built a little island in my head. I'd jump onto it like it was a diner or some other refuge. There I wasn't scared. I was just shut down so I could walk through the door into that place I had to call home.

By the time I'd graduated from Valley High, I was more realistic. I did want to go to college. The Navy seemed like a good way to get there some day. By then I looked just like

Ned, had a thirst and a wanderlust as bad as his, and, with a drink or two in me, could seduce more girlfriends than I could handle. *They* loved me. I had a lot of lost love to make up for. When I was tired of one I'd take another drink and jump to the next.

The Navy would make that even easier. I'd go to sea (my raft on the River), have a girl in every port (real idyllic islands) and a girl on shipboard. Life would be so simple. My mother had written me off, Round-Eyes one through four got ruder every day. There wasn't a thing to stop me. I'd been working at the Uptown in the kitchen part-time and the Navy recruiting officer said he was interested in my skills. Culinary, that is. Good hands and a tireless tongue were not what the Navy was looking for.

I put on one of those old dinnertime dresses and enlisted. I'd cover up my gayness in the Navy if I had to, just like I'd learned to do at home. Women officers, it turned out, were just like my mom, wedded to what they got from men: money and protection. If I followed the rules, I could blend in so no one noticed me. But it all took its toll, hiding a big sailor-woman like me in broad daylight, under the blazing sun.

Once in, I tried to make myself so reliable they'd take me for granted. I never asked for awkward leaves; I was always around when they needed me. I drank, but in the Navy they'd have thought I was weird if I hadn't.

Unfortunately, I still somehow pulled women to me. Because I'm good-looking in the way my father was, because uniforms became me, because I could whittle a tune out of air on my whistle, because I grew up soft-spoken to avoid notice and inherited the suave Casanova manners of my dad, women seemed to find themselves drawn to me. Some liked feeling drawn. But others got scared. I don't know if my looking so boyish triggered a panic button in them, or if they were scared of how they were feeling. It had been hard enough back in Morton River.

If a lady officer noticed me, I sure knew about it. They'd watch me. Stalk me. Everywhere I went I'd feel eyes on me. I tried to unlearn habits like standing by my chair till everyone had been seated. Even so, the higher-ups would ask the other seamen about my social life. I had to be so careful. One wrong move and I'd be punished for being attractive to them. It never occurred to me, at first, to neutralize them by giving them what they wanted. Not to slip up and get put on report, but to open my arms and pull them in.

I began to be scared again. Scared of losing the Navy now. Here I was on North Island, an island where I was supposed to be safe, and it hadn't worked. I spent more and more time in the bars in Coronado, drowning the fears and the self-imposed loneliness. Drowning the part of me that screamed for love.

Now I feel like I've come full circle from the Navy. The Queen of Hearts, as long as she was still a dream, was an island of safety too: my own business. The closer she gets, though, the easier it is to see that there is no safety. No matter how many sets of rules you learn, and learn to break, you're always jumping in feet first, free-falling. I guess the only thing to do, Rosa, is close my eyes and jump.

CHAPTER FIVE

Elly met Grace shortly after moving in with Dusty. She'd literally bumped into her in the library. In the midst of Elly's apologies, Grace had reached out to silence her.

"You're from Tennessee," Grace said, voice hushed in wonder.

It had taken Elly no more than three seconds to realize, "So are you!" They'd thrown their arms around each other and established a ritual of meeting at the library once a week.

"Come hell or high water!" Grace had said. "I want to hear that down home voice real regular!"

Grace, at forty-two, had tight-curled, pearly-grey hair that gave off a glow even under the library fluorescence. "This is Seeker," she said that first day, gesturing to a German

Shepherd by her side. "I keep her for company more than to be tugged around this weeny town like I don't know where I'm going." Her accent was as broad as Elly's was mild. To Elly she seemed braver, stronger, wiser than anyone she'd ever known. Life, she told herself, was hard enough without being blind.

"How's the Southern belle this week?" asked Grace now, two weeks before Dusty's Queen of Hearts Diner was scheduled to open. Her smile brought up the edges of a cupid mouth wedged between cheeks Elly had claimed Grace had inherited from a chipmunk ancestor. Elly had puffed out her own cheeks, held Grace's hands to them to demonstrate.

Twenty years earlier, Grace had left Tennessee to visit her cousin LuAnn, who'd migrated North with her husband's job. She'd been so impressed with the services for the blind—a local politician had raised a blind son in Morton River Valley—she had stayed. She rented two rooms in LuAnn's garreted Victorian home. "My suite," she called them.

"Life," Elly replied now, "is grand." She sighed. "But things are surely hoppin'."

It was late January. They trekked down a steep street toward the River, dirty snow piled to either side of them. Elly walked first along the narrow path, resisting the urge to check Grace's progress on the ice patches. At first she'd been terribly self-conscious walking with Grace and Seeker, not knowing how to help, or if help was needed, and embarrassed to ask. She was also aware that Grace attracted even more stares than Dusty because of her blindness.

"And how's the budding dyke?" she asked as they reached a wider walkway. She slipped an arm through Grace's and squeezed it against her coat.

Grace's cheeks were bright red. It could be the cold, thought Elly. Grace answered gruffly. "Still budding."

As they entered the Sundae Shop, Elly felt that wonderful thrill that coursed through her every week when they treated themselves in the cool, dim shop. It hadn't changed since opening decades before: marble soda fountain counter, black and white checked floor, red booths, wrought iron chairs and tables in back. Memorabilia of the Valley hung everywhere; pictures of the sandbagging operations in '28 and '55, to supplement a never-adequate dam. Even a photograph of the Queen of Hearts when she'd been delivered in 1946. Eliy had offered to buy the picture over and over, but the owner wouldn't break up his collection.

Grace rearranged the library tapes in her bag and pulled out her crocheting. "You sound tired," she said.

"The opening's next week, Dusty's crazed with last-minute details, and I'm scared to death!"

Her friend laughed. Seeker settled with his head on Grace's feet and sighed. "You mean nothing is new, you're just running out of worrying time, honey."

"It's like Christmas down home. When the grandmas and grandpas and aunts and strays were due to pay a visit, Mama would say, 'There's more to be done than the day is long!' " She slipped off her fur jacket. "I have to get my hair trimmed," she said, feeling the panic return. "And buy a new uniform, and pick up apron material."

"Whoa, girl," Grace said, her needle dipping up and down in the wool. "Take a deep breath and let it out slowly. Do not forget that you are the most determined and competent woman I have ever known. The kind of woman who dreams so hard it comes true. And that is rare."

"And—" Elly rushed on between breaths. She had no time to be listening to mumbo-jumbo without breathing.

"Just do what I say, Elly Hunnicutt," interrupted Grace. "Not to distract you from the subject, but LuAnn and I tried that gay bar I told you about."

Despite herself, Elly's attention was caught. "When?" Since meeting Elly, Grace had decided she might be gay. "What happened?"

36

"LuAnn's other half was out of town last weekend, so I sprang her." Grace's laugh was like a waterfall, starting high and tinkly before it fell to churn somewhere deep in her throat. "We were both so nervous you'd have thought someone had just announced they were hijacking that bar down to Cuba!"

"Did you dance?"

"Only with LuAnn."

"At least you got on a dance floor. My social life is about as lively as a fiddle without strings. Sometimes I'd swear Dusty's seeing someone else. She's surely not interested in me."

Grace lay her crocheting in her lap. "But why didn't anyone ask me to dance? I thought it'd be different with women."

Elly appraised her friend. She could have been one of a dozen women who hung out at Marcy's except for her unfocused eyes. "It was only your first time, sweetie. No one gets asked their first time. I never have been unless I got out there and flirted up a storm."

"A red-hot mama like you? Damn, I'm a good dancer." She leaned across the table, hands in fists, tears filming her eyes.

"Your time will come," Elly said to console her.

"I'm sorry," said Grace. "It's not that I expected a miracle. I just get so mad—it's why I took up meditating. So I'd stop yelling *I'm just like you!* in my head." She picked up her needlework. "I'm just so sure about being gay. I feel like I lost so many many years being scared of being any more different than I am." Grace breathed till her large breasts under their heavy grey sweater heaved, and heaved again. In a moment a smile lifted the corners of her lips once more.

A waitress delivered their shiny silver sundae dishes with three rounded scoops of ice cream each.

"Anyway," said Elly after a first smooth mouthful, "you don't need miracles. Just exposure."

"I wish there was a place we could go where there's no liquor. So Dusty's not tempted."

Elly set her spoon down. Dusty's name could engulf her in gloom these days.

"She's not drinking, is she?"

"No. But she acts like she is. I don't understand it. I never smell anything—I'm *sure* she hasn't touched any, but she's just like a drunk. Hurtlin' ahead at full throttle, caution to the winds, going, going, never resting, like a woman possessed who doesn't have to worry about the consequences."

"Maybe you should teach her to breathe."

Elly laughed. "Maybe you're right," she said, calmer just from saying it all, from being with Grace. Why did she trust her so? Just because she was from down home? Because she was blind and felt less dangerous than someone whose every defense was intact? Or was it some inner peace that meditation really brought? "What I wish I could give her is a little of your magic."

"Magic?" asked Grace, chasing melted ice cream with her spoon.

"Heck, girl," she went on, twisting a lock of hair as she talked. "It's like Mama said after Pa died, 'If you're going to put all your eggs in one basket, make sure there's no holes in the darned thing.' When Dusty bought the restaurant, instead of bein' scared of losing her job, I thought we wouldn't have a thing to worry about."

Grace was plying her needle again. "But now you see the hole in the basket. With your own business you feel more at risk than ever."

Most of Elly's ice cream had melted while they talked. She spooned up a few mouthfuls. "Dusty's always worrying about that neighborhood. The families, if they found out we were gay, could make us fail. The church across the street could run us out on a rail."

"Nobody can make anyone else fail."

Elly toyed with the red enamel bracelet on her wrist. "Nobody?" she asked. "How about Dusty?"

CHAPTER SIX

Dusty had installed a woodstove to keep heating costs down, and its warmth felt like love on that cold February night. It enclosed them with their friends in just the kind of circle Elly had always wanted to create in her home.

Wearing a flowered lounging robe Dusty had given her for Christmas, she sat at the old oak coffee table, cutting aprons and curtain panels from partial bolts of white cloth dotted with red hearts. After yards of the stuff her eyes were blurring.

Jake spoke from a deep arm chair. "I don't know about all these hearts, girls." He stroked his beard as if in consternation as he examined a finished apron.

"You *love* them," teased Dusty. She sat in her favorite chair, an ancient brown leather of the kind doctors once used.

Her faded black cords, her white shirt over a black turtleneck jersey, made it hard for Elly not to go sit on her lap. "Don't get all macho on us," Dusty warned Jake.

"Macho? Do you really think I could be macho? How happy Dad would be," he sighed. He was short, with a broad chest and narrow waist. Blond hair gathered densely where his shirt opened. His thick thighs in his jeans looked powerful.

Grace, wearing the jeans and flannel shirt Elly and Dusty had given her for Christmas—so she'd look more like a dyke—began to pick out the tune *Macho Man* on her banjo. Rosa gave Seeker a treat while the cats watched the dog's every move. Rosa danced around the room, out of uniform for once, wearing red jeans and a Boston Red Sox sweatshirt. Her two kids were asleep in Dusty and Elly's bed.

"*Macho, Macho Man,*" sang Jake and Elly and Dusty, as if to encourage Rosa's dance.

"Is she a good dancer?" stage-whispered Grace.

Elly tried for a stern tone. "If you weren't doing such a beautiful job with that banjo, I'd come over there and slap your hands. I *told* you Rosa's straight."

"So was I, once." Grace pouted good-humoredly and began to play *But Not For Me.*

"And I don't want to hear that darned ol' banjo feelin' sorry for you either."

"Yes'm," replied Grace. A devilish smile crossed her face. "You'all 'bout frighten me to death with your threats."

Rosa picked up a new apron and settled at Jake's feet, leaning against his knees. "It's nothing personal," she said, "but I *do* like boys, even my *mamasota* here."

"She's always borrowing my beefcake mags," Jake said. "And *our* song is—"

Together they sang the first line of *Someday My Prince Will Come.*

"But he won't teach me the dirty lyrics," complained Rosa.

"Nasty girl," Jake said.

Dusty rose from her chair and put on her slippers.

"Need more to sew, you big beautiful butch?"

Dusty sat beside her on the couch. "Need more girl," Dusty said, leaning to plant kisses on Elly's bare arm.

"Never mind you," Elly said coyly, glad of Dusty's playful mood. "Show me your last apron."

Dusty held it up.

"How in the world did you let Duke get paw prints on it? But you're getting much better. A few more aprons and you'll be ready to do the sewing for the household."

Jake laughed, a sound somewhere between a guffaw and a titter.

"Shut up, you," said Dusty. "I'll bet *I* could impress your dad."

"You surely could," said Elly.

Jake looked Dusty up and down. "I'll bet you could too."

"Humpf," Dusty replied, grabbing a curtain panel and sauntering back to her chair. As soon as she sat, Duchess's brother Duke jumped to her lap.

"Watch this, girls," Jake said. "How to be the complete butch in fuzzy slippers with your sewing and your kitty cat in your lap."

Dusty glowered while the others laughed.

Elly worried that Jake would deflate Dusty's mood, but saw a wink pass between them. She sat on the arm of Dusty's chair and ruffled her hair.

"Why don't you play us a Valentine's Day song, Grace?" asked Rosa.

"No!" Dusty grabbed Elly and pulled her onto her lap. "I don't want to be reminded of opening day."

"Dusty," Rosa said, "the opening will go just fine." She looked to Elly like a cheerful bundle of hope, bright-colored, smiling. "You're just what the neighborhood needs. The diner can pull it together. The retired factory workers from Italy, the new workers from Puerto Rico and the ghettos, the Valley U. grads, people from the church, the teenagers with moms on welfare—you'll see." She gestured toward the woodstove. "It'll be like that, a hot spot they can all hang around, to share the warmth, you know?"

"It's not the opening I'm worried about," Dusty said. Her face seemed to gather shadows as she talked. "It's *after* the festivities, when real life starts up again. Hell, I could get spoiled like this, not working at the plant or the Queen of Hearts."

"When did you quit the plant?" asked Jake.

"Two weeks ago."

"Trying to get out before they fired you?"

Dusty's laugh was bitter, scoffing. "They were going to decide whether I'm queer or not at my hearing. The steward was planning to do me a favor and convince them I'm not." She jabbed at her fabric, got her thumb. "Ouch!" She'd been trying to sew with Elly on her lap.

"Just an extra red spot, lover," said Elly to reassure her. "Don't worry about it."

Dusty's eyebrows shot up. "Look at the sympathy I get around here, would you? I'm bleeding to death and she tells me not to worry about the curtain." She sucked at the hole in her thumb.

"Love you," said Elly, laughing as she kissed Dusty's cheek.

"Is it legal to decide if someone's gay at a union hearing?" asked Grace.

"The government has a rule about queers being security risks."

"What are they so scared of?" asked Rosa. She added another to the stack of curtain panels. "That you'll smuggle helicopter screws out to your girlfriend?"

"It's no state secret," Jake said, "what kind of screws she smuggles out to her girlfriend."

Dusty's bawdy laugh filled the room. "I don't know what they're afraid of. I've never seen the plans to one of their precious choppers. I riveted, I welded, I inspected, I kept my mouth shut. I've never tried to make more sense out of them than I could see in green and white—after I cashed my pay check."

Rosa held up a cigarette, Dusty lifted a table lighter toward her. "I don't understand," Rosa said, the cigarette hanging from her lip as she picked up more fabric, "how it got so out of hand." She squinted against her own smoke. "Thanks," she said to Dusty. "What did Rita do, post a notice on the bulletin board?"

Elly stopped herself from making a number of nasty comments, but her cheeks burned with them. Her needle flew in and out of the fabric.

"Didn't have to," Dusty answered. "Her work was so bad during and after the breakup they had her up on her second verbal warning. She broke down. Threw herself on the goddamn mercy of the foreman—a Morton Valley redneck who idolizes George Wallace and all those other bigoted Southern politicians. Rita cried in the foreman's arms from what I hear. Told all."

"She knew damn well she could get you fired," Elly spat. She wiggled off Dusty's lap.

"I don't exactly blame her for not having my best interests in mind, lady," Dusty quickly, and sharply, countered.

"Why do you defend her?" Elly asked with equal sharpness, sitting at the table again. Dusty looked as if she would answer, but closed her lips with a sudden firmness. The lamplight flashed across her glasses. Elly crossed her legs tightly.

"How come *she* didn't get fired?" Grace asked. She played *Dueling Banjos* very quietly.

"Her job doesn't need a security clearance."

"She's femme; doesn't do the screwing," quipped Jake.

"Talk about nasty, Jacob," Rosa chided him.

Elly couldn't keep silent. "She knew about your brush with the feds before," she said, her voice sullen even to her own ears.

"You mean our Dusty really *is* a spy?" Jake asked in a hushed voice.

Dusty smiled. Elly watched the far-away look come into her eyes that announced the advent of a story. Elly remembered how much she loved this woman and wanted to take back her anger. But Dusty did have some last ties with Rita that were infuriating.

"Did you get caught doing it—I mean—with someone?" Grace asked, strumming faster. Her face held a look of embarrassed fascination.

"No. I got out just in time." She cleared her throat. "It was my friends who weren't so lucky."

"Hot chocolate for everyone?" interjected Elly before Dusty got going. She headed to the kitchen. Duke was sniffing the very tip of Seeker's tail while Seeker watched. Elly scooped the cat up as she passed. She could hear plainly even from inside the kitchen, but stood at the door to wait for the water to boil.

"It was pretty awful," Dusty started. "I'd just gotten back to Morton River from the Navy and was staying with my mom and step-dad." She explained the relationship with her family. "The three little round-eyes were in heaven when they saw these two six-foot, crew-cut CID men—Navy cops—at the door, figuring I'd gone AWOL probably. I was terribly hung over—the shakes, dry mouth, that feeling of wanting to run and hide from the world. This was the McCarthy era, remember? I knew damn well what these guys were after, but what could I do? We had all been terrified of investigation. They'd finally caught up with me. I led them into the living room."

" 'Do you know . . .' " one CID man asked me, naming five girls from the base. 'Are you aware of any homosexual relationships among them?' I knew my stepbrothers were listening and I could feel my face redden. 'We're investigating an allegation that these five women, along with you, consistently and repeatedly engaged in deviant sexual activities while in the service of the United States Navy.' I'll never forget those words." Dusty paused, as if even the memory was oppressive.

But Jake asked, "Do you think *I* could get in the Navy?"

Dusty laughed.

"And leave me alone with my kids?" Rosa said. "You are beached for life, *mamasota.*"

Grace asked, "What could they do to you? You were out of the Navy."

"You mean besides get me in trouble at home? Besides mess up the application I had in at the plant? It wasn't easy for a woman to get a good-paying job like that. And I was this close to being hired." She held her needle between two fingers. "They could only make my family relationships worse and then ruin my career."

"It makes me ashamed to be straight," said Rosa, stubbing out her cigarette. "These days they're arresting Vietnam vets who sit in at the Statue of Liberty. Did you hear about that?"

Elly sliced a loaf of banana bread out in the kitchen. Rosa had nothing to feel guilty about.

"To make a long story short, I denied everything about any of us being gay. Then they changed their tactics and told me, point-blank, that they knew I was up for a job needing security clearance. And started asking questions not about me, but about my friends." She fell silent.

"You told them," whispered Jake, his voice filled with the heavy tones of one who knows what it is to be betrayed—and to betray.

Elly poured the water into mugs as Dusty's silence stretched out. "Well, no," Dusty finally said. "I never actually

46

told them my friends were gay. What I said was, I could only speak for myself. So instead of asking me about lesbian relationships, they asked me if I'd ever known this one to date a man, that one to have a boyfriend back home. The sort of thing that didn't seem awful to answer. I felt very relieved that I could tell them the truth. It was only later that I realized how damaging my answers could be made to sound as evidence. It was like they knew just how far I'd go to cooperate, to save my own skin. I didn't betray my friends by what I said, but I didn't help them enough to keep my record clean. I should have stuck up for them more, been courageous then, and got it over with. Because now, of course, that slightly grey record is exactly what the plant is holding over my head along with Rita's confession." She expelled a loud breath. "You get back what you give out in the world, that's for sure."

"You can't punish yourself forever," said Elly, reentering with hot chocolate and banana bread on a tray.

"Did your friends get discharged?"

"Les did. Not by my statements, though. She'd been the careless one who'd led them, with evidence they got from her, to us all. But two of the others had been planning to make a career of the Navy and never got a promotion again. Another asked to leave for health reasons and the other—" Dusty's voice trembled, "—she's still, I understand, in and out of VA hospitals to detox. Chief Lil. And I still feel like a shit. I was scared enough to lie for me, but I was too scared to lie and save them."

"Elly's right," Grace said, accepting her cup and plate. "You can't punish yourself forever, Dusty. It would all have happened without you. Even the woman in the hospital. For whatever reason, this had to happen in these lives."

"Maybe," said Dusty. "But I'll tell you one thing. I had a hell of a hangover again the next day. And the next and the next."

Rosa moved to perch on the arm of Dusty's chair. "No wonder you're so paranoid about the Queen of Hearts' neighborhood coming down on you."

"Paranoid?" exclaimed Dusty. She thrust her sewing down and looked at Rosa. "You think I'm a coward, don't you? Scared of the CIDs, scared of the neighborhood. Hell, would I be doing this whole diner trip if I was a coward?" She stood, hands on hips, as if challenging them all.

"The fire needs tending," Elly said, feeling a need to chase the chill that had settled in the room despite the hot drinks, the warm bread, the caring friends.

The smell of wood smoke reminded her of a dream the night before. As if Dusty's fear was contagious, she'd dreamed that the Queen of Hearts' reds were flames, a hooded gang of boys fed the fire, the priest fanned up the fires of hell, and the neighborhood stood by while the Queen of Hearts burned to the ground.

Grace began to play again, a faint, but light-hearted version of *Country Roads,* as if to reheat the house. Dusty strode heavily from the room; Elly feared she wouldn't return. But she did, with a pennywhistle. She accompanied Grace.

Jake got up and tied a finished apron around his waist. He began to sing along with the banjo, kicking his short sturdy legs high as he did. Then he pulled Rosa up and danced her in circles.

Feeling the pall lift, Elly kept the beat by clapping her hands and jingling her bracelets. Seeker barked, the cats hissed and Elly moved behind the chair where Dusty had settled. She leaned over to massage Dusty's shoulders and neck muscles.

"El!" whispered Dusty when Elly's hands strayed around to her chest, "Jeeze, I *never* had a girl like you."

"You glad things worked out the way they did?" Elly asked in a seductive, teasing way. "Even if I get a little fresh in company?"

Grace ended her song. "Enchanted," said Jake, curtsying to Rosa with the edges of his apron outspread.

Elly moved her hands up to Dusty's shoulders, laughing to watch the heavily bearded, handsome pharmacist perform so incongruously. She rose and went behind him, retying the apron with a fancier bow. "I wouldn't want you to feel left out. Why don't you take this one home?"

"Oh, ladies," said Jake, mocking, but obviously pleased. "You really know how to treat a girl right."

Dusty laughed heartily with the rest, but Elly was worried. Would she punish herself forever, holding onto her fear like an untreated wound, simply because the pain was familiar?

CHAPTER SEVEN

Opening day at the diner was like navigating a river gone wild. The very feel of it grew from a rumbling undertone to, at noon, a roar, a reverberation, a wave that swept through Elly like the Grand Opening of the World. And it was. This was *her* world, and with Dusty she controlled it.

Dusty, like a runaway skiff, zig-zagged through Elly's day in white pants and chef's jacket over a red turtleneck, a confident smile fixed on her face. Nothing was automatic for them yet, each step must be thought out and performed very deliberately. Elly guided herself by the blur of Dusty's whites, the particular pattern of a section of equipment, the white squares and rectangles full of hearts, Rosa humming and darting around her like a little bird.

Red balloons and red streamers bedecked the diner. Every full-course meal was served with a tiny heart full of chocolates. The Queen of Hearts was mobbed, the pace dizzying. What a triumph to be attracting so many people to a business owned by gays. That theirs was a brave gesture was obvious. The neighborhood people trained inquisitive or downright suspicious eyes on her. She was glad she'd painstakingly painted her nails at midnight, glad she'd risen early to do her makeup right.

For support their close friends and Dusty's Navy pals, as well as Rudy from the bar, co-workers from Dusty's plant and from Elly's old diners, all came to wish them well. They told Elly she was a knockout. A basket of flowers had been delivered. Elly's level of excitement rose still higher at the sight. Who had been so kind? GOOD LUCK, the card read. It was signed by Rita.

Elly stamped a foot in anger. What did that bitch want? First she'd cost Dusty her job, now she—Dusty stepped out of the kitchen and leaned, big as life, against the shiny milk machine. Elly thrust the basket at her and returned to her customers. When she glowered back, the flowers had been set by the register and Dusty was gone. Some nerve, she thought, and dismissed Rita from her thoughts as best she could with that basket staring her in the face every time she rang a sale.

"How's it going?" Dusty asked later when Elly stepped into the kitchen for clean spoons. "You look like a million dollars. And you've got the front running real smooth for a first day." They grinned at each other in excitement and triumph, but just briefly. John the dishwasher returned through the swinging doors with more dirty dishes.

"Feels like home to me," she told Dusty. "How about you?"

"It's been a long time," said Dusty, "but the work is coming back easy." She wiped grease spatters from her glasses.

51

"Look, only three burns so far." She showed off the red weals on the insides of her wrists as if they were battle scars.

"Poor baby," mouthed Elly, wanting nothing so much as to take the wounded wrists to her lips. "You'll be a mess by the end of the week."

"It goes with the territory. I don't feel a thing."

"You couldn't look any better," Elly whispered, "in your whites."

Dusty glanced toward John, a neighborhood kid she'd decided to hire for reasons of diplomacy. His back was turned. She looked at Elly then, from head to toe, her gaze relishing the tight-fitting white bodice, the short skirt of her dress under its heart-shaped apron, her legs in nylons. "You're so short without high heels."

John swung with a steaming tray of glasses. Folding her arms, Dusty asked skeptically, "Are those really clean this time?"

John was Dusty's height, thin, with longish hair as fine and wavy as a baby's curling over his ears. He looked as Irish as Dusty—and with his wide blue eyes, pouting lips, hairless cheeks, his willowyness, he seemed younger than seventeen, different from the rest of the corner gang.

"Sure they're clean. Have a look," he challenged her, chin forward, tone not quite polite.

Elly laughed to lighten the animosity between them. "I'll bring them back if they're not," she promised.

"Won't be a problem," John mumbled, passing them. He reminded Elly of her seventeen-year-old self; she too had been certain no one had ever done it right before her, had been too proud to learn by listening.

Dusty shrugged. "He'd like to be boss," she explained. "First job, first day. He'll learn."

Elly smiled in sympathy, but noted the not-quite real smile of Dusty's which had reappeared. "I'll leave this war of wills to you Irish," she said. "You know how I *adore* the Irish." She moved through the swinging doors to the customers, who still came and went in waves.

Cigarette smoke, sweet syrups, smoking oil. Steaming frost rising from the ice cream bins. Taking a moment to pat her hair and redraw her lips in the bathroom mirror, she sashayed back to work, selling slender smooth packs of gum to customers already sucking minted toothpicks, fitting aluminum high chairs beneath babies' rumps, reciting the specials over and over: Dusty's Braised Beef, Fresh Biscuits, Liver and Onion, Baked Apple, Dusty's Pepper Steak. The grill sizzled out in the kitchen and Elly dreamed as she worked of the unique future the Queen of Hearts would have—a place where people flocked for the house specialties and for the warm welcome.

Rosa appeared beside her to ring up a check. They bumped hips as they used to at the truck stop. "Two o'clock and still piling in!" Rosa cried. Her hum had turned raspy. "Will you be okay when I leave, *mi amigita?* The kids get out of school at three."

"Night shift will be here by then," Elly said, sipping a warm Coke whose bubbles had long ago disappeared. "You hanging in there, sweetie?"

"This is how I love it," Rosa replied. "Busting ass with friends, working my job, living my life. Dusty won't retire on me for a good long time!"

Elly laughed as Rosa went off to present another check. Then she saw a priest, probably the one from across the street. He sat alone, taking up the whole of a booth, jowly-faced, short and wide to the point of straining his clerical garments. A chill ran down her spine. She was glad he was in Rosa's section. She picked up an order of Braised Beef for two women in the end booth.

"I can't tell you how changed this place feels already," one of them told her. "I love Sammy, but this business had been running him down for years, ever since his operation."

"He'll be cookin' on Dusty's days off," Elly told them.

"Just so we won't have to do without his perfect ham sandwiches!" She was well into her seventies, with flushed round cheeks and a boyish manner.

Her companion spoke in a barely audible voice, looking at her plate. "This is how we remember diners. Inexpensive, cheery—with personality."

"Thank you," replied Elly.

"I'm Gussie Brennan," said the shorter, livelier woman. "And this is Nan. We live in that little stone house across the tracks. We can see the diner plain as day from our back windows."

Elly peered past the unsteadily pointing finger to a narrow house perched not quite at the edge of the cliff across the River from the diner. "I hope we'll be seein' a lot of y'all, then." She wondered about the women as she left them. Had they always lived together? Could they be . . .

Rosa caught her arm. "Father Grimes wants to talk with you when you have a minute." She was looking at the floor.

Her body tensed. "A problem?"

"I should have remembered to tell you. Sam always fed him free. He only went to church once a year at Easter, but he thought this was good for public relations."

Elly wiped her hands on her apron. "How can I help you, Father?" He looked to be in his sixties and suffering from chronic indigestion.

"Hello, young lady," he said. He had a good voice, deep and woody, which contrasted oddly with his body. "I've always had, ah . . . a *special* relationships with the owners here."

His manner was a mix of imperiousness and subservience. Elly felt both implored and insulted by the time he'd finished his pitch.

"I'll have to talk to Dusty," she told him. "We didn't plan on anything like this. If you'd like to order lunch today I'll give you an answer tomorrow."

His sour look returned. "Mine is a poor church," he said, his palms up before him, his voice hypnotically smooth. "I came out without a penny. If I could know before—"

Lunch hour on opening day, muttered Elly to herself as she hurried to the kitchen. *Customers practically hanging off the ceilings, and he has to know now.* She asked Rosa to take him coffee on the house. His parish might be small and poor, but she didn't want to make enemies with the only church in the area.

In a quick whisper she explained the situation to Dusty.

Dusty's tone was indignant. "No! Who does he think he is? We're not even Catholics. Those priests get enough out of their parishes, including, I thought, someone to cook." She shook her head as she flipped a dozen biscuits from their pan and shot a glance at Elly. "What do you think?"

Elly grabbed a biscuit. "Just like Mama's," she said. "But I'm a little worried about turning him against us. He acts about as Christian as a hungry mountain lion."

Dusty was moving at top speed. "That would be blackmail!" Her tone allowed no argument. "Tell him we're thinking about a senior citizen discount and that's all."

"I don't know, Dusty."

Dusty's smile stayed in place, but her eyes were hard. "I do," she said.

Father Grimes set his cup down with such a bang that Elly thought it would break. He stomped out on his little legs, nodding curtly to those who greeted him.

"What's with him?" Elly heard behind her.

"Jake!" she cried, hugging him. " 'Pon my honor I surely am glad to see you. You look so respectable I hardly recognized you."

He was dressed in a well-pressed pin-striped suit, bright white shirt and red tie, his hair freshly cut and brushed back in a style from an earlier era. He smelled like aftershave mingled with the flowers he carried. He also held a chef's hat. "I tried

55

for the Early Diner look," he admitted, posing. He offered the flowers. "These are for you."

She knew the gift was as much for the public offering from a male as for the flowers themselves. It would keep neighborhood suspicion at bay a little longer. "Why, Mistah Bonner," she said, dipping her nose into the petals, "thank you so very much. These are lovely."

"My pleasure, Miss Hunnicutt," he answered in his deepest voice, with a fluid bow.

Elly tried not to giggle. Jake's moustache twitched with contained laughter. She kissed his cheek.

"Didn't the priest like the specials?" Jake inquired.

"The prices," Elly answered. "He's used to a free ride."

"May I go into the kitchen and present this to the Chef?"

"Wait till I can get a picture," begged Elly. She ran to fill coffee, deliver an order, take another, grab her instamatic.

She focused over the swinging door as Jake ostentatiously presented the hat to Dusty. Elly turned to Rosa beside her. "I swear that big old butch of mine just wiped a tear from behind her glasses."

"She has half an onion in her hand," said Rosa. "You'll never prove it. Uh-oh. Look what Jacob just noticed."

Inside the kitchen, Dusty was making introductions. "This is our dishwasher, John."

The boy stared at Jake. Later, Elly would remember this scene in the kitchen over and over. Jake transfixed by the willowy Irish boy. John's pouty lips opening with a sensual air of surprise. Along with Dusty and Rosa she watched as the Queen of Hearts began her own life, hurtling along her own diner-channel beyond their control after all.

The look between the men had lasted only seconds, but Jake seemed to turn from John with an effort, like a statue coming to life. Dusty had put the hat on and Jake walked around her, surveying its effect.

Back at the counter Elly served him coffee. She was curious about the exchange with John, but had neither time nor privacy to pursue it. Just as well, she thought, pouring Coke for herself. Why add fuel to a fire that might be no more than a momentary spark?

Jake's eyes were bright. "Lemon meringue!" he said. "Just like a real diner!"

Even as she answered, "This is about as real as you can get," she knew it was the beginning of a tradition. Jake at the counter, winter and summer, she, with more time, smoking one of her long cigarettes as she stood across from where he sat. John brushing gracefully by, as he did now, to pick up, deliver dishes. Dusty a white whirlwind behind her, grabbing orders off clothespins hung on a line across the kitchen window. The day crew tired, ready to go home, the night crew drifting in. John working behind the counter again, experienced, swiftly and quietly handling dishes, his long-lashed eyes on Jake. The customers, coming and going into the dark, the twilight, the late afternoon sun, a stream of them as long and full as the River.

"I thought you went off duty at three," said Elly.

John started. "Just making sure everything's clean."

Good, thought Elly. But why the sudden conscientiousness? Why not 6:00 AM or 10:00 AM or noon? She watched Jake watch the tight young ass stretch the fabric of John's now dirty white pants. John was a neighborhood tough. He couldn't be gay.

She readied the night waitresses, cashed out the drawer. When she finally went to the kitchen for Dusty, John had left. Dusty, talking to the night cook, was still grilling hamburgers, as if reluctant to give up her ship.

"Can't you make her stop?" asked Earleen, a spare small black woman who had been known for her power-packed batting on the softball circuit. Now she was close to fifty. "Don't you trust me with your grill, child? I've been spreading grease for close on thirty years now."

"Come on, Dusty, Earleen's got our number in case the vegetables mutiny."

Dusty handed her spatula to Earleen with a ceremonial gesture. "I don't know what I'd do without you, El."

"Work yourself to death, most likely. You're as stubborn as a volunteer crop of potatoes, as Mama would say."

Dusty's face looked worn, her lines multiplied. She left slowly, her eyes seeming to feast on the sight of the Queen of Hearts. "I keep thinking it's going to disappear," she said, looking back one last time as they reached the Swinger. "It can't really be ours, can it, lady?"

Twilight was turning to dusk. Someone inside switched the new red neon sign on just then and it answered, like a challenge written on the sky:

DUSTY'S QUEEN OF HEARTS DINER.

CHAPTER EIGHT
Dusty's Tales

Come on in, Rosa. Pull those milk crates over and sit down. Jeeze, we've been so busy with this place, it's the first slow day we've had. I owe you another installment on my life story, don't I?

I need to wipe the sweat off before my glasses steam up again. This is the only part of kitchen work that gets to me, this heat. I sweat sometimes till I can't see for the drops rolling into my eyes, till my clothes are damp and my glasses steamed up. It's not working at the stoves, or the weather, it's me, how I can't hold back at all, but throw myself into everything I do like I have to prove I'm worth something.

Elly says since I stopped drinking I'm a workaholic. But I'm not. I'm just giving the Queen of Hearts what she needs. And right now she needs all of me. I couldn't have done this when I was drinking, either. Imagine yourself coming in here at 5:00 AM with a hangover, or starting to drink when you leave, trying to stay high till you go to sleep at night and handling the Queen the next day. No way.

That's how it was in the Navy. I guess I drank so the life I was leading would look good to me. I remember the night even Chief Petty Officer Joswick looked good.

I'd been hitting the bars pretty hard. I'd get to a place after a few when I could feel this big charmer of a smile spread itself across my face and wipe out all thought. It was like I stepped outside of me and became someone smoother, happier, more interesting. Next thing I knew I'd be hopping out of my booth and shining that pennywhistle on my pantleg, if I was someplace where I could get away with wearing dungarees.

But that was as far as I'd get. In the Navy you didn't make yourself too conspicuous or you weren't in the Navy very long. I'd get into that place and then be left high and dry, with no place to take a girl even if I was courageous enough to find one.

Hand me those carrots, would you, Rosa? I have a beef stew to put together for tonight.

All that ended on the night of the Chief. She wasn't exactly a light in my life, but she lighted the way for me afterwards.

The base kitchen had a cooling system, but the room was so chock full of personnel that week it was like putting an ice cube in a boiling pot. I was glad I was just a galley slave and not a cook. I'd spent the afternoon outside dreaming of women, missing their bodies, looking at a day and sky so bright my eyes still felt seared. The dimness of the kitchen, instead of being a relief, brought new shocks. The stainless sink and cooler doors became little suns that got bigger with the hot yearning inside me. I felt half-blinded.

Chief Lil worked beside me, a CPO pitching in because two seamen were on leave. She must have been about twenty-six. I'd barely noticed her before because she blended into the military so well. She was your cartoon officer, female or male—short-haired, burly, bowlegged, a barking bulldog. She never acted like she noticed me, wasn't one of the officers after my ass, I thought. I was all of nineteen, and dreaming about her when we were apart. We'd never made it together, the lovely seaman-galley slave and me. We couldn't find a place to be alone long enough. But we made out whenever we could, hot and passionate in the walk-in cooler. She kept my smile muscles in shape.

As I worked that day I noticed the Chief. She might not have been pretty, or even femme, but she was fast as lightning, neat and organized. I wasn't exactly clumsy, but I knew she had skills to teach me in a kitchen and the kitchen was all I still had of me. I didn't see it then, but I was terribly homesick for Morton River, and ready for any place, anyone, that would feel like home. So I watched her with the food—and with the crew, amazed to see that when she was working with us, not over us, she didn't bark at all, but was soft-spoken, listened when we talked. Maybe she was actually happier that way. I liked her for her shy smiles and rough humor, but she was definitely not my type.

After clean-up I lingered, fooling with my pennywhistle, not admitting my curiosity. It was cool there, I told myself.

The Chief stayed and we got to talking.

"Eight years," she told me she'd been in the Navy. "I was one of the first to enlist when they opened it up to women in 'forty-two. Eight years, six months and three days," she went on.

I was impressed, but her tone sounded flat, not proud. "You counting time till you get out?" I remember thinking a whiskey and soda would make this talk feel easier.

"I'll never leave," she said, real quiet, almost sad.

I didn't push her. It was so peaceful, all of a sudden, after the way we'd torn through dinner. And I was lonely, so lonely I sometimes felt like the only tree on a hilltop, wailing wind blowing through me. I felt a great wave of affection for this woman who seemed like someone I could lean on. I looked up at the stainless steel, but it still held its glow and I needed darkness. I turned from the glare to look at the Chief's lank blonde hair grown out unevenly over her collar, at her blunt nose and thin tense lips. She raised her head and I recognized the all too familiar brightness in her normally expressionless brown eyes—the brightness I'd been avoiding so successfully in the upper grade seamen and the petty officers. So much for being pals, I thought, as I felt those familiar bubbles of excitement invade my gut.

Listen, I told myself, *you don't want to do it with her.* I couldn't face what was in those eyes. Or what was in me. I turned away.

"How about you, Seaman. You a lifer?" she asked me.

"You make the Navy sound like prison."

"Nah," she said, smiling that winning smile again. We were on stools at one of the counters, drinking the last of the coffee. Two sailors came in, rattling their buckets. "I like it. This is the only life I could lead."

I nodded, understanding in a flash why a lot of people stayed in. "It must get to be a kind of habit," I mused aloud.

I was trying everything on in those days, to see what would fit. Did I want a habit like this? I saw the Morton River, full and fast and powerful. I saw the huge dam that stopped it up. I imagined cracking the dam and letting that River flow. I wonder if that was the moment I fit the first piece into the puzzle which would make my later life, which would lead me home. I swore then that no habit like the Navy, no creeping indolence would trap me. Like the River, I'd hurl myself against my dam.

The Chief sipped some coffee. "You say I talk like I'm in prison," she challenged, eyes narrowed. "Maybe that's okay. Maybe I'm one of those people who feels safer with the gate locked."

A few minutes earlier, my brash nineteen-year-old mouth might have told her she was keeping herself in the dark and didn't have to. But sitting inside her aura of resignation, I saw how easy it must be to get caught up in surviving that she couldn't see her choices any more. Fear, pain, ignorance, comfort—I wondered which of these was the Chief's gatekeeper.

"What would I do out there? Where would I live? Alone in a tiny apartment, without even a base to hang out on. What would I wear? How could I earn a living? They don't hire women out there to march around parade grounds. I'd end up washing dishes in some greasy spoon."

I grumbled, "Nothing wrong with that."

"And where would I meet people?"

I knew she meant women. "Pluck 'em off trees!" I cried, standing and doing a little jig, like I'd had a few whiskeys already. I laughed at the picture she'd make, nude on a tree-lined lane, timidly gawking at the beauties lounging in the branches. Damn the woman, I thought. One minute I liked her, the next she seemed to disappear behind a cloud and irritated the hell out of me.

"There are places," I suggested cautiously.

Our eyes held.

It had been so long for me since I'd had any but the hurried and frightened touches of my seamen. I knew CPOs were assigned single rooms. And there was something in the Chief which stirred me. I wanted to dazzle her, dazzle any woman, for the ways dazzling made me feel good. I wanted a woman to take places, to give a good time, but I didn't want to be

63

seen in public with Chief Lil's burly body and uninviting face. How she looks doesn't matter, I told myself, then thought again. *The hell it doesn't,* I answered myself. But I wanted someone, by that time, anyone. Period. Loving hands, laughing, sharing eyes. Release.

"I've got a pint stashed," said the Chief.

That did it. With a pint I could do anything. We sauntered casually through the late night heat then, trying to appear separate. As if either of us could be doing a thousand other things and had chosen to do this one thing for no particular reason. It was how we had to appear to others; it was how I wanted to appear to myself. If I wanted out, I knew, it had to be now. Once we started, there'd be her hurt to face. Or to avoid.

The base seemed hushed. The stars were like suns retreating, but ready to blaze again come morning. I remembered a night on the bank of the Morton River, Katrina against my shoulder, stars blinking up there like they couldn't believe how bold we were. Would tonight be a pleasant surprise? I kept walking.

After lights out, I went into the bathroom, hid feet up on a toilet seat till the dorm sounded like a tomb. Then I slunk through the halls to her room. The light overhead blazed, but I killed it and stood a flashlight upright on her foot locker. The room became shadows around an umbrella of dim light. We sat side by side on her cot and drank till the pint was gone. *Now, Dusty,* I told myself, *get out while the getting is good.* Get out to what? To my own hand, on me? I wanted to make love to another woman so bad I was trembling.

My ears strained for sounds of watchful officers all the while we worked our way inside each other's clothing. We were in uniform dresses, of course. Hers rode up those short bulging legs I was trying to ignore. But hot damn, the shock of bare soft thigh is something I'll never even try to resist. I knew what I'd find next: damp regulation cotton briefs, even damper hair matted beneath them, those tender pinkish lips all swelled up with need, that thick clitoris standing attention for a mere apprentice seaman's practiced hand. Every woman is pretty down there.

"Yeah," the Chief whispered with reckless enthusiasm into the tent of light.

"Shh," I whispered fiercely, clamping my lips over her open smiling mouth to muffle her. I was confused to find her so passive in bed when on the base she seemed one hundred percent all-American butch.

Her teeth caught my lower lip and I tasted blood. I hurt while she came, but the pint had numbed me and I was doing *it*, making love, at last.

The summer took on a pattern after that. The Chief had something I needed real bad and her whiskey made it easier. And we liked each other, even if in time all the sneaking and tension, the lying and fear, twisted what we had and made it ugly, like some addiction. I went back to that shadowy cell over and over as my hand went back to her slippery saluting parts over and over that night.

Looking back, it seems as if the Chief and I had descended to an underground space that was real only in our minds. Everything and everyone else became background for our frenzied meetings. I'd drink with my own crowd at the Enlisted Men's Club, watching women dance with men while I longed to wrap my arms around a girl who'd follow me. Part way through the evening the Chief might stop by my table to slip me a note that the coast was clear and, with our smuggled booze, we'd sneak off to have sweaty secret sex till we passed out.

The sweat in my eyes then felt like tears. There was no romance in what I had with the Chief, or with the others like her. I'd fall for sweet and pretty seamen I couldn't make love to, then get involved in affairs with superiors who had privacy and liquor. My soft words were more to get me in the mood than because I meant them. To this day I am ashamed to have abused my body, my soul, that way. It took each morning so long to come, took the stars forever to melt back into the big broad sun when I was locked in one of those drunken, erotic nightmares I craved.

Poor kid, I can think now. Young Dusty Reilly, going with the officers from lust and loneliness, with the help of liquor. From the distance of the Queen of Hearts kitchen, Elly out front like a second heart beating in my life, I know I have what I always wanted. No more confused Dusty, dreams buried under all that darkness. I don't even need a bottle to dull reality now, Rosa. I like my life straight up these days.

CHAPTER NINE

Summer birds loudly cheered the early June morning, cool and damp with night dew. Someone had been mowing a lawn at twilight the night before and the smell of cut wild onion stalks made Elly tingle. She loved seeing the world before most of the neighborhood was awake and peering out windows, noticing the odd women in their garden. Usually Dusty fed the ducks while Elly stayed inside and put on her makeup, but they'd celebrated their first anniversary, quietly and tiredly, last night, and she wanted to keep feeling close to Dusty. Sleepy-eyed, she'd followed her outside. The pond was purplish at this hour, wisps of hovering mist holding in the tranquil night.

Last night had been nearly perfect. They'd put away their worries about the Queen of Hearts and Dusty had seemed more present than she had in weeks. While Dusty disappeared for half the afternoon to find an anniversary present, Elly had fixed the chicken the way her mama used to for special occasions, rubbing it with mustard, then shaking it in flour. She'd diced crisp bright green peppers, sliced red-skinned potatoes and peeled plump small white onions.

Dusty had arrived home bearing a long white florist box, bowing as she presented it, then taking Elly, box and all, into a swooning embrace. At dinner, she'd carried on so about the chicken that Elly had finally written the recipe out for her to use at the diner. She wrote while balanced on Dusty's lap, with one of Dusty's hands where it hadn't been in so long—well up under Elly's skirt.

Her thighs squeezed together now, almost involuntarily, remembering those insistent, exciting fingers playing with her labia. Her hungry body's welcome had been unrestrained. There was a year's familiarity in the touch of those fingers, and as Dusty separated her outer lips to pull gently at the long inner lips, then stroke them with her index finger, Elly's handwriting on the recipe card sprawled more and more until Dusty noticed and laughed that deep creaming laugh that meant she, too, was turned on.

"Your handwriting's trying to lay down, lady," said Dusty.

Elly's voice caught in her throat, came out half purr. "Do you blame it?" She ground her buttocks into Dusty's crotch and felt the pleasure of her own tightening muscles. Dusty kept right on stroking till Elly lay the pen down and collapsed back against Dusty's strong shoulder and firm-tipped breasts.

"I bet I could carry you to bed," Dusty whispered.

"*I* bet a bushel barrel of warm Cokes I could come right here in your lap."

Dusty wet two fingers with saliva, then slid them back down to graze her lips, one finger, then the other, over and

68

over. Elly's legs spread bit by bit to either side of Dusty's thighs, leaving her wide open to her lover. She crooked one arm back to caress the short hairs at the base of Dusty's neck.

"Jeeze, El. You're the most exciting woman in the world, you know that?"

Elly won her bushel of Cokes, both arms cradling Dusty's head, crying out, arching up from Dusty's lap, lifted pelvis craving more of Dusty's circling fingertips. Then Dusty carried her, not with ease, but not without grace, to bed. Elly tried immediately to go down on her, but Dusty asked for her hand, and took its vigorous thrusts so readily into herself that Elly forgot to try again. It had been good, so good, to have Dusty moving again like that, singing like that beneath her, to the light quick touch of her fingertips.

They'd slept close and deeply, awakened with loving words, and now, outside, Dusty crouched, her silent worried self again, luring Angelica closer with scraps. The duck's limp had disappeared and she waddled at high speed toward the food, quacking. Helen of Troy flapped her wings in the water one last time, then launched a complaining assault toward her companion, as if fearing the other would eat her share. From the looks of Angelica, Helen was right. Dusty laughed at their antics as Elly brushed out her hair on a bench under the willow tree, well back from the scene she watched.

Duchess and Duke, in their splendid white and black fur suits, pretended indifference as one washed, the other pounced on low-flying bugs. But Elly had watched many times before as they followed Dusty like this, refusing catlike to miss a thing. They treasured Dusty too.

"Mornin', lady," called Dusty from the bank.

She just smiled in reply.

"Looking forward to getting back to the grind?"

Duchess rubbed Elly's leg. "It doesn't seem so bad after last night." She petted the cat, thinking how grateful she was that Dusty had been able to snap out of her slump for a little while.

"You're right." Dusty stood, loose-limbed, and came toward her, stopping to pull her up. "I love you, El. Once we get over the hump at the diner things will be like this all the time. You'll see."

In the grey light, they walked past the flower beds where irises had recently replaced tulips. At her vegetable garden, the first she'd put in since childhood, Elly paused. "Look at that moist top soil, just ripe for plantin'."

"Like you last night?"

Dusty stepped back so that Elly could walk ahead on the path. Elly's short uniform skirt brushed against her nylons as she walked, making a rubbing sound that always make her feel sexy. She'd pinned her hair up and felt the cool morning breeze on the back of her neck.

"Let's celebrate something once a month," suggested Dusty.

"At least," whispered Elly, watching as Dusty locked the house.

In the Swinger Dusty was still smiling peacefully, driving with one hand on Elly's thigh. They listened to the early morning news, Elly waiting for the weather forecast as if for hints of the hours ahead. Only an all-night gas station was open, lit up like day; other lights, yellow, homey-looking, came on in bedroom windows. Gordon Lightfoot was singing "If You Could Read My Mind." Over the old Morton River Bridge they clanged, not another car in sight. Elly felt the River's rush of power in the cooler air.

Dusty had the car cigarette lighter pushed in before Elly had finished taking a cigarette from the pack. She pondered whether she should make a reference to Dusty's recent moodiness and inaccessibility, or whether she should leave well enough alone. Before she could decide they were pulling up to the Queen of Hearts which still slept under her darkened neon sign.

Rosa, a bright red scarf around her hair, was hurrying down the hill.

"You're early!" called Dusty with a cheerful smile. She held the door open for both women.

Rosa looked at Elly, widening her eyes. "*Somebody* got up on the right side of the bed today." She made a face. "And it wasn't me. Every day it gets lighter earlier and earlier. Am I getting old? I can't sleep through it any more. I wish the weatherman would save it and tack it onto winter mornings when I'm slipping and sliding down that hill to work. But it's just as well. Jake's up grunting and banging his weights around on his days off now. I think he wants to get his muscles *before* he goes down to that gym to show off to John, never mind going *there* to get them. I swear, since John joined up, Jake's at the gym every day."

Dusty gave them a troubled look as she left for the kitchen. Elly felt as if her stomach would fall right to her feet. Last night, undone in a moment!

Rosa turned to face her and clapped a hand over her own mouth. "I wasn't supposed to say anything!" she whispered in horror.

The Queen of Hearts, with only the counter lights on, didn't shine. She smelled like day-old, locked-in cooking. But the second shift had set everything up last night and within minutes the scent of fresh coffee had invaded the front, while Dusty's first batch of cinnamon rolls soon joined it. The milk truck drove up, then the pie woman, the soda man, the ice cream salesman. Elly switched on the overhead lights and let the first customers in. The Queen's stainless steel gleamed. Rosa began to hum. The day, whatever it would bring, had arrived.

As the sun began its trip around the windows, recorded bells signaled six o'clock Mass across the street. As always Elly

71

was surprised to see that anyone went to hear Father Grimes. But she had no time now to worry about his appeal for the neighborhood. She lost herself in the frenetic familiar details of feeding, pleasing, ordering, organizing, paying and taking money. Lately she'd had trouble finding the smile she needed for the truck drivers, the laborers, the saleswomen and clerks and businessmen of Morton River Valley. The smile designed to help them forget their troubles and return to the Queen of Hearts for coffee and serenity. The smile that hid her own concern about losing Dusty to this business, losing the laughing, swashbuckling Dusty to the fears of failure that seemed to be drowning her. But that smile was second nature; it came on with the lights.

By 10:00 the breakfast rush was over. She took some trash out back rather than let it wait for John; he was slow as a creek in a dry spell these days, trying to avoid more breakage. She'd never seen anyone with such poor coordination, but he was trying. And he had finally mastered the art of being on time.

Across the tracks Nan was pinning wet laundry to a clothesline from her little back porch, and Elly could hear the squeak of the pulley as each item floated toward the diner. She waved and Nan, who couldn't see well at that distance, but was used to the daily exchange, waved back, smiling widely.

Elly moved inside and poured herself some Coke. Dusty was shelving supplies in the kitchen while John dreamily worked at cleaning and stacking dishes. Motes lazed in the bright sunrays. Two firemen from the nearby station cracked jokes and drank iced tea.

"What's the Special?" asked Rosa.

"Fish and chips."

"Great. I'll take some home for supper. The kids love it, and Jake can heat it up later."

Elly groaned. "I'd almost forgotten about Jake."

"I blew it, huh? Dusty'll be mad as heck."

"Not mad. Just more scared than ever."

"I spoiled her good mood. She's turning into a real grump."

"You hit the nail on the head. She walks around here—and home—paying no more mind than if we were all a flock of chickens."

"What can happen in a gym anyway? All these straight men around."

Elly laughed, remembering her old roommates Rudy and George, and the stories they'd brought home from the gym. "All those straight men sometimes go to the gym because they don't have to *be* straight there, girl."

Rosa looked astonished. "Sometimes I think Jacob protects me, I swear." She snapped her gum. "My ex-husband works out in one. My brother goes."

"Not *all* straight men," Elly assured her. She pushed hair off her face, rearranging her bobby pins. "But it does make you wonder."

She straightened the pastry displays, put more coffee on, made sure the orangeade dispensers were full. Father Grimes was coming up the street for his free morning coffee. She'd never got up enough nerve to charge him after that first day, and he never ordered anything he had to pay for. The chip on his shoulder against the diner seemed to grow heavier every day. She wanted to run and lock the door in his face. But he came and went without incident this morning, glowering, and the day moved on punctuated now and then by a steamy jolt of memory from last night's lovemaking.

After lunch, Rosa stopped at her side. "I've been thinking, you know, about my ex and my brother." She paused to put another cup on her tray. "No wonder I get along as good as I do with my *mamasota*—Jake. I'm used to faggots."

Elly's laugh was cut short by a loud crash, certainly the loudest yet of John's accidents. Rosa leapt back from the

73

swinging door, almost losing her dishes. The priest, who had returned to swill lunch coffee, looked like a vulture waiting for carrion. Elly and Rosa peered into the kitchen over the door.

"You all okay back there?" Elly asked. "They could hear that one clear across the River."

Dusty stood, back to the grill, fists clenched. Her face was nearly as red as her turtleneck; she'd flung her chef's hat to the floor. "*I'm* all right," she said in a tight voice. "But someone's about to lose his job."

"Go ahead," John shouted, "fire me. You'll be sorry." He sounded close to tears.

"Is that a threat, Mister?"

Dusty, Elly wanted to say, *stop, Dusty, you're only making this worse.* She looked toward the priest from the corner of her eye. He was not hiding his attempt to listen.

"What are you going to make of it?" John moved as if to roll up his sleeves and ready himself to fight, only to find he'd worn a short-sleeved shirt. When he made fists of his hands, his wiry biceps bulged.

"Out," said Dusty in a growl. Her arms were folded. Elly knew she wasn't budging.

John's face lost its anger, turned surly, sulky. His hands hung limp, helpless. "You got to be kidding."

"Listen, Mister, I can't *afford* you. I can't keep up with all the breakage. And half the time you don't even get them clean."

"I'm better than I used to be," said John, defensive now. "I'll *replace* them."

She saw why Dusty had kept him on, aside from fear of his gang. A boy like that, who could swallow his pride when he was wrong—

"No," said Dusty, eyes glazed. "Out."

But now Dusty was wrong. She hoped the priest hadn't heard much of the exchange. She couldn't get rid of the sense

74

that he had some connection to the gang, beyond being parish priest to most of their families. Would he interfere? She turned back to the counter, John's curses in her ears. Father Grimes brusquely signaled Rosa to him. Rosa shrugged at his questions. He stared all the harder toward the kitchen. Waiting for a chance to oust these owners who didn't pander to him? The shift whistle blew down at the factory. In a few minutes they'd be mobbed.

Rosa shared a quick cigarette with her, looking at her round-eyed. "He's not a bad boy. Not like those other kids from the neighborhood. I've watched him since he was a little guy, wondered what it cost him to act so tough."

Dusty leaned over the doors. "Would you call in the night dishwasher, El?"she asked. Her voice had a forced cheerfulness, her eyes looked blank, that fixed first-day smile was back. "And then Job Service? Tell them we want experience, references, maturity, will you?" She turned, then turned back. "Good riddance, right?"

Elly didn't answer. Dusty hadn't talked to her about firing John and obviously hadn't considered any consequences. Now she wanted support. Well, she could go to, to—*Rita* for her damned support. God, she was disappointed in Dusty. The kid was trying to back out of the track he was on toward the life his gang was destined to live, was trying to *come out*, damn it. What was a few dishes to that? She'd bet anything Dusty was just scared of having him around and not willing to admit it. Elly had never met anyone with so profound a fear of being found out—or was it a fear of being gay? Right now, whatever Dusty's conscious or unconscious motives, Elly felt bruised by her gruffness, felt like nothing more than Dusty's head waitress. "I wonder," she said angrily to Rosa as the first workers came through the door, "why today, after four months, Dusty all of a sudden has had enough of John?"

"You don't think," Rosa asked, puffing quickly as the workers settled on their stools, "it's because I spilled the beans about John and the gym?"

Elly was watching the priest talk with a booth of workers; he was gesturing toward the kitchen with a grim look on his face. She looked at Rosa, and wanted to tell her that was exactly what she thought. Tell her she was remembering Dusty's Navy inquisition, her cowardly, if unintentional, part in the lesbian purge. But her loyalty spoke. "Of course not. John may be a good kid, may even be one of the club, but you have to admit he was a lousy dishwasher."

That evening, as she drove home with Dusty through the beginnings of commuter traffic, Dusty seemed calmer, more placidly silent than ever. Their anniversary might never have happened, John might never have infuriated her. The River glided smoothly under the bridge as they crossed, as if its waters didn't carry within it a leashed power. Half a dozen times Elly started to ask about John, but this large solid silent mass beside her didn't seem made of the same quivering flesh she'd caressed last night.

They were on the poor end of Main Street. Old wooden tenements sprawled along the River there. This was where she'd have to live if she stayed in Morton River without Dusty. Yet her own silence, she decided, wouldn't help either of them.

"Did you fire John because he's seeing Jake at the gym?" Her heart began immediately to pound.

"Of course not," Dusty answered quickly, not looking her way. "You know how hard I tried to keep him on."

"It's just funny it should happen today."

Dusty yawned. How could she be so unconcerned? Didn't she know what she'd just done? "I forgot all about the gym," Dusty said. In the same flat tone—or maybe there was just a teeny bit of enthusiasm in her voice, she added, "I hope it didn't spoil last night for you. I really should have gotten rid of that boy long ago."

Yes, she decided, studying Dusty's profile, she did believe her motives were practical only. "But don't you see the connection? You're more scared of having John around and gay than you are that the gang will try to get back at us for letting him go. You fired him for bein' *gay*, Dusty."

They stopped at a traffic light and Dusty looked over at her. There were beads of sweat on her forehead. "Don't be silly, El," she said, shaking her head. "No, El. You're wrong. I'm the last one who'd do that."

Elly squeezed her eyes shut. "It's *scary* how you can deny what's going on with you, Dusty. I'm not criticizing you. I love you. Remember last night? But you're wrong this time. Dead wrong. Sure John's no expert, but what are you expecting for minimum wage? For seventeen years old?"

"He's not cut out for dishwashing, El."

"That's not the *point*."

Dusty's jaw was set. Her knuckles were turning white on the steering wheel.

"Shit!" cried Elly. "Living with you is like living next door to floodwaters. You're so dammed up that when you break everybody gets hurt."

They were at the big shopping center. Dusty pulled in and parked in a space far from the stores. Her chest rose and fell noticeably. Her fists were in her lap. A Sears sign loomed above them, its neon sleeping in the late afternoon.

"What—do—you—want—me—to—*do?*" Dusty asked, staring straight ahead. "Tell you you're right? I know why I fired him. You don't live in my head, El."

Elly felt her own breathing quicken. "I don't know what I want you to do, Dusty, except *see* what's going on. *Say* what you're feeling. I get scared and mad when you explode like you did today. And don't hide away in your head, lover. Stay out here where I can reach you. Please."

Tears fell from Dusty's eyes, ran down her cheeks, her neck, onto her whites. Her glasses got steamy. Elly lay a hand on one of the tight fists, tried to open it, hold it. After a long while, Dusty let her, saying, "Don't leave me, El?"

"No. Oh, no. Never. Want me to take us home?"

Dusty nodded. They exchanged seats. Elly drove slowly home, glancing now and then at her gradually relaxing lover. They pulled into the driveway. Elly pried her own tense fingers off the steering wheel.

"Look!" said Dusty, her voice raspy from crying.

Occasionally, traveling ducks visited their pond. A flock had settled in since morning.

"Maybe," said Dusty, her voice excited, her eyes bright now, "maybe we'll get some ducklings out of this visit!"

Elly slumped in her seat. The ducks. Angelica. Helen of Troy. Rita had named them. Maybe Dusty should have stayed in that soft, comfortable life with Rita. Maybe Rita was more what she needed. She sighed and then said as a gesture of peace, "I don't think those tough old ladies will let the drakes near them." She felt so tired. Wrung out.

"You don't think so?" Dusty watched the flock feed on leftover scraps.

Then she admitted, out of the blue, "Maybe you're right. Maybe I *was* scared to keep John around. Maybe hanging out with Jake was just one too many strikes against him."

Elly closed her eyes in relief. Dusty *saw!* She let her head rest on the arm Dusty stretched across the back of the seat.

"I wasn't thinking good," Dusty went on. "I shouldn't have done it like that. Next time—well, there won't be a next time. I'll be more careful who I hire."

Someone not gay? Elly wanted to ask as she watched Dusty walk down toward the pond.

She let herself in the house. Dusty hadn't understood after all. But at least she'd admitted she was wrong. "Besides," Elly said to herself as she unpinned her hair and began to wash up for dinner, "she doesn't beat me, she doesn't spend all our money, or drink. She doesn't chases after other women." She smiled at her soapy face in the mirror. "And she makes love like an angel sent down just to pleasure me."

CHAPTER TEN

When the trouble began two weeks later, Dusty seemed to relax more than she had since Valentine's Day. The enemy no longer crouched in the shadows of the river bank somewhere, or lumbered noisily in on a freight, jumping the train at Main Street and slinking along the tracks up Railroad Avenue. The enemy was visible, showing its shape right in their backyard.

"There's a fire at the Queen of Hearts," she told Elly, her words clipped.

Elly lay on the bed, awakened from first sleep, hearing fire, seeing fire, smelling fire. Her throat hurt and she felt a weakness in her legs as she tried to rise. Dusty had swung her long legs out of bed to pull on last night's chinos and her lightweight black turtleneck sweater. Her calm, intent hurry bolstered Elly.

In the car they sat close and Elly willed herself to think they were a unit strong enough to survive anything. She pushed pictures of catastrophes from her mind, as well as her new fears about Dusty's behavior in a crisis. It was a cool night, but she opened the car window for breathing air. When they went over the River it seemed to roar louder than ever.

It was just past midnight when they arrived; the factories slept, their dark windows framed by the ghostly outline of red brick. Dusty parked the Swinger on the wrong side of the street, in front of the church. The world was filled with the sound of idling fire trucks and the River. The fire engine lights swung around and around on their shiny staring faces, and on the Queen of Hearts.

Elly had a glimpse of Father Grimes standing with four neighbors in a grouping which seemed welded together in judgement and reproach. Ever since George Wallace had been shot in May, the town seemed even more closed, more suspicious.

She could taste the hot charred smell in the air. Dusty looked at her as they crossed the street, and smiled a wet-eyed smile. The Queen was standing; the firemen were putting their hoses away. It was going to be all right. Elly swallowed tears of relief.

"It probably wouldn't have amounted to anything anyway," said a tall, dark-coated fireman, chewing gum slowly and deliberately as he watched the other men work. "These dumpsters contain flames pretty well. But one of your neighbors spotted it early and called."

Elly carefully avoided catching Dusty's eyes again, hid the fear and joy she felt. But they stood close, their jacket sleeves touching, and she felt comfort from that slight contact.

"Usually," the fireman went on, "dumpster fires start from emptied ashtrays that smolder a while, then flare; or a cigarette thrown in by a passerby. Other times you get kids looking for excitement, figuring this is a harmless way to get it. I'd say that's what we've got here for two reasons." He seemed to be enjoying his analysis, as if he lectured school children. But Elly was so grateful that the fire was out and no damage done to the diner that she felt comforted by his drone in this pocket of time between night and day, work and home, crisis and calm. Her adrenalin flow was ebbing; everything would be all right.

The fireman continued, counting on sooty fingers, "One: there's no kids at the scene. I *know* there's usually a gang out here till all hours. Two: your neighbors saw someone run away."

Elly glanced toward the priest. Surely *he* couldn't have done this? He was waving his arms as he talked, more animated than she'd ever seen him.

The tall fireman seemed to have noticed where she was looking. "Unless you know of someone who might want to harm you," he said, stumbling over his words, staring at Elly.

Elly shook her head. "No. I had a thought, but that's impossible."

"Father Grimes have something against you?"

"We refused him free food," Dusty answered.

The fireman jotted something down in his notebook. "Priests are human too. It wouldn't be the first—"

Another firefighter came up to them, spoke quickly to the man with the notebook. "We're all set here."

"Come on in for dinner sometime, guys," said Dusty. "On the house."

"Thanks," said the tall firefighter. "But this is our job. We do it whether you like us or hate us, thank us or complain. We do it no matter who, or what, you are." He paused long enough for Elly to wonder if he was telling them it was okay with him, at least professionally, if they were queer. "I'll report this as an arson and it'll be thoroughly investigated."

82

Dusty quickly told him about firing John. Elly looked beyond the dumpster and across the tracks. The three flat narrow houses stood darkened, except for a dim light in one upstairs window. She remembered how her gramma had slept less and less at night. Had it been Nan or Gussie who'd called the fire department?

The engines pulled noisily away. Standing across from the Queen of Hearts, Elly became aware of the River again, like a song of life going on. The neighbors had disappeared.

But Father Grimes was still there, talking to a cop, rubbing his hands. The cop shrugged and got into his cruiser. They watched as his tail lights moved down the street and around the corner. They were alone in the dark with Father Grimes. He approached them, shoulders and head bent forward, hands in fists at his sides. "Good people could have been hurt if your fire had spread," he said.

Dusty and Elly looked at each other. Did he think they'd set the fire? Elly was too stunned to answer.

Dusty shoved her hands into her pockets. "What are you trying to say, mate?"

"You know very well what you are and so does everyone else. I knew something was wrong from the day you took over Sam's place."

Elly felt as if war was being declared.

"Sam sold it to us," said Dusty. "It's ours now. I haven't heard any complaints."

"I have," said the priest. "You came out of the gutter somewhere and into our street, but you won't last. People won't stand for you around innocent children. You'll be back in the gutter with the rest of your kind soon enough." He pivoted and stomped off toward his church.

Dusty's whole body leaned toward him. "Hey, *Father!*" she yelled. Her hand sought Elly's arm, as if to hold herself back. "You won't get rid of us, Father. Just you try!"

The words sounded childish to Elly, but she was glad Dusty had said something. Had stood up to him. Had taken a stand, for both of them, against the fear he inspired. Was this how it had felt to be Dusty in front of the investigators? Out at the factory about to lose her job? No wonder she was so scared.

Elly shivered. She hugged herself, but her teeth began to chatter. Dusty put her jacket over Elly's shoulders and led her to the car.

CHAPTER ELEVEN

Gussie and Nan appeared at the diner the next day at exactly noon. Although the place was crowded, Elly noticed that they waited for a booth on her side. Nan seemed quieter than usual, while Gussie fussed more, unable to choose between soups, then sandwiches, and finally ice cream flavors.

"Thank goodness it's only our little hometown diner," she told Elly, laughing at herself. "When I could take Nan over to Rossi's Bienvenue Restaurant they dance around like they have ants in their pants waiting for an old fusspot like me."

"I don't care if you're slower than cold molasses, sweetie," Elly chided her. "I'd rather wait ten minutes for you than serve half the people who come struttin' in here all rude and messy."

Gussie looked significantly at Nan, then grabbed Elly's hand and pulled her closer.

"We saw the fire last night," she whispered. "Come on over after you get off here. With your honey." She slipped a scrap of paper into Elly's hand, then looked around like a spy in enemy territory.

Nan whispered, "We hope you won't think we're meddling old ladies."

"Not a chance," Elly assured them.

When next she got to the kitchen, she opened the paper and read Gussie's address. Dusty was rubbing mustard into great quantities of chicken. "Getting ready for our new special," she said. "Elly's Mustard Chicken."

Elly clapped her hands together happily. She whispered the invitation.

"We'll be there for sure," Dusty said.

Elly checked on the new dishwasher, Rosa's cousin Hernando, just arrived in the States. He was rattling and scraping and singing too loudly to hear a thing.

Cautious of the ladies' safety, they drove after work away from the diner as if heading home, then turned back and parked near the fire station as if that was where they were going.

It had been a long time since they'd walked down a sidewalk together, visiting friends. Dusty walked on the outside, and Elly resisted the urge to slip her arm through Dusty's even in broad daylight.

"What a funny little place," she said, patting back her hair and repinning it as they drew near.

Made of stone, designed to fit on a narrowing plot of land wedged between the River and the tracks, it looked like a gingerbread house. Nan greeted them at the door and led them to the kitchen where oscillating fans swept breezy swaths across the room. The River flowed outside the open window, louder than the fans. The house smelled open, sunny, clean. One of the kitchen windows overlooked the tracks and had a clear view of the Queen of Hearts. Elly wondered mischievously if there were only one bedroom and whether it held a double bed.

"Do you worry about being so close to the River?" asked Dusty.

Nan shook her head. "I was here for the flood in fifty-five. We were so high it never got near us."

"You'd think," said Gussie, "that they could learn to control the darn thing. After all, we just made our fifth trip to the moon!"

Nan shook her head. "If we get another flood I'm afraid it'll take out the rest of the factories. That'll kill this town better than a superhighway."

"And the Queen of Hearts' business," groaned Dusty.

"Iced tea?" Nan asked. Her front teeth protruded when she let herself smile. "We haven't anything else but sherry."

Dusty spoke a little too emphatically. "Tea is fine. I don't drink."

As Gussie remained standing until the others were seated at the kitchen table, Elly realized that Gussie must once have been nearly as tall as Dusty. Had she been as good-looking? She'd certainly aged handsomely and carried herself with something of a swagger. Gussie caught her curious stare and Elly felt herself blush. Gussie winked. *Why,* thought Elly as she recognized a definite attraction to this woman, *she's butch!*

Gussie cleared her throat. "We feel a certain affinity with you young women," she said in her deep, weathered voice. She wore a crisp short-sleeved men's shirt and shorts over her thin, somewhat bowed legs. "After Mr. Heimer died, Nan here decided she'd prefer my company to staying on alone."

"I've never been sorry," said Nan, face flushed, eyes on her hands which fidgeted with her silverware. She picked up the iced tea and topped off every glass. "I needed Mr. Heimer then, but it's Augusta Brennan I need now."

"Thank goodness," said Gussie.

Elly simply grinned. These women were coming out to them! What if—she realized she'd never even seen lesbians their age before, that she knew of.

Gussie went on. "You can imagine my surprise to find myself still eligible at *this* ripe age. After I got out of the convalescent home I thought I'd be alone the rest of my life, except for Mackey here." A very large cat had lumbered onto Gussie's lap.

Elly glanced at Dusty. She looked positively gleeful and clapped one hand against her thigh, saying, "Hot damn!" Elly jumped up to hug Nan, and then with an extra squeeze, Gussie. The latter patted her bottom and Elly blushed again.

"I like your taste in women," Gussie said to Dusty.

"Me too!" exclaimed Dusty. She scraped her chair closer to the table. "I'm sorry trouble had to bring us together," she said in that formal manner she put on when she was embarrassed. "But I'm very pleased to know you both."

Pale green curtains lifted as the fans' breezes touched them. Over a carefully mended cotton tablecloth printed with bright baskets of flowers, Gussie and Nan smiled at each other. Nan rose to serve big bowls of blueberries over homemade shortcake. Elly imagined herself years hence, retired, leisured, preparing meals for Dusty, sitting in a kitchen with new friends. Dusty met her eyes and nodded, as if to confirm her vision of their future. Suddenly they had a long, long future!

As they ate, Gussie began to talk. "There was something that kept me awake last night. My age, for one," she said, laughing, hands folded over her little belly. "I was restless, got up to go to the bathroom a few times, woke Nan a half dozen times snuggling against her. Then we both came wide awake. There'd been a crash and another sound over by the diner.

We rushed to the window. The first thing I noticed was how dark it was by the diner. I called Nan over, but she's had cataracts and can see less than me. Eventually I made out a form, then another. They'd thrown back the cover on your big metal garbage bin and smashed your floodlight."

"El had me replace that today."

"Good. Then one of them set fire to some paper and flung it into the bin. I could see the glow growing inside and called the firehouse."

"Did you recognize them?" Dusty leaned over her folded arms.

"Only by style. Neighborhood toughs. The ones who make snide remarks when I pass the grocery store wearing bermuda shorts."

Nan patted her hand. "You always look dapper to me," she said.

"That's all that matters to me. I've never dressed for a man in my life and I certainly don't intend to begin now."

Dusty laughed and stuck out her hand. Gussie shook it firmly, laughing too.

"So John's taking his revenge," Dusty said, leaning back till her chair teetered on its back legs.

"John?" asked Gussie.

"The dishwasher I just fired. He's part of that gang."

"No," Gussie said. "No, it wasn't him. It was two of the harder ones. I could tell by their walks."

"Leon?" asked Elly.

Gussie shook her head. "His grandmother lives next door. I probably would have recognized him. He's so big he stands out."

"John must have put them up to it," suggested Elly.

Dusty's voice was worried. "I'm not sure it's that simple now."

"Why else would they bother you?" asked Nan quietly.

Elly nervously pulled a cigarette from her purse. "Do you mind?" she asked Nan and Gussie. Elly cupped Dusty's hand, taking comfort from its strength, as Dusty lit the cigarette.

"Listen," said Dusty. "Elly and I have talked about this. If it was retaliation for letting John go, I think it would have happened right away. And come directly from John, with maybe a couple of cronies. But two weeks—this seems planned. It could be a combination of John's anger and his gossip about us, about what he's seen at the Queen of Hearts. And what passed between him and Jake."

They explained the men's attraction to each other and repeated Father Grimes' harangue.

"If Leon works the gang up to hysteria about queers because of his own fears about himself," said Dusty, "they could make life miserable for us. At the least."

"And at the worst?" asked Gussie.

"Drive our customers away."

Gussie slammed a fist on the table. "They won't drive *me* away."

Nan added, "And we've been telling our senior group about how good your food is."

"Thank you," said Dusty with a smile, "but between that poor excuse for a priest and the pious neighborhood families, your friends may feel very lonely in the Queen of Hearts."

Nan was fidgeting again. "I've lived here for thirty-five years," she said. Though she appeared to be younger than Gussie, her voice had a quaver to it that made her sound older. "That priest hasn't done his flock much good. Before he came here there must have been two to three hundred people going to services; you couldn't find a place to park. This was before they built the big church out River Road and gave it to the fellow who used to be the Father here. As soon as they brought in this Father Grimes even the most loyal of the Railroad Avenue parish began to drift away. And there was some sort of scandal a few years back; he was behind some dirty work the street gang was up to. Mr. Heimer was so sick then, poor thing, I hadn't my wits about me enough to follow the news."

Elly and Dusty were holding hands across the table. "Funny painted lady," Elly said. "Our Queen of Hearts. How did she get in the middle of this long story of hate? How could anyone want to kill her? Last night I couldn't help but notice how her red stripes are like ties, red ribbons tying us to her. She seemed even more precious, attacked."

"She's not just a diner, El, is she?" Dusty asked. "Last night, to me, she looked like a ship at sea, proud and built for waves and storms."

"Then," asked Gussie, "you're sailing her more than just to make a living, aren't you?"

Elly met Dusty's eyes. She willed herself to believe in Dusty's strength again.

"Yeah," answered Dusty. "I don't know what it is, but we have something important to do in our little restaurant. I can feel it."

CHAPTER TWELVE
Dusty's Tales

Look at me, Rosa, flipping meat patties and lining up strips of bacon like I haven't got a care in the world. I don't, do I? Nothing's happened since the fire a month ago except name-calling and a little graffiti out back. So why do I feel like there's something out there, circling, closing in for the kill? Should I give in and feed the priest? Somehow I don't think that ever would have helped, much less now. Maybe I should offer some peace deal to the gang like Kissinger would?

Trouble, Rosa. You can't live dreams without trouble. First there was Dad—and he left. Then there was Mom's diner—and she abandoned it, and me. Then the Navy—dry land and dead romance. Rita—everything I'd come to need, as long as we drank. Now Elly and the Queen of Hearts—who knows what'll happen? Elly's mad because I fired John, mad because I'm too damn tired to do anything when we get home, mad because Rita's started hanging around here. But I guess I'm like the River, I keep going on and on, trying over and over.

Even when I looked the Navy square in the eye after I learned what it wasn't, I didn't give up. I stayed in another two years, hanging onto my memories of the stories I'd read as a kid. Stories of wharves, of sailors coming off ships and being sucked into the crowded waterfront dives. The drinking, the fighting, the roaring of sea shanties, the women. My lusty romantic imagination swarmed with exotic uniforms and good times. Maybe men really do live like that, but women sailors do most of their drinking in cocktail lounges just like civilian ladies. Who could raise hell anyway in one of those damned regulation skirts?

Jeeze, Rosa, sometimes I wish we had a liquor license. Wouldn't it be nice to sit down at the end of the day with a beer before I went home? Shoot the breeze with Earleen. Relax. I miss it, that's for sure.

I don't miss the Navy. But then Navy was still a glamorous word for me and when I finally gave up my binges with Chief Lil and her cohorts I got what glamor I could from it. In my last six months of enlistment, I used my leaves to head for town. Sooner or later, I figured, I'd find what I was hungry for—skirt or not.

Of course, we had to be careful. Women on their own even in San Diego weren't as commonplace as now. And in uniform we were watched. The fifties were no picnic, believe me. It was hard for a group of high-spirited girls to go to a bar in Coronado, the closest watering hole, and keep the military men away. Just like it was hard to eat in the mess and not have some dumb guy stick love notes in your mashed potatoes. It didn't get any easier to hold back my smile when I was head over heels with the femmy young seaman across the table from me who wore my favorite perfume and ran one smooth nyloned foot halfway up my calf now and then. There was nothing more frustrating in the world than to go out with a "straight" girl who was begging to be turned and have no place to dance, no place for the in-between mating rituals that led to the hotel door. So more and more my only release, also totally against regs, but a lot more common, was to get drunk.

But, hell, hadn't my life been a series of challenges just like this? Isn't it still? "Hey, Dusty," Life calls to me. "You wanna be a dyke? Handle *this* one if you can!" It takes I don't know what to stay gay sometimes: stubbornness, guts, a rebel streak.

So I learned how to leave the base, and the island, all innocence, like whichever girl I was going with was just sightseeing with me.And I learned how to sidle unnoticed through a Navy town, to find a place to stay that offered privacy so no one would notice or report us if we were locked in a room for only two of the twenty-four hours I'd paid for.

If it wasn't for the whiskey and soda I might have noticed what an awful life I lived then. But at least it was still predictable. In the Navy, even getting past the rules was an unchanging game you could learn. I got a charge out of becoming an expert at outwitting the authorities, outsmarting the straights. Gay may be hard, but I thought it also made me a damn sight better than anyone else.

It's still true today. Half the time I feel like a turd because I'm queer. The other half, especially when I'm drinking, I feel sure I'm superior. Of course, I'd be happier just to be me, openly, like I'm not a skeleton rattling in my own closet, but that's impossible.

So in the Navy I'd get all smug about breaking the rules. Was it worth it? If the straight world had set out to stunt me, it couldn't have done a better job.

Superior! Sure, once free—the door locked, hiding us, the alarm set so we wouldn't overstay, a bottle open so we could relax fast and keep it light—I could touch my lovers. I never knew I was bypassing the rest of the dance: love and trust. It never occurred to me that I might deserve to love by the light of day. My solution was to blame the girl, not the world, to drop this relationship that was not worthy of respect in anyone's eyes.

And listen to me now, Rosa. Haven't I learned a thing? I still let the straight world make things so hard I surrender anything I've got going for me. Can I keep it all? Elly and the Queen? It's like I spend my life walking a tightrope, hugging everything I care about close to me. But always blaming what I'm holding for unbalancing me. Ready to jettison it all to keep from falling. Isn't there a way I can get off the tightrope and live without the terror of falling?

I finally exploded. My cruising buddy Les, the crazy one who later blew it for our whole crowd, worked in the laundry. She had a scheme to smuggle out a couple of men's uniforms and go out on the town drinking, maybe picking up girls. Sometimes fear itself drives me into a berserk kind of courage, a wildcat challenge to the world. This was such a time.

We rode the Nickle Snatcher, the ferry that went over to San Diego, and checked into a hotel where we could change. Then we took a cab past the neon signs: rose-colored, turquoise, blinking gold, to the seedy part of town. It was a summer night, but damp and foggy. We must have combed our hair ten times each. Les was cute, small and trim-looking in her clean white razor-pressed uniform. At the base she wore her hair in a Dutch bob with bangs. I'd smuggled her a jar of vegetable oil and she'd slicked her hair back tonight into waves and a ducktail.

95

The women's bar was dark and crowded, a hole in the wall on a scruffy street. No military personnel came here, it was too dangerous. Fans were the only ventilation and they turned real slow, as if the fog and the cigarette smoke had combined to create smog that was like sludge. There was a mildewed, sour smell, like the clothing section of a second-hand store. We lounged on stools, our whites crisp as fresh air, checking out the girls, ordering drink after drink. I was desperate to hide my terror of the place from Les, from the bar, from me. Les was jumpy too. The more we watched, and were watched, the move obvious it got that this was not a good-time place, at least not tonight. My pennywhistle was in my back pocket, but I could more easily picture myself playing into the base PA system at three AM. Maybe it was the weather making me so cranky—I could see half the couples were fighting and the other half seemed to be cutting in on one another's partners. The liquor was nasty and watered down, more overpriced than usual. Our uniforms felt more and more like a bad idea. We got noticed, but not welcomed; the military police could bust in there any minute, and this was the kind of bar whose shadowy patrons, like people in a crowd scene in a second-rate movie, could afford even less than most gays to clash with the cops. I began to see us in their eyes: two callow, good-time butches in peacock drag, off limits, asking for trouble.

One woman seemed to welcome us, though. Her butch sent her up to the bar for a drink, and when the femme brushed against me with pointy, uplifted breasts, the butch winked as I looked over. Oh shit, I thought, the last thing I want is trouble. When they got up to dance I saw they were dressed in bargain store clothes, the femme's set off with tinsel-like jewelry. She had a tarnished air about her, like one of those mock wedding cakes left till it was dusty and faded in the window of that bakery down on the back of Morton River's Main Street. Her makeup was thick, but I could still see the unhealthy color, the dark circled eyes like her lover's.

After a while the butch came up for another round, squeezed beside me and when I turned down her invitation to join them, bought me a drink anyway. I thanked her, and not wanting to be rude, made conversation about the unending fog. She was missing a couple of teeth in a smile that pulled the left side of her face into a snarl. Her clothes were men's, or boys', overlarge on her scrawny frame. Her shaking hands lit an unfiltered Camel. When our drinks came she slapped a bill on the counter with a macho flair that made me suspect it was the last of her money. "Hey, sailor," she said. Her voice was a kind of natural whisper, and she talked ghetto black though she was stark white. She gave me chills as bad as the fog did. "You want to buy some reefer?" she asked.

The chill turned to distaste. I was too drunk to gracefully dismiss her and also too drunk to think clearly. Dope was for criminals back then, for the scum of the earth. I was as respectable as a queer could be—wasn't I? The thought came into my mind, enormous, as thoroughly convincing as alcohol thoughts usually are, that this was where my queerness, no matter what I wanted, would lead me. Just like Father Grimes said, Rosa. Do I still, somewhere inside me, believe what I thought that night? I told the butch no thanks, making my tone as rough as hers. I was sober enough not to show my shock. This was her territory and I'd let myself in for such an offer.

She leaned closer. Her breath smelled like she badly needed dental work. "Some smack?"

The term was so new to me I didn't get it at first. "Not tonight," I said, all innocence.

"A girl?"

I looked at her. "A girl?" I asked. Of course, I wanted a girl. Wasn't that why I was there? "Who?" I asked, stupid with drink.

"Jeanine there," said the butch with a jab of her thumb. "She thinks you're cute."

"Jeanine?" I repeated, turning to look at her femme's brassy smile. Weren't they together? Hadn't they acted like they were? I looked back at the butch and noticed her eyes for the first time. They looked strange. Glassy. A sweat had broken out on her forehead and her complexion was sicklier than ever. What else had the Health Officer lectured us about besides homosexuality? It clicked. I realized what smack was and turned from her to hide my confusion. I downed my drink and signaled for another. All I'd really wanted was a peaceful night of getting high.

"Twenty-five for the night. The whole night. In advance." She winked again. "She'll take you round the world, you'll see."

I must have gone into some kind of shock at that point. What did she mean, around the world? and did women really sell their bodies to other women? Did *I* look like someone who would buy a woman? Did that mean this runny-nosed squirt was a pimp, selling her own lover so they could get a high?

Like air fills a balloon, moral outrage filled me. There I was, in full drag, in the dive of my dreams, high on my own drug, alcohol, half-hoping I would meet a girl for some casual sex—and I was angry that this woman thought I was like her. I wasn't, was I? The priest isn't right, is he? Will I end up the kind of monster my stepfather said I would? Is that what I hear when Leon and the gang taunt me?

My tears were too close for comfort. I concentrated on the butch sipping her drink, waiting for my answer, looking evil and ridiculous and vulnerable all at once. What had brought her to this? Was it being gay? Had she started out like me? No, I told myself, controlling my tears by telling myself what a picture I'd make, big Don Juan Dusty Reilly crying in her whiskey.

Yet, my mind went on, was I any better, the way I was using the Chief and the other officers? Or seducing the baby booties fresh from basic training and dumping them when I started feeling itchy? In a flash, as I stared at the tired lines on that woman's face, I saw myself as I really was. Another human being just like her, making it the best I could waist deep in my own desperate, selfish, fearful needs. But I couldn't face the truth of me any more than I could keep looking at the butch's face. Her face was breaking down before my eyes, falling apart in a naked plea. How could I get rid of that vision of her, and of me in her? I did the only thing I knew to do. I downed my drink. And shifted into that place that made me smile. No more thinking, no more fear. My body knew what to do.

I'd *show* her I wasn't like her. I swung round on my stool and hit her with all the anger I could muster. But in my haze of drunkenness I didn't even manage to deck her. She ducked and fell against the woman on the next stool.

The butch became like a fighter whose face had been splashed with cold water. The sad lines disappeared, the skin tightened, paleness turned to angry red and she seemed to come to with the blow, remember who she was, that she had some self respect left, too. The swing I'd expected when Jeanine had flirted came now. It had all taken about thirty seconds from her last words. I found myself, tailbone bruised, sitting upright under my barstool.

Les was always ready for trouble. Quick and wiry, she was at my side, and at the butch with a bevy of sharp jabs.

The femme, now an enraged defender, clawed them apart.

I'd stood and watched it all, my head humming with liquor, my smile muscles stretched tight, just as if I hadn't started the fight. The bar had come alive, taken sides despite the fact that the others knew nothing about what was going on. The persistent fog, the tight-pressed throng, the frustration of being gay, all came out in curses and blows. Just like in the movies, the fight seemed to take on a life of its own, to control the women, to compel them to insult one another, to hit and push.

I don't know, maybe they'd all been wanting at one another for a long time and I'd given them a chance at last. Maybe it was part of a night's entertainment. For me, it was another glorious dream lived: I was a sailor fighting in a drunken brawl. But this wasn't what I'd imagined at all.

I found Les' eyes. My head cleared when I saw her bloody nose, how scared she looked. How would we explain bruises, breaks? We both looked toward the door and started shoving our way out along with a few other women who weren't interested in trouble.

"The sailors!" we heard when we reached the door. "Get the sailors!"

We flung ourselves outside and tore off as fast as we could, racing along the side streets and alleyways Les knew so well, outrunning the barwomen and, I hoped, my visions of myself—the monster I never wanted to see again.

I ran, taking in great gulps of cooling night air, my head more and more clear. I was high again, but not drunk. We slowed to a job, a lope, a walk, then stopped and leaned against a warehouse close to the docks. I looked up at the stars jiggling overhead, and realized I hadn't even gotten to dance. Grinning a real grin, I grabbed by buddy Les, hugged her, laughed like a fool and danced her around. We whooped, on that dark empty street, spinning, then moved like a couple of vaudeville dancers down another dark street, singing some loud pleased song, swinging around lampposts, leapfrogging hydrants. This part of town was empty of people at night and the world was our own. We were free of the Navy, free of that tawdry underworld, free for the moment of our scared bottled-up selves.

Eventually we started to deflate and turned toward the hotel. Quieted, we walked briskly through a crowded residential district that looked like home. It felt good to be there.

Home. I'd felt it pulling at me ever since I'd left and thought myself mad to miss my nightmare there. But I couldn't keep living like this. At that moment I was certain I wouldn't be a Navy lifer.

Home. I tasted the word and it was not, for once, bitter. Because of tonight? Partly. But I also found myself thinking not of my stepfather's house, but of the Valley itself as home. The grand green Valley and the Morton River rolling, streaming, cascading into it, powerful and certain where it belonged, where it was going. Would I ever be as sure as the River? It needed no one else's rules and had found its way safely longer than all the generations of Valley people. As a kid I'd walked its banks, swum its waters, watched its ways. Now that I was grown, did it have more to teach me?

Jeeze, I could use another high like that, the kind that clears away the cobwebs and makes the road ahead clear. I knew without a doubt that if I came home and lived a respectable life I'd leave the monster behind. If I followed all the rules I wouldn't turn out like that butch in the bar. I'd be able to prove that gay and gutter weren't the same.

I came home and climbed out onto this tightrope where I'd be safe and above it all.

But how in hell do I stay up here, Rita?

CHAPTER THIRTEEN

It was a hot August day. The air conditioner had broken down twice, but was working at the moment. Dusty was off for the day and Elly was just as glad. One day her lover would act like everything was fine, coming out of her kitchen to joke with the customers and play the jukebox; the next day she'd be listless, dispirited, as if it exhausted her to put on such a cheery front. Elly never knew what to expect.

Bandy-legged Sam, the former owner, was cooking. He maintained the same exuberance and aggressive friendliness with the customers that he'd always shown. Twice a week, his high spirits exorcised the shadow of fear that hung over the Queen of Hearts.

It was that slow time between breakfast and lunch. Rosa was handling the customers, Elly was tallying vendor bills and half listening to one of Sam's stories from his days as a cook in the Navy.

"Hiya, Admiral!" called Grace as Seeker led her through the door.

Sam looked up and said, "Two eggs over easy, rye bread and ham with a side of grits comin' up!"

"Grits!" cried Grace. "You're making grits now?"

"He's just teasin' you," Elly said. She looked over at Rosa for the wave that would tell her Rosa could handle it if Elly took a break now.

"Come on to our booth," Elly told Grace, dumping the ashtrays and wiping the table. Rosa hummed by, Hernando stacked dishes, the few customers murmured and laughed. Someone was playing *Sweet Georgia Brown* on the jukebox; the song always gave her a lift.

"You know," said Elly, glad to have Grace to talk to, "listening to Sam makes me understand why Dusty's so mad at the Navy. He got to do everything she wanted to."

Grace, all in white, drummed her fingers on the edge of the table.

"You nervous or something?" asked Elly.

Grace's face held a high color. A smile kept slipping across her lips and disappearing, as if she could catch it and hide it away.

"Grace?"

"Did you hear the news?" Grace asked, her tone light and offhand. "George McGovern is running for president. Maybe we'll get some sanity back in the government!"

"Grace," said Elly sternly. "You're not tellin' me something."

She could see the very deep breath Grace took. "Jo Ellen came over last night."

103

Elly felt flickers of both excitement and fear for her friend. "And?" she prodded.

Grace's smile would be banished no more. It gleefully pushed up her cheeks till they lifted her dark glasses.

"Somethin' tells me you went and *did* it last night."

Grace nodded.

"And only three months after the first date. Come on, Gracey-girl, I want to hear it *all*!"

A great ray of sun streamed from the back windows down the aisle and lit Grace from behind. She spoke as if picking and choosing words worthy of her experience. Her voice, breathy and slow, sounded as if she was speaking from a dream.

"It wasn't like a man at all. There was so much holding and breathing together, asking each other if we were okay. She was familiar to me; I knew what her body was saying." She paused, then asked shyly, "Does it sound like we were doing it right?"

Elly laughed. "Sounds to me like you did it exactly right. Those are the parts I love best." She lit a cigarette. "Not that I'd give up any little bit of it. Tell me more!"

"You mean details?" Grace's shocked expression faded to embarrassment. "I couldn't—I wouldn't know how to describe all those things."

Elly smiled and took Grace's hand. "Well, it did you good, sweetie, that's as plain as the hand before my face."

Rosa brought Grace's breakfast, Elly's sandwich, a pot of mustard and some Coke. Elly noticed that Leon had swaggered in and swung himself onto a stool not far from the booth.

Grace's face had gone dreamy again. "She's so beautiful. Every place I ran my hand there was another long smooth curve. I know just how much Jake must have wanted John."

"Shh," she said, whispering who was nearby. Then she continued in a low tone, "Look where that led, anyway, Jake and John. And I'm still worried about Jo Ellen being married."

Grace washed down a home fry. "She's made it real clear that I'm an affair. She and her husband are trying to have an open marriage."

d"Just don't you get caught when it snaps shut in your face tight as a turtle's mouth."

Grace laughed. "I'm not expecting much, honey. I just wanted *out*. Don't fret it. Has Dusty's gloom and doom finally got to you? Anything happen here last night?"

"The daily question," Elly replied, twisting a lock of hair. "So far, so good. At least with the neighborhood."

"What else could go wrong?"

"Rita."

"Uh-oh."

"Dusty finally agreed to go to dinner with her last night."

"And?"

"And came home in a good mood."

"Is that so terrible, honey?" It was Grace who pressed Elly's hand now.

"It's somethin' I can't do, Grace—put Dusty in a good mood. She's hardly ever interested in anything, even what you did last night. What if she runs away from the diner and me? And back to safe secure borin' old Rita and the bottle? Just a week ago she said she never wanted to see her again!"

"El, are you letting it eat you up?"

"No, but . . ." Even Sam's once-a-week perfect ham tasted like wadded up paper towel in her mouth. "Of *course* I am! Why *shouldn't* I be? I don't see a thing wrong with jealousy, damn it. It's like having a big red flag that says DANGER! Shoot, Rita's dangerous—to Dusty and to me. And I'm helpless. I've just got to wait this thing out. Dusty could be with her right now."

Elly caught herself waiting for advice, sympathy, but Grace only nodded, said nothing. Maybe Grace's silence was her wisdom. Elly was stuck with her own pain on this one.

Sam loudly greeted the mailman, then strode the length of the diner, walking as if it were a deck, to present Elly with the mail. "It's all yours!" he said. "And I don't miss those bills one darn bit."

"A bill," said Elly. "Another bill. An ad. What's this?"

Sam had returned to the kitchen. Two early lunch customers arrived. Leon still sat, but was no longer hunched over. Elly had the feeling he was listening.

She opened the envelope. "I spoke too soon," she said to Grace, feeling as if she had taken a blow to the gut.

"What's wrong?"

She read aloud. "*We know about you two. We don't want your kind around here.*"

"Is it signed?" whispered Grace.

"No," said Elly, weak with fear. She passed the letter to Grace who ran her fingertips over its surface. "It's those damned scary-looking cut-out letters. Oh, God, Grace." She put her face in her hands. "Who would do this just because we're gay? That priest? His church? What harm do they think we'd do anyone?"

She'd forgotten all about Leon. He got up just then, clapped some change down on the counter and swaggered out, tugging at the front of his jeans as he walked. She watched out the window as two more gang members met him across the street. The three slapped hands and walked around to the back of the rectory. Had he been waiting for this?

Though Grace hadn't uttered a word, Elly answered, "You're right. It's just a bunch of kids trying to find someone weaker than they are. And it's not even them I'm afraid of. It's my own lover."

She wiped tears away with her apron. "I don't know *how* she'll take this. What if she falls apart? Is that selfish of me, being afraid I'll have to hold this life of ours together? It's been like coming in out of the rain for me." She could hear her own voice growing strident, her accent getting thicker and thicker. Rosa was looking over to see what was wrong, probably wondering why Elly wasn't relieving her for lunch. "Grace, I need Dusty. I need her to stay together for me."

Rosa hummed up busily, retying the red scarf at her neck. "I won't let that postman back in here if he brought you bad news," she said, then picked up the letter. "So that's why that damned *varón* was in here," she said. "Sneaky little cowards, aren't they? Sending mystery notes." She laughed. "You're not letting them get to you, are you?"

She felt ashamed of her fears. First the jealousy, now this. Was her world really so fragile? A challenge in her voice, she asked, "How can you be so sure it's the kids?"

"Of course, it's them," Rosa said. "No one in their right minds would want to chase a good restaurant out. They're just troublemakers."

"But" she started to reply, then sighed. Straight people, no matter how sympathetic, didn't understand that it really could be dangerous to be queer. Didn't even want to know about it. She took a deep breath. It wasn't Rosa's battle.

She smiled at Grace, squeezed her arm. Dear brave woman to come out so late in life, to take such a risk for love. She stood, took a quarter from her pocket and poked *Sweet Georgia Brown* onto the jukebox. "It's time for your lunch, sweetie," she told Rosa in a normal voice. Propelling her into the booth, she said, "Keep Grace company while I get your sandwich." She turned back to joke, "And you all better pay those damned bills while you're there, will you?"

She took an order, cleared a table, all the while feeling desperate inside. Leaving wasn't an optionshe knew that as well as she'd ever known anything. She was a Hunnicutt; she'd fight to the end. Slowly, the everyday tasks calmed her. *Just let Dusty be home tonight*, she prayed as she worked. I can get through this if every church in the world condemns us. If we just stay together.

CHAPTER FOURTEEN

No hurricane had hit New England for years. At dawn the sky had a murky look which gave the red brick of the factories a yellowish cast. As Elly and Dusty drove in toward town the air was so moist that fat raindrops fell now and then on the windshield, unattached to any shower.

"It's spooky," Elly said.

"Exciting, though," Dusty countered. "I remember hurricanes when I was a kid. Branches, leaves, electric lines across the streets so you couldn't go anywhere even if you were crazy enough to try. Families kind of huddled and close—us against the world. We're due for one."

"I was too far inland. It's my first." She was nervous, but Dusty seemed so calm about it, seemed even to feel affection toward the storm.

"What the hell, lady. You have everything else hitting you this year, you can handle Mother Nature."

"I have my limits," Elly said. She knew Dusty had seen Rita a few more times, but so far had always come home at night.

At the Queen of Hearts, Elly kept tuning the radio from one station to another, as if the various weather forecasters would bring reassurance, not the panic that hooked their listeners. Outside, the trees grew more and more frenzied in the eerie light of day. They flailed their branches as if to signal distress—which of them would succumb to the storm, which bow to its windy strength without breaking?

The customers chattered nervously or strained to hear the radio. Each had a different worry: this one's boat moored up the River, that one's elderly mother staying alone through it with her cats. Elly studied each customer—second nature now—for signs they knew of the anonymous letters.

A new letter had arrived the day before, the sixth in six weeks. Dusty had sat on the couch in their house reading and rereading the letters as if in their text she'd find a way to silence the senders. They'd put the first five in a bundle and given them to the analytical fireman as evidence. Finally Dusty had said, after three hours of silent depression, that it could be worse—let them stick to paper threats. This new letter felt like the hurricane's early threatening winds: there was a chance the impulse would exhaust itself into a tropical storm.

Business was slow. By two o'clock most people were not venturing out. Rosa went home when word came that schools were closing. Elly, ever alert to the howling winds, lingered in the kitchen whenever she could.

Dusty was cleaning behind the grill. "This is the first day in weeks I've been able to do this. Night crew tries, but it's not Earleen's strong point." There was a gentle fever in her eyes as she looked at Elly, as if the storm had released her from everyday worries. "I love this kind of work. I'm so glad you're good at handling the front. By myself, I'd run us out of business in a week."

A polka played on the jukebox, its rhythms strangely harmonious with the storm. Elly whirled between the counters in the kitchen while Dusty laughed and turned to grab her.

"I knew you'd get over being scared of this weather," Dusty said.

"There *is* a kind of high it gives you. Like a holiday. Or," she whispered, tugging away from Dusty's hands around her wrists, "the kind of storm that takes *you* when you've got yourself into a passion."

Dusty's face was soft, her eyes downright hot-looking. "I could grab you right now, lady."

Elly laughed and pulled away. With the Queen empty of customers, she went out onto the back stoop. The sky had grown even darker. At the narrow little house across the tracks there were no clothes on the line, but Gussie was rescuing the plants in their brightly colored pots and handing them in to Nan. Waving, Elly tried to shout to them over the wind, but neither woman saw or heard her.

She felt frightened again. It was only she and Dusty now, cut off from everyone by the riotous winds, as if this was some kind of test of what they had together. Could all her anxiety just be new relationship blues? Maybe things weren't all that bad and the buoyancy of new love had simply hit its first waves. At some point you had to realize that even your greatest love is only a stranger become dear.

She wished she could be at home, but at the same time realized that someone might need the Queen of Hearts. Restless, she wandered to the front. She'd already cleaned every ketchup bottle twice, and all the sugar containers, the salt and pepper shakers, the ashtrays. If no customers came she'd have to begin polishing the ancient jukebox selectors, with their intricate, fan-like grooving. When she saw Jake's little red Beetle pull up she could have crowed for joy. Family at last.

The car seemed to glow in the dark moist air. She watched Jake, so blond he glowed, too, walk jauntily toward the diner, poking a furled umbrella at the ground with each step. Rudy, his ex, was beside him. The wind came at them from behind, pushing, but the rain had let up for a few minutes.

"Am I ever glad to see you," she cried, hugging Jake tightly.

Jake squeezed back. "Nice weather we're having," he said, wiping her lipstick from his cheek.

She had the urge to hide him from Dusty's sight to keep the peace. But Rudy, balding, slender, batted his eyelashes over Jake's shoulder from the vestibule. There would be no hiding the two of them when they got going.

"I wasn't sure," said Jake as he removed his rain jacket, "if you girls had it in for me. Rosa told me John's friends have been hassling you."

"Nerds," said Rudy, rolling his eyes. "I *love* your decorating scheme. What did you do, hire a couple of designers who hit their stride in forty-two?"

"*Rudy*, this is an original," Elly protested.

"Then I shouldn't run down to Marcy's and redo it in Art Deco before it's too too chic?"

"You might start a revival," said Jake. "I can see the headlines in the Upton Herald now—*Aging Barkeep Brings Back the Bad Old Days*."

"This place shouldn't be a restaurant. It should be a museum. A relic."

Elly poured them coffee. "I take it you like the place."

"It's perfect. Not a tacky tile out of place. And your uniform says it all. You've always had a good touch."

Jake had settled at the counter. She watched him exchange a silent wave with Dusty. But Rudy pushed right through the swinging doors for a hug.

"Is this what happens to people who buy businesses out here in the Valley?" Elly heard him ask. "They vanish off the face of the earth?"

Dusty laughed and clapped him on the shoulder. "If it isn't the Grand Dame of Upton."

"No! No!" Rudy shrieked. "Don't touch me with those gross paws. You look like a chimney sweep, not a cook!"

Elly turned away to greet two soaking wet firemen. "Guess the rain started again, fellas," she said as she set down her cigarette to serve coffee.

One laughed. "We thought we'd come over for a bite *before* it got any worse." They took their coffees to the engine company's customary booth at the far end of the diner.

"Looks like you two need to dig in for the ;ight," she told Jake.

"I have my trusty umbrella."

"Sweetie, if you think that thing's going to do you any good in this wind—"

"I can fend off falling branches with it," Jake suggested.

"So long as you don't carry it open. The wind will whisk you off to—"

"Emerald City? How marvelous!"

She cut him a slice of lemon meringue pie. "On the house," she said, "if you give me the scoop on John."

Dusty slid two plates through the window and came out wiping her hands. Elly delivered the firemen's order.

"I have a feeling it's going to be a long night," said Dusty, leaning with arms folded against the milk machine. The diner itself seemed to tremble as wind shook the Queen of Hearts sign. "So where have you been, Jacob?" Her eyes were narrow behind their glasses.

"He was about to begin," Elly explained, trying to keep tension from her voice.

"Begin what?" quipped Rudy. "A collision with a Mack calorie?"

Jake ignored him. He'd asked for chocolate ice cream and was spooning it over the meringue.

"Yuk," said Elly.

"What can I tell you," Jake said. "I have str-r-r-ange tastes." He was looking toward Rudy.

"Like dishwashers?" Dusty inquired in a sarcastic tone.

Jake looked sharply at her. "John won't be a dishwasher forever."

"Why?" asked Dusty, her expression unchanging, her tone baiting, "do they use paper plates in prison?"

"Oomph!" said Rudy.

Elly held her breath.

"She's right," Jake said, patting his beard with a napkin as Elly whisked the empty plate away. "He was a little shit. I knew it the first time I laid eyes on him. But it only weakened my resistance."

Dusty unfolded her arms and disappeared into the kitchen. Elly worried, but Dusty returned with four red milk crates and made herself and Elly seats behind the counter. A major gust of wind made Elly jump. "It's okay, lady," said Dusty. "We're safe here."

How could Elly tell her that her fear came from Dusty's coiled anger at Jake?

"What a gentleman," said Rudy. "You never brought *me* a chair."

Jake smiled, cackling in a wicked way. "Who needs a chair when he's on his stomach?"

"Come on, you Yankee fairies, I want to hear this story," Elly said. She leaned across the counter, chin in her hands.

114

Jake wiggled a bit on his stool, asked for more coffee. "I may as well," he said. "You always get your way in the end, El, I can tell." He took a sip of coffee. "Not two days after I joined the gym, who should show up there."

"Surprise!" said Elly, in a mocking voice.

Jake glared at her. "A very pleasant surprise," he said with an innocent expression. "In spite of his terrible body, poor boy. His chest is so close to sunken you don't need a treasure map." He timed his pause for laughter. "So I showed him how I built mine up."

"Yeah," said Rudy, "doing pushups over a prone body."

Ignoring him, Jake went on, "One thing just seemed to lead to another, and before I knew it, he was telling me his whole life story, week by week. It's hard growing up gay in a tough neighborhood like this."

"He *is* gay then," Dusty stated, as if that settled something.

"Honey, that boy trades his fair body for safety on the mean streets of Morton River. He said it started when he was about ten. He's gone from one gang leader to the next as they were drafted or married. It was always kept quiet, never talked about in the group, but he was one perk of the guy willing to be toughest, willing to risk his neck stealing a car for joy riding, copping drugs. And John got the picture right away. If he wanted to be accepted, not tormented and ostracized—and he worshipped these tough guys—he'd cooperate. But with this leader he admitted to himself that he was enjoying it and fell hard."

"*Leon*?" said Elly. "How could anyone love Leon?"

"So he cried on your shoulder about the juvenile delinquent he's in love with?" sneered Dusty.

"The boy needed love along with all that sex. He always hoped for more than he got. Of course, the leaders knew the rules. Men might do sex with a john, but they sure as hell didn't love one."

"And you were a kindred soul," Dusty said more kindly.

"He hadn't seen me anywhere but here, acting straight." He caught Rudy's shocked look. "Relatively. He hadn't known a gay man could have muscles, wear suits. He thought to love men he'd have to act like a drag queen. He sensed I was gay, but I looked like a normal man to him."

Rudy made a sound as if to stifle a giggle.

Jake looked up from his empty plate to Elly. "This is hard work, you know."

She moved to the pie server, willing to indulge him. So far Dusty seemed to be taking it in calmly.

"How could you expect me to resist him, Dusty?"

Dusty didn't answer; she was looking out the window. Up the street, Leon and some gang members were slashing at one another with fallen branches. The storm had stirred them, too. The rain came ever heavier, as if bucket after bucket were being flung against the windows. Elly hoped the gang wouldn't get it into their heads to shelter at the diner.

"I am sorry," Jake said finally. "About the fire, the hate mail. I really don't think John's engineering it, though. I think it would have happened anyway. You know how popular gays are in Morton River Valley. In the world, for that matter."

Dusty's laugh was more a grunt of disgust. "So he's in their clutches," she scoffed, "forced to clip words from newspapers—"

"—at scissorpoint," finished Rudy.

Jake said nothing for a moment. The gang stood at the top of the church's steps under a shallow overhang, looking toward the diner.

"Somebody," he said, staring across the street, "or all of them, beat the shit out of John."

The collective gasp was louder than the storm.

"But *why*?" asked Elly. This gang had seemed merely mean, menacing. Beating one of their own now made them downright dangerous.

"They found out he was meeting me at the gym."

The wind and rain pummeled the windows; there was a loud crack. They rushed to booths to watch a huge old tree shed a branch. Twigs lay across the red beetle and the Swinger, leaves were plastered against the windshields. Behind the shelter of the back of a booth, Dusty's arm stole around Elly. It felt solid, strong, protective.

Across the street the church doors opened, a dark maw offering shelter to the gang. Father Grimes pushed the doors closed against the wind with Leon helping.

Dusty's one bitter word said what they were all thinking. "Sanctuary."

Rudy implored the ceiling light. "If you're up there, you heavenly beings, close down the churches! Look what they protect! Who they attack!" Elly had never before noticed the inroads age was making on Rudy's face. "Who do we hurt?" he asked.

The firemen, forgotten in their corner, sauntered to the cash register, helped themselves to mints and toothpicks. Rain smashed against the windows, like waves assaulting a ship. Joking with Elly, they fastened their slickers and ventured outside.

"Look at the wind push them around," said Jake.

"Those big strong men. And they could have stayed right here where it's warm and cozy," Rudy purred, his anguish of before pushed out of mind.

"Now you want to bring out the whole Fire Department in our diner!" complained Dusty, but there was laughter in her voice. She lit Elly's cigarette and smiled into her eyes, mouthing the word love.

Rudy rose. "It's time, dear ones."

"You leavin' us?"

"We're on our way to try that new bar in Crossby. Morton River is beginning to sound a bit too much like Pansy Place, New Hampshire, for my tastes."

117

"Good luck bucking the storm in your Bug," Dusty said.

"I hope you're safe in this glorified boxcar," Jake countered. "Maybe the steeple will draw the wrath of the heavens onto itself."

"Speaking of heaven," Rudy said, "I almost forgot why I came by. Marcy's Bar is having a Reunion Thanksgiving Dinner. Tell the world. We want all our old friends there. Bring your pennywhistle, Miss Dusty."

Dusty was frowning. "I don't know. I gave up drinking a while back and haven't been in a bar since."

Rudy's mouth fell open. "No *wonder* you vanished. I'll make sure there's plenty of cider. Unfermented."

Dusty looked at Elly.

Elly thought of Rita, also an old friend at Marcy's bar.

"It's up to my girl, here," said Dusty. "She always knows what's best."

Elly breathed deeply, trying to imagine what Grace would advise. "Oh no, you don't, you ol' butch," she chided. "It's not for me to decide. If we go I'm going to have fun, not ride herd on my wild rooster all night."

Dusty shifted her feet, rubbed the back of her neck. She looked at Jake and Rudy. "What the hell, fellas, It's been over a year. I can handle it. If my girl wants to go—we'll be there!"

CHAPTER FIFTEEN

"Dusty, lover?" Elly asked. "Aren't you *ever* going to go down on me?"

It was a hot, moist, blue summer with noisily bedding birds singing a love song out the window. Dusty peeled her big-boned naked body away from Elly and stared anxiously through the smoke light at her. Without glasses, the last of Elly's makeup seemed like smudged dusk. "You mean . . ." she faltered, unable to say the words she needed.

Elly twisted close again and smoothed back Dusty's hair, tonguing an earlobe. "I mean with your mouth," she whispered, rubbing a sharp hip across Dusty's belly. "You know, like this," and she sucked on the earlobe, then flicked it back and forth with her tongue.

"I never did that before."

Elly stopped. Her body was always a surprise to Dusty. Those fragile-looking, slender shoulders glowed in the dim light, sweaty from humidity. The shock on Elly's face began slowly to fade to her slow, teasing smile.

Dusty dove, belly down, under a pillow. Partly to escape that knowing smile. Mostly to hide her humiliation. She counted. They'd been together one year and five months. She'd been making love with women for twenty-three years.

"How could you never do that, an elegant ol' Romeo like you?" Elly asked in astonishment. "Though I can understand not wanting to with prune-face Rita."

In all the seventeen years she'd been with Rita, Dusty had only tried it once, after her old Navy buddy Les had brought home some postcards from Denmark. She'd slid down Rita's body, getting as far as rubbing her lips across her pubic hair. Rita had stopped her.

"I guess," she lied to Elly, her head still under the pillow, "it just never came up." What a gap in experience to admit to this dynamic new lover. Especially now, when she sensed that Elly was disappointed in her about the diner, and especially in the way she'd messed up by firing John.

All that seemed to be the farthest thing from Elly's mind now, though. She hung over Dusty's broad back so her breasts just grazed it, and said, "Do me, lover?"

It was Elly's favorite phrase, said with her Tennessee drawl exaggerated, a sure-fire way to turn Dusty on. But *did* she want to do it?

"Don't you want to?" Elly asked, her breasts tracing double patterns on Dusty's back.

She shrugged, half hoping Elly would give up. The room was growing darker. Outside there was lull in the birds' chatter and she could hear the ducks quack across the little pond.

But Elly knew ways to overcome Dusty's attempts to avoid what she feared. Thank goodness, thought Dusty as Elly

120

stretched against her so her longish brown hair tickled Dusty's neck. Again, Elly whispered into her ear. "Then let me do you."

"Elly . . ." Dusty complained, her tone half-aggrieved, half pleased and excited.

Elly began to tickle her in earnest, giggling. "Don't you hide your face from me all night, you old butch. You come out here and get yours."

Dusty twitched and held her breath to defend herself from Elly, but the woman was unrelenting. So she heaved herself up and pushed Elly back downward on the bed. The gold chain Elly wore around her neck gleamed. What an incredibly exciting woman. But—

"I can't," she said, breathless, kissing gently the hollow beneath Elly's throat. There was nothing like a few hours alone with Elly to make her forget her role in the world as a competent, hard-working cook and restaurant owner, and bring out the shy uncertain kid in her.

"Why not?" asked Elly, apparently perfectly happy to lie beneath her and grind her pelvis upward instead of down. Their hot damp bodies made a sucking sound each time Elly broke contact. "Here," she said, gripping Dusty by the buttocks, urging her forward with hands. "Scoot up over my mouth."

"El!"

Elly laughed at her shock. "Why not?"

"I didn't even have time for a shower today!"

Minutes later, she found herself under a hot shower while Elly sat on the closed toilet seat repainting her nails.

"You sure are taking your sweet time," said Elly. "If we don't take more time off, my nails are going to look like I do them with a rose clipper!"

Dusty turned off the water and dried every available inch of herself, twice. She even passed a hand between her legs and smelled her fingers.

Elly was laughing when Dusty, trying to control the fluttering in her stomach, stepped aside to let her leave the bathroom first. Outside, a car started. Dusty wished it were somebody stealing the Swinger. Then she'd have to bolt out the door, pulling clothes on and—"Be home by midnight!" called a mother in a shrill voice. No chance. Elly pulled the curtains shut.

"You're so dry now I could start a fire with you, lover," Elly said, passing a hand over her skin.

Dusty narrowed her eyes to hide the secret half-smile trying to sneak across her face. This woman sure knew how to keep her mind off work.

But Elly had become dead serious. She switched on a bedside light and slowly, deliberately untied Dusty's white terry robe. "Yeah," Elly said, her voice deep, slow, "and that's exactly what I'm planning to do."

In the heat Dusty lay still, robe spread open, long fleshy legs gently urged apart, her lover's mouth breathing hotly on her skin still warm from the shower. "Can't we turn the light off?" she asked.

Elly had parted her outer lips and was blowing between them. She looked up. "But you're so pretty!" Her laugh, sometimes, was like glass windchimes.

"Pretty?" She squirmed as Elly studied her.

"Pretty. Even butches are pretty down there."

As well as Dusty knew that, she'd never thought it of herself. "You could at least close your eyes." She hesitated, remembering a time—"And put your heels back on."

"Why, Dusty," Elly said in surprise, but said no more. She quickly bent to the floor and slipped into her black patent leather high heels, giving Dusty time to admire their effect on her little feet, her long, shaved, shapely legs. Then she nestled between Dusty's legs once more and her tongue licked, flat and hard, the length of Dusty's inner lips.

She gasped at Elly's touch. Nothing had ever felt like that.

"You like it, lover?" Elly asked, talking into her, starting a new rush of feeling.

She no longer minded the light being on. The sight of Elly's delicate fingers holding her apart, of her tongue touching her *there*, of her soft moisture-smeared lips pursed above her—it was as if some bright hot star shone on them, illuminating Elly for her further pleasure.

Elly pulled her inside her mouth. All of her. Dusty felt the flood of her excitement immerse the tongue that entered her. Then the flood spilled out and out till her thighs were wet, the bed was damp, till she came against Elly's soft warm tongue.

Elly lifted her shining, smiling face and moved up beside her in bed, kissing her all wet like that. "You've got the sweetest smell," she told Dusty. "And you taste like—"

"Sex." Dusty finished happily. Her love for Elly became palpable, made of this warmth and smell and pounding in her veins. Her whole body felt as if it had just sighed a great sigh, stretched a great stretch. Surely the glow she felt showed. She was high, as if Elly were some rare wine. She propped herself on one elbow and looked wondrously at Elly. "You smell like the bed after we've been doing it for hours."

Elly kissed her wetly again."No, lover, I smell like *you*. This is what you smell like." Leaning back, Elly asked, "Hand me my cigarettes?"

"No." She was wondering what Elly smelled like. "El," she began, thickly, clearing her throat, but the words were too hard. Gently, she pushed Elly back on the bed. It was Elly's turn to grin. Slowly, she moved where she could begin to kiss Elly, as if her mouth was merely meandering over her moist skin, as if she had no particular purpose in mind. This was like the way she'd close her eyes and jump and whatever she feared to do would be done. This time she'd jump tongue first.

As she kissed all inside Elly's thighs she could hear Elly's breathing change. "Lover," she was saying to Dusty, from deep in her throat.

Dusty breathed in, through her nose. The smell of sex was everywhere. It was intoxicating. She floated on it, in it, wishing she'd had the privacy in the service to explore like this, the self-assurance to have tried again with Rita. She was resting her head on Elly's thigh, breathing her in.

"Lover, lover," Elly repeated, twisting toward her.

The high hot flush of her contentment fled. Give her a kitchen and she could perform culinary miracles. Give her a house, a diner, anything in disrepair, and she could fix it. But give her a girl, and some sex right now—what should she do next? It all seemed so awkward.

But Elly's hands pulled her closer. All that curly hair tickled Dusty's nose. She pushed her tongue through it, found the parting of the lips, but was stuck there, couldn't get further.

Elly reached down and opened herself to Dusty's tongue.

The boldness of the act sent another rush through Dusty. Her tongue all at once knew its way. Elly moved beneath her, already awash in a sea of her own making, her hands in Dusty's hair, twisting, curling, grasping, then falling limply to the bed as she groaned—no, cried loudly in a way Dusty had never heard a woman cry out before.

Elly pulled her up, her eyes barely open, her mouth faintly, contentedly, smiling. "You *sure* you never did that before?"

Dusty wrapped her sturdy arms around Elly, pressed with a hand her lover's head against her broad shoulder. Elly always seemed to know how to help her to feel good, how to help bring her confidence back. And did it in such a gracious, unselfconscious way that even Dusty's pride would fall.

The hot night trapped their fragrant heat around them; they lay content in the glow of it. Darkness had fallen completely and with it silence. A breeze pushed past the light curtains. Dusty let her eyes close. As she fell asleep she thought: I don't want to be afraid any more. Look at all I've missed.

Some time later, Elly switched off the light. One small bird cried out in the night. Elly kissed Dusty's forehead. Half-dreaming, Dusty wondered if stars ever fell through bedroom windows. How the white glare would glow, turning dark to dusk, waking the birds to sing their love song once more.

CHAPTER SIXTEEN

What would I do without you to talk to, Rosa? I hope you don't mind me stopping by the house, I feel like my head's a whirlpool. What with the priest threatening damnation, El and her needs, the gang and their threats, I've been walking by the River, listening and listening for what it can tell me—and I can't hear a thing. We need a flood so it'll roar at me so loud I'll hear it.

I feel like flotsam the River is battering and buffeting all the way out to sea. I'm so damn tired of fighting. I was remembering back to when I left the Navy, to the energy I had then.

I'll never forget June 27, 1953. I came out of the Navy like a rocket, powered with hope, resolutions, and the certainty I knew how to do this right. I stood listening a while as the train hissed and rumbled away from Morton River up and out of the Valley. I stared down the tracks like they were the road to paradise, like I was standing on a mountaintop looking at a panorama of the world—and it was mine to claim. Then the train was gone and the traffic, the River, kids' cries, the slam of car doors, rushed into the silence. Sunlight winked at me off the empty tracks. Everything smelled warm, looked bright. My chest was so full of excitement and promise it hurt me to breathe.

Freedom! I thought, tasted, dreamed. Like my dad before me I was ready to plunge into life. Despite the summer heat, I stopped at an Army-Navy store to buy myself the peacoat the Navy refused to issue to women, and the dark turtlenecks sailors wore in winter. And I picked up a pair of flashy white bucks for dancing. I remember promising myself that I'd dance through the soles. I even thought I might stop drinking. Then I walked up the hill toward home. I planned to live there, get part-time work, go to school on my benefits. At home, hiding who I was would be easy after the Navy.

But nothing inside those lace-curtained windows had changed. Old Round Eyes and his sons gaped at me like I was AWOL from some zoo. My mom cried a little, but I couldn't tell if it was because she was glad to see me, or because of the conflicts I'd brought back into her life. They all spent a strained hour opening the souvenirs I'd brought back and then they drifted away. I felt like I'd escaped Korea only to come home and be wounded. I went for a walk down along the River, and decided then and there to put off school for a while. My first priority would be a place of my own and a job to support it.

The Morton River Valley, in the eyes of a traveler come home, had filled up with charms I'd never seen before. I relearned the River's banks and walked Morton River's streets, listening to great old trees who whispered leafy secrets as I went. Could they, who'd watched generations build these

127

solid graceful homes, teach me what I wanted to know to be comfortable in this world? Could they teach me where I belonged? Or did they agree with the priests and my stepfather and the Navy—that homosexuals just didn't belong?

It seemed I walked a hundred summer streets, a thousand hot but shaded miles, waiting to hear if the plant would take me on or if my hands were too queer to be trusted with their helicopter parts. Knowing it might take the rest of the summer, I settled for a graveyard shift cooking job at a nearby diner and, owning no car, rented an apartment in a converted attic nearby. Its refrigerator was big enough for a few six-packs, its bed for the full undress parade of baby-bootie types who marched to it.

Finally, I could have my fill of luscious bodies mine for the taking. Not once did a Chief climb my narrow steps. Not once, stubbornly, did I close the ragged shade that would have sealed out the witnessing church spires and skies of Morton River. I laughed as loud as I wanted at our bawdy antics, held the groaning girls as they came, lounged for hours in steamy clouds of fragrant sex. And told myself this was joy.

On the nights I had to work, I'd have the luxury of a day filled with stacks of used paperback and library books. Since I couldn't go to school yet, I set about to educate myself through Willa Cather and Charles Dickens, Carson McCullers and John Steinbeck, Thomas Wolfe. Especially Thomas Wolfe, who knew about rivers. But I longed for someone to talk to about my teachers. I longed and longed in general, just like I had in the service.

One morning toward the end of summer, when fall was so near a hint of it cooled even my close loft, I lay hungover on my rumpled sheets watching a sweet firm ass, creamy-white, disappear into hot pink bikini panties. I was hit with the realization that the sight no longer thrilled me. As a matter of fact, I couldn't wait for her to go. Before the clatter of her sandals died on the wooden steps I was prying open a cold can of beer and taking stock.

I'd learned three things since I'd taken off my uniform. One: that when you were a woman the world was the same in the Navy or in the Valley—as Rita was to tell me over and over. Everyone was equal out there, but some of us were more equal than others. Two: that if I was going to make a living, it didn't matter who was blowing the bugle—the base PA system or my own alarm clock set to the head cook's time—I had to live by the rules or sink. Three: that by the end of the summer a girl a week was not my style.

The illusion of freedom had turned me on a lot more than those willing bodies who'd close their eyes like it didn't matter too much who I was either. Impersonal sex left me feeling dirty, too close to the gutter of the world's prophecies. It was time, Rosa, to once more run from the monster I was afraid of becoming.

I walked again that day, feeling cleansed by too much liquor. Restless, anxious about the decadent years that could pile up on me like so many starched uniforms, one layer on top of another till I wouldn't be able to move at all, I looked curiously into the wide old front windows, wishing one of these homes was my own. I listened to the trees, shot here and there with yellow or red, and I heard them sing with happiness at their fate: *Roots*, they seemed to whisper. *Roots* give us life again and again. But who'd ever heard of someone like me rooting? People like me went from girl to girl, home to home, job to job, and died lonely and poor.

What are you rolling your eyes at, Rosa? I'd convinced myself it wasn't true, but now, again, I'm not so sure.

The next night, from lack of other ways to fill my time, I accepted a ride to a party. After enough drinks, I felt the grin take over my face, and pulled out my pennywhistle. But I couldn't get interested in anyone who came to me. I stopped playing and let them all drift away.

A short, dark-haired woman, seated on the other side of the room, appeared in my sight only after the curtain of listeners had parted. Intent and watchful, she rose wide-hipped, black-skirted, in a pearly-grey blouse, to cross the room to me.

"You look just plain weary," she told me, her interesting face opened by a friendly smile that made me forget her watchful look. She seemed a few years older than me, built solidly, as if she'd stay steady on her feet no matter how many times she emptied the wine glass in her hand.

"Yeah," I agreed, nodding, uninterested except by the word weary. Unusual in this crowd. Did she read a lot too? "Guess it's time for me to go crawl under my haystack."

Rita—yes, Rita—laughed. I got the feeling she didn't laugh often. "Will that help?"

"No," I admitted, suddenly certain that she'd know what would.

So I stayed a while longer, drinking myself silly as we talked books for hours. And stayed again at the next party, this time exchanging books and phone numbers. One Saturday afternoon I went over to visit and we discovered our parallel lives.

"I can't believe you went to Hilltop Elementary too."

"And graduated from Valley High only two years behind me."

"Did you know Janet Ellendorf?"

"And her weird brother Sid?"

"How about that hoody Mike Thompson?"

"Oh," Rita said—Rita Collins, a good Irish name—"that whole crowd. He married that vixen Nancy Tinker and you ought to see her now. Only our age, but with five kids, none of them quiet types."

You know the kind of talk. Like coming home. "How do you keep up with all these things?" I asked her. She'd baked a chocolate layer cake and I was on my second piece. Lunch had

130

been a welcome change from the truck stop meals I'd grown used to.

"Roots," she answered.

And I froze with the cake halfway to my mouth. I heard the leaves lift and fall, lift and fall outside her windows. It was a grey day of damp blustery breezes. "What do you mean?"

"Just that—roots. They keep me going." She was standing before her black pained bookshelves—shelves!—not just stacks of books. "If I can't have kids, if my family won't talk to me—" Was that a bitter tone? "—then I'll send roots down into what I have."

"And you have—"

"This town, these old schoolmates, the people I work with out at the plant. I really hope you get the job. It's like family out there, as long as they don't *know.*"

"Don't you think you can make a home with a woman?"

Rita's tone became caustic. "Name me two gay girls that have."

I couldn't. And here I'd had a flicker of hope—but a home and roots seemed tantalizingly out of reach for me. My face must have fallen.

"Dusty," she said passionately, sitting across the table now, "don't get me wrong. I want that more than anything on earth. A lover to grow old with, to ride back and forth to the plant with, to raise pets with, to putter with when we're old folks in our yard."

I'd managed to polish off the cake. "Sounds good to me. When do we start?"

Rita looked demurely down. "Start what?" I stood and walked around the table, wondering with every step if this was right. Did you simply, in the end, walk in and *take* your place in the world? When I pulled her close she didn't lean, didn't collapse on me. She even felt capable of holding me up.

Her lips were quite nice, well-shaped, soft, responsive. But after that first kiss there was, on her freckled, sharp-nosed

131

face, a look of satisfaction that almost scared me away. Yet that face, something like my grandmother's, something like my mother's, was familiar. And her eyes lacked a certain hungry intensity I'd had enough of; her hands, with their strong grip, hadn't any touch of hunger or restlessness in them.

Rita seemed to know what life was all about, Rosa, and what she wanted. That night, after a couple bottles of wine, in her crisp-sheeted bed, under her alert, protective gaze, as agitated leaves stirred shadows around the streetlamps outside, I slept better than I had all summer.

CHAPTER SEVENTEEN
Grace

Grace and Seeker moved slowly down Railroad Avenue toward the Queen of Hearts. The fall air was as cold and clean-tasting as mountain water, and Grace breathed great mouthfuls of the stuff, smiling with the pleasure of it after the summer's humidity.

She thought back to all those years in school when she'd been given bad grades in comportment—comportment! As if she would ever be, or want to be, a Southern Belle like Elly. She'd defied their continuous warnings about smiling to her blind old self in public places. It was the sort of thing her teachers called a *blindism,* but she'd asked them just who the heck they thought she'd be fooling if she tried to hide who she was. As a kid she'd never known what to believe. People told her on the one hand that she was as good as anyone, then acted as if she had this gross defect to hide. Even at school age she had a lot more things going for her than some of these sighted people. Like honesty. So she smiled.

She hadn't felt much like smiling since Jo Ellen had backed off. Thoroughly modern Jo Ellen, she chuckled to Seeker, had folded under the stress of her husband's nights with other women. The rejection hadn't broken Grace's heart, but she missed the intensity, the companionship, the touching. And it wasn't likely she'd find all that again soon in Morton River Valley.

She sighed, and was hit by the most godawful smell she'd ever breathed. She indulged herself in what she imagined to be a grimace horrendous enough to ruin her comportment grades forever. "What *is* it, Seek?" she asked. He sneezed, as if in protest against the stuff, but then he sneezed when he was happy too. And he generally began to sneeze as soon as he realized they were headed for the Queen of Hearts because Dusty always fed him treats.

She could hear a scrubbing sound as she climbed the steps. Inside, coffee almost replaced the awful smell, but what about everything else? There were no yakking customers, no onions frying, no register drawer sliding shut with a little ping. Wasn't anyone here at all? She calmed her anxiety with deep breathing, but couldn't stop a sense of that priest clearing the place with a squad of righteous reformers.

"Elly?" she asked, hesitant to move forward. Seeker waited patiently.

"Hi, sweetie." The words were sad, whispery.

"What's wrong?"

134

"What's right is more like it," Dusty growled. Her voice was angry. Poor Dusty. If she were a man she'd be the most respectable member of the community.

"Are you trying to make me guess?" Grace asked calmly. She'd at least refuse to mirror their distress—there were enough bad vibrations in the diner.

She heard Elly's bracelets jangle. "Come up to the counter, girl, no one's here. We sent Rosa and Hernando home for now."

Elly smelled like a saleslady in a Memphis Five and Dime, a smell Grace could not resist. If that Dusty hadn't snapped Elly up like a treat all for herself . . . But it wasn't all perfume. Not many sighted people in her life had sensed so immediately her painful impatience to know the shape and feel of things. Like the heart-shaped aprons that night before the diner had opened; Elly had made sure Grace knew what they were making. And now poor Elly sounded like someone had torn her heart-shaped apron in two.

"Good dog," said Dusty. Grace heard the crunch of a dog treat. Then Dusty explained, "The smell is the solvent the guy's using to clean up." She sat down on the stool next to Grace and swung a leg back and forth, the fabric of her slacks catching over and over. "Some bastard wrote *QUEER OF HEARTS* across the front of the diner."

"How horrible for you all," Grace said, reaching for Dusty's hand. It was stiff and sweaty.

She could hear Elly expel smoke as if it were fear. "In black spray paint," Elly said. "Huge letters. They must have used two cans."

"More like two gallons," added Dusty, making a sound like a fist hitting a cupped hand.

Grace had a swift sense of Dusty in the bow of a ship, standing against the wind and mist, the roar of water the only sound, wearing the coarse wool sailor suit someone had held up for Grace's inspection during a school museum trip. Grace

135

remembered feeling its flap of material, loose across the back, striped with a raised ridge of smoother material and the flare of the trousers with their double row of buttons. Legs wide, arms folded, Dusty moved up the Morton River, a conqueror from some Amazon land.

"I don't understand how no one saw them," Dusty went on in her voice of doom, dispelling Grace's vision but not her sense of Dusty. The atom bomb might have fallen on Dusty's kitchen; there would be no chance of reconstruction and a nuclear cloud was seeping out to the counter. Didn't Dusty *know* how she sounded? Was she trying to make it worse?

Gloom froze further talk. She missed the sense of hurry-up urgency that drew her to the Queen of Hearts, the confusion of lives that she felt in the air in such contrast to her own pacific life. Loneliness was her bane; and she never felt alone when the jukebox beat right up through the floor, when the kitchen doors swung open and closed. The diner had become her focal point and she scrimped in spending her government checks so she could take her meals in the Queen's warmth. She'd tried to increase her income, decrease her loneliness with jobs over the years, but available work had been such drudgery that she's chosen instead to live simply, even in poverty, rather than tolerate a life she abhorred. At the thought of what she might now actually lose . . . She breathed deeply, searching for calm.

"Maybe *you* all think this is the end of the world," she said. "But my stomach thinks it's lunchtime. Dusty, honey, would you feel like whipping me up one of those enormous burgers of yours with lots of Russian dressing, extra pickles—"

Elly interrupted with a laugh, "—and extra crispy French fries—"

Together Grace and Elly drawled, "—*Southern* style!"

That had forced a reluctant little laugh from Dusty. "Watch out or I'll dump some of mah southern stahyl white gravy on them."

Once Dusty was out of range, Grace asked, "How you doin'?"

"Just about like you'd expect," answered Elly.

"*Real* big letters?"

Elly took Grace's arms and moved them far from each other. "Damn big letters."

"It'll be gone soon."

"I have to agree with Dusty there, girl. We can erase it from the diner, but not from people's minds." Elly's voice rose. "Thank goodness, here comes Gussie Brennan. She's about the only one who'll be able to cheer Dusty up." She poured Grace's Coke with a whoosh.

Grace took the familiar squat glass and turned it in her fingertips, running her index finger along the bulge at the top. When she lifted the glass, bubbles jumped against her nose, the sweet syrup smell preceding the Coke taste.

"Good morning, gorgeous," called Gussie.

"Aw, shoot," Elly answered, a shy smile in her voice.

Gussie hugged Grace from the side, squeezing her shoulders.

Dusty swung open the kitchen door and walked, heavy-footed, to Elly's side.

"Nobody, but nobody, makes these things like you do, Dusty," Grace said.

"A lot of good it does me."

"Humph," Gussie said. "Don't bother to compliment that one. Would you look at the puss on her ! You'd think somebody wrote you-know-what on her forehead in indelible ink."

"Just like they tattooed people in Nazi Germany," Dusty blazed out. "Don't think these people wouldn't stoop to that if they could get away with it."

"*Hog*wash," said Gussie vehemently. "This is one of the few countries in the world where we have a fighting chance. I wish I could be around to see what happens in the next

137

fifteen, twenty years. By nineteen-ninety there'll be laws on the books protecting you. And no thanks to the likes of you or me, Reilly. I used to be just like you, hiding under my bed at the slightest threat. It'll be Elly and Nan who win our battles for us: our backbones, while we huff and puff and go round in circles. Maybe when you're my age you'll see how silly all this fuss is."

Dusty remained silent.

"Is this how you're going to treat your loyal customers? I haven't seen a frown that ugly since . . . " Gussie seemed to think a minute. "Since my mother caught me with my best friend Kathleen."

Grace could smell fresh coffee. Elly clinked cup onto saucer and poured. "Don't stop there," Elly urged Gussie in her flirty purr of a voice.

Gussie stirred the coffee. "She was a cutie, that Kathleen. A little like Grace with all those curls, but hers were long and all fluffed up. I loved to get my fingers into them. And you can stop looking at me like that, Dusty Reilly. I *mean* the curls on her head. I knew a sexy story would get your attention." Gussie was playing with Grace's curls while she talked. "It wasn't easy those days, to get close to much below the chin, what with the long heavy skirts and the high-necked blouses. We'd just discovered, though, what we could get away with in broad daylight if Kathleen sat on my lap while I pretended to brush her hair. You couldn't tell from the front if her skirts were up or down in the back! It's one of my favorite positions to this day. I love Nan's flannel granny gowns."

Grace grinned to imagine it. She heard the click of Dusty's lighter and Elly's intake of smoky breath. "Mama walked in and there she was," asked Elly, "your hand up her—"

"At exactly the wrong moment. I picked the brush up quick, but Kathleen's face must have told its own story!"

138

Despite Dusty's big laugh, there was a wariness in her voice, as if she feared to let her guard down. "How'd you get out of that one?"

"Why," said Gussie, suiting her actions to her words, "I just jumped up, dumped Kathleen off my lap and started yelling, 'You spoiled it, you spoiled it!' at my mother."

"You *what?*" Grace asked, giving Seeker the last French fry.

Gussie's laugh was as hearty as Dusty's, and Grace could hear Gussie slap her thigh. "I told her I'd slipped a spider I'd made of knotted threads up under Kathleen's bloomers. Kathleen hadn't known what to do with herself, but now she started hooting and hollering around the room, slapping at her skirt, while my mom, whose sense of humor was just like mine, almost keeled over laughing. I just stood there, covering my mouth with my hand as if to laugh politely, but really I was sniffing Kathleen on my fingers. Every time Kathleen looked up and saw me doing it, she'd hoot and holler more to cover her embarrassment!"

"Gussie," said Elly—Grace could hear a loud kiss on Gussie's cheek—"you're somethin' else. I never knew girls carried on back then."

"Oh, weren't we the devils! You would have been proud, sailor girl."

Dusty agreed. "But I wish I'd known when *I* was doing it, that you'd been at it forty years before me." Without the wary tone, she asked, "Where's your lady today?"

"Not doing well at all," Gussie said. "I took her over to the doctor and he thinks there might be a new flu bug making the rounds. But she's demanding a Queen of Hearts danish and some of Elly's coffee, so I'm to bring them home after you feed me lunch."

"Coming up," said Dusty. Her step sounded a little lighter.

Elly removed Grace's dishes and slid a new plate toward her. "Boston cream pie?" asked Grace, sniffing.

"Can you hear me in there, sailor?" called Gussie.

"Yeah!"

"I wanted to let you know my old pal Dale's coming to town. The one I told you about from the midwest."

"Jailbait?"

"It was twenty-five years ago that we were lovers. She's forty now, in Berkeley, California, raising a ruckus about gay rights and what all. She might have some ideas on how to straighten out this neighborhood."

"They're straight enough!" called Dusty.

Later, the solvent man came in to be paid, and Dusty went out to inspect his work.

Elly asked when she came back in, "What are all those cars parking across the street for, lover?"

"El Creepo the Priest is blessing another straight union."

"A wedding?" asked Grace, excited. There was something about weddings that never failed to make her feel sappy. "Tell me what's going on, El." They moved to a booth.

Dusty followed. She hissed toward the window. "Go ahead, cheer 'em on, El Creepo! Tell 'em what a service they're doing your parish every time they get into bed to make babies for your side!"

"Oh, Dusty," Elly said. "They're not all our enemies. You're actin' close-minded just like you're accusing them of doing."

"Is it a big wedding?" asked Grace.

"Ten or fifteen cars," Elly answered with relish. "People all dressed up. Women with their little purses and gloves. Men holding car doors open for the women, just like Dusty does for me."

"Does she?" asked Grace, a little envious. The funniest things sometimes made her wish she was sighted. To hold doors open for Elly Hunnicutt . . .

140

"And look!" Elly went on. "There's John, all spiffed up. And Leon, lookin' almost human in a suit except for those crawly sideburns."

"Hot damn," said Dusty. "No wonder they sprayed us last night. They thought they could show off their handiwork to this big crowd and all the gawkers who stop by."

Grace felt Elly growing more tense beside her.

"Just try and come in here afterwards for coffee, for anything!" threatened Dusty.

"El," Grace said. Maybe today wasn't the time for watching a wedding. She wished Gussie would join them, but she was at the counter with the paper and her lunch.

"The bride is here now," Elly went on. Her voice was hard and flat, defiant, as if she was determined to talk on over Dusty's protests. "In a white dress, white hat. They're rushing her inside so the groom doesn't see her before the ceremony."

"I know," Grace said. "Because it's bad luck. It's one of the great advantages about being blind." Her joke seemed to do nothing to lighten the atmosphere. She was hearing the rush of the River, the sharpening of a saber, the flap of Dusty's sails in the wind as she bore down on Morton River.

"You know, I think *Leon's* the groom? My lord, who would want that ape? How in the world will he support a wife? But he's the center of attention all right. Dressed to the nines. I wonder if that's Rossi the realtor next to him. Leon's pointing over to the diner, his arm around Rossi senior's shoulders. They're laughing—"

Dusty's fist slammed the table so hard an ashtray leapt. "We were a wedding present for that turd!" she cried out. "And no one over there condemns what they did! How can you go on about their fucking fertility rite when we haven't had a half dozen customers in here all day because of them?"

Grace held onto Elly's own fisted hand. "I'm not doing it to offend you, Dusty," Elly said tensely. "Why don't you leave it alone?"

"Christ," spat Dusty.

Elly stood. "Dusty Reilly, you're acting crazy over this thing. If I didn't know better I'd think you've been drinkin'."

"Crazy? After what *they* did, I'm the one who's crazy?" She was shouting back at Elly.

"Dusty," said Gussie softly, at Grace's elbow.

Like a pouting kid, Dusty asked, "What?"

"You're not mad at Elly. It's them. Out there."

"How the fuck are we going to live? Them out there won't give us a chance. How am I going to stop the sons of bitches from wiping us out just because we love each other? They're the crazy ones, not me. What do you want from me?"

"Fight the right people."

"HOW?"

Grace's heart went out to Dusty's broken cry. She knew, all at once, what was wrong. Dusty had taken the straights' hatred and swallowed it whole. How could you spend your whole life hearing you're no good without believing at least some of it? That doubt, that self-condemnation, had festered inside Dusty. Gussie may have been right about Elly and Nan standing up to the world better, supporting Dusty and herself, but of course they'd need to. It was Dusty and Gussie who were the ones the world saw as queer, because of their walk, their dress. It was Dusty and Gussie who bore the brunt of abuse while the Ellies waited at home to give comfort. It was the Dusties who broke. And were too proud to ask for help.

"You could start by asking us for help," Gussie suggested quietly, simply, but with a tremor in her voice.

"What can you do? What can anyone do to help?"

No one answered.

"That's what I thought," Dusty said. "There's no way to help. It's been like this for thousands of years and it'll always be like this. I was nuts to buy this hunk of tin and think hard work and caring would succeed. I had no right to risk everything for a dumb dream. You were right, El. I'll try and get back on at the plant."

Elly moved away from Grace, toward Dusty, crying softly.

"I'm sorry, El," Dusty went on. "I know I risked a lot of what you wanted too. This is the end of the line for me, though. I won't throw good money after bad."

"Go ahead," Elly said through her tears. "Go ahead and sell the Queen of Hearts. Go back to the plant. But if you do, you better make sure Rita's ready to move back into your house. 'Cause I won't be there."

CHAPTER EIGHTEEN

Dusty made inquiries at the plant, and tried to persuade Elly to her point of view. But Elly was a stubborn Hunnicutt through and through. And so Dusty stayed on at the diner. Elly watched her drag one foot behind the other, depressed over their swift descent into financial trouble. They'd budgeted for a slow start which had not happened, and now they had a slight cushion to ride out the hard times—if they were brief.

The Saturday before Halloween Elly persuaded her lover to go to the party at Jake and Rosa's.

"You are gorgeous," Dusty said as she escorted Elly on her arm up the stairs to the second floor flat. Elly wore a floor-length yellow ball gown made over from an old summer dress and some curtains. "My Southern belle." Dusty was all courtly manners tonight, like a solicitous groom leading her bride down the aisle.

"Shoot, lover, it's just little me," Elly answered, doing her best to look coyly up from under her eyelashes. Someday she was going to try those fake ones. Mascara wasn't always enough. "And I was only tryin' to be fit company for you."

As late as that morning Dusty's mind had been too fragmented with worries to plan a costume, so Elly had decided to take charge. Half an hour later Gussie appeared at the diner with Nan's old riding habit on her arm. Now Dusty wore the black pants and green jacket with black velvet collar, and she moved elegantly beside Elly.

"Don't you go kissin' too many of these Yankee girls," Elly half teased. "You'll knock your moustache off."

Dusty stroked it while she looked pointedly down the front of Elly's dress.

"That is not how a southern gentleman acts, Dusty!"

"Caught you!" said Rudy as he came up to them. He wore a homburg and oversized bow tie with what looked like Jake's blue suit. "I'm just leaving for work," he explained.

"Wait!" Elly said. "Let me guess who you're dressed as." She pretended to concentrate. "I know! You're supposed to be that hunky bartender at Marcy's!"

"*That* tacky place?" Rudy said, and hugged them goodbye.

The room, red-curtained, was lit with ruddy glow of orange paper lanterns; a trail of them led to the kitchen where most of the guests carried on noisily.

Elly sashayed toward the kitchen with Dusty's arm lightly encircling her shoulders. In the dining room three young lesbians in granny glasses, long hair and jean jackets, obviously visiting from the larger, more sophisticated Upton, were dancing to a Pink Floyd record like one on the jukebox whose lyrics seemed to be animal-like grunts and growls. "What are you?" Dusty called in a friendly voice.

145

The dancers looked at one another. One shrugged. "We didn't dress up," she said, and offered a joint to Dusty.

Elly drew Dusty back a little too quickly. "No thanks," she answered for both of them.

Outside the kitchen door, Dusty looked down at her. "Jeeze, El," she said in an aggrieved voice. "You know I never touch that stuff."

"I know, lover. I'm sorry. I'm a little jumpy."

"Well, well, look who's here," called a mocking voice in the kitchen.

Elly felt her insides constrict.

"Hi, Rita," said Dusty. She hooked her thumbs in her belt and narrowed her eyes. Rita smiled widely at her. Dusty asked, "You two ever meet?" She stood very erect, but her words were mumbled.

"Not formally," Elly said, drawing the words out. "How do you do?"

Rita held a drink. Her face was flushed. She seemed terribly small to Elly. "Glad to meet you," Rita said without expression. "This is America, Rosa's cousin. She works at the plant."

Dusty shook America's hand. Elly wondered if this woman had gotten Dusty's job along with her girl. The foursome fell silent. Elly ground her teeth behind a polite smile.

Rosa, wearing one of Jake's hospital uniforms, pushed past some people in the doorway. She was neither smiling nor humming.

"What's wrong?" asked Elly, fearing for the Queen of Hearts.

"Gussie just called. They were going to try to come, but Nan's worse. Gussie says they've got her all doped up and she's spooning chicken soup down her gullet."

"Could she—" Dusty broke off.

No one wanted to consider the possibility of death.

146

Quickly Rosa offered, "The doctor said the infection got a very strong hold on Nan, but her constitution is good. She can fight it."

"Do you think that's the truth?" Elly asked. Rita had slunk away with her drink and her friend.

"Who knows? I'm sure Gussie doesn't want to spoil the party." A smile changed Rosa's face. "Hi, friends, speaking of the party! Welcome to our annual bash!"

"Dusty!" came a call from inside the kitchen.

"It's Grace. Will you ladies excuse me?" Dusty asked, smoothing her moustache again as she bowed. "This may be another Southern Belle in distress."

When she was out of hearing, Rosa pulled Elly to her. "Listen *mi amigita*, I'm sorry about America's date. She didn't know about Dusty being here, and she never told Rita who was throwing the party."

Elly rearranged her flowers. "It wasn't a pleasant surprise, but I don't blame you, Rosa. This town's just too small for both her and me. If she goes near my Dusty I'll be glad to tear that skimpy mouse-brown hair out of her head."

More guests were arriving. "Try and enjoy yourself," Rosa said before rushing to the door.

Elly could see Rita in the living room. A full glass in her hand, she sat slumped on the couch, squeezed between America and two drag queens. Elly realized that Rita was wearing all black, but couldn't guess what she was dressed as. She certainly wouldn't give her the satisfaction of asking. She went into the kitchen.

Grace was cutting up a large chocolate-frosted sheet cake with orange cat decorations. Dusty was arranging each slice on a paper plate with candy corn.

"I hate myself for this," Elly whispered to Dusty, "but I want to stick real close to you tonight." She was behind Dusty, her arms around her middle.

"Must be my moustache," Dusty joked.

147

"You know perfectly well what—or who— it is."

"What's going on?" Grace asked.

Elly explained in a whisper. Grace whistled low. "I finally get Dusty out dancin'," Elly said, "and look what happens."

"Oh, El, nothing happened," said Dusty, turning to feed her a little orange pumpkin candy. "And nothing's going to happen."

"Apple dunking!" called Jake. He wore a skin tight muscle shirt, brief gym shorts and his heart-shaped apron.

Grace jumped up. Seeker leapt after her. "A game after my own heart," Grace said, rolling up her sleeves.

"You actually like gettin' all wet?" asked Elly.

"No. I like playing against blindfolded competitors!"

Jake herded everyone into the living room. Luis and Lisa, Rosa's children, were dropping apples into a washtub full of water, slopping it on the garbage bags that lined the carpet.

"*Mamasota!*" Rosa cried to Jake. "What are you letting them do?"

Elly watched Rita over the washtub. The woman had yet another full glass in her hand. When the contest began she seemed to absently watch, her only animation coming in the form of weak applause when America dunked. She did not participate.

It was Dusty's turn next. "Sink your teeth in!" called Rita. When Dusty rose, moustacheless, face dripping, Rita was ready with a dry hanky.

Elly watched as Rita lured Dusty to the couch. What was the bitch trying to prove? She worked a lock of hair around her finger till it hurt her scalp.

Rosa's kids took forever to catch their apples. Elly shifted and squirmed in her gown, seething with rage at Dusty's all too frequent laughter.

Grace went last. She knelt, hands behind her back, and found the last apple, pushed it against the side of the tub, brought it out immediately.

148

By this time, Rita had a hand on Dusty's knee. Didn't Dusty have a will of her own? Didn't she give a damn about Elly's feelings?

She forced herself to applaud. Jake awarded Grace first prize—an impossibly tall witch's hat.

"Hey!" Dusty called. "We ought to sit you on top of the diner Halloween night. You'd scare anyone in that thing." And where, Elly wondered, did all this cheer come from all of a sudden?

Grace bent to Seeker, but the dog edged backward, growling. "Even my own dog!" cried Grace.

My best friend! bemoaned Elly. Didn't Grace know Dusty was all smiles next to Rita? Then shame came to her. Of course, Grace couldn't know. No one knew. Elly simply wasn't the end all and be all for this whole gang.

"Now that's not a bad idea," Jake said. "Setting a guard Halloween night. I could watch after I get off work at eleven."

"But girlfriend," said one of the drag queens, "you'd miss the ball at Marcy's!"

Jake put his hands on his aproned hips. "The sacrifices a girl has to make. I owe this to Dusty, Miss Thing."

Elly found herself able to forget Rita for a moment. "What a lovely gesture," she said.

"I'd volunteer too," said Hernando. Others said the same.

"And you all know Grace's Dixieland Banjo is at your service. Guaranteed to keep you awake if I have to hit all flats!"

"But where?" asked Elly. "If we guard her from inside nothing will happen."

"Isn't that the point?" Rita asked.

Elly didn't even look at her, this woman whose intentions she could *feel*. "The point," she said carefully, "is to catch someone red-handed. To have witnesses." Like I do, she thought, to your slinky paws all over my Dusty.

Those who had stayed in the room consulted with one another. Jake produced a sign-up sheet. Elly wondered if perhaps they could set up their observation point at Gussie and Nan's, and if Nan could handle the commotion. She wanted badly to discuss it with Dusty.

"You could use our attic," offered a straight couple. "We're across the street, right next to the church."

"Perfect, hon!" said Jake, hugging the woman.

Dusty stood, hands shoved in the slash pockets of her riding coat. She took to Elly like a young Thomas Jefferson about to orate. "Wait a minute. This is awful nice of all of you, but we can't put you out like this." What, Elly thought, had happened to Dusty's promise to her to accept help if it came along?

Then she noticed that Dusty held an open beer can. She gasped at the sight.

"But we want your restaurant around here," someone cried.

"We want to see a gay business make it!"

"We want to run that gay-hating priest out of town. It's nineteen seventy-two, not the Middle Ages."

Elly looked from the beer can to Rita. Did Dusty realize what she was doing? Could drinking be so natural, especially with Rita by her side, that she wasn't even aware of it? Dusty took a swallow. Rita smiled and nodded.

Rita or no, she crossed the room, holding her yellow gown away from the washtub spillage, and stood beside Dusty. "Of course we can accept, lover," she said. She slid a hand under Dusty's jacket and around her waist, pulling her slightly farther from Rita. "These are our friends. How about free dinners for all the volunteers?"

A cheer went up. Dusty lowered her head and grinned.

"Just say thank you," Elly told her, trying to keep the anger from her voice.

"But America and Rita offered to stand guard all that night with me," Dusty whispered. "What do I tell her?"

150

"All night," Elly said, pulling away. "All night with you? Do you really think America would show up?"

"Yes, I—"

"And even if she did, you think it's a great idea to spend the night with your ex?"

"I hadn't really thought of it like that. I just appreciated the offer." She still held the beer in one hand, the other hand in a pocket.

Elly hissed. "Dusty, you said you'd let people help. Just say thank you to your *real* friends, will you? Rita will understand all too well."

Dusty did so, and raised her beer can as she spoke. She seemed to notice it for the first time. Elly watched her look for a place to set it down, then draw it back toward her mouth, and finally place it on an end table.

Jake shouted out at that moment, "God save the Queen!"

CHAPTER NINETEEN
Dusty's Tales

I never used to get sick when I drank, Rosa. Up, up, up I'd go, to that place where I was a good as anyone, then better.

Where, like my dad would say, I could charm the pants off a nun. Where I knew, for a little while at least, the secrets of the universe.

But I'll tell you, I wrestled with the devil all night long after the Halloween Party last week. I didn't sleep worth a damn thinking how close I'd come to drinking again. I'd almost forgotten what drinking had been like these last years—more like a medicine I swallowed than growing liquid wings. It put out my lights, didn't turn them on.

And if my years in the Navy were lit by blinding white light, then my last years with Rita were a long dark tunnel. Not pitch black, no, but dark like we were living submerged in the Morton River. I'm glad we're not together, but I think we could be friends now. I feel comfortable with her.

The only bright spots, I'm ashamed to say, were the few times I got drunk enough to cheat on Rita in quick steamy affairs that might last a minute or an hour or three weeks. I don't know if Rita did the same, but she never seemed to notice any of mine. Of course, once the passion of those had worn off I felt like a louse, full of guilt and shame, damning myself worse than a thousand priests would. After years of this I felt sour inside, I felt like a big river churning before a storm.

It had been coming a long time, a tidal wave building, and it crested the weekend we spent with Craig at Mystic Seaport on the Connecticut coast. He'd rented a place there for about a month before the season started.

Wham! Like this, Rosa, my life was like some vegetable sliced in two. Whole one minute, severed the next, then chopped into little pieces I could never put together again.

Craig was twenty-three and single, still living with his parents, but earning what we did out at the plant where he worked in Rita's department. He was a baby still—slight, shy, down-cheeked, and Rita had adopted him, she said, because he seemed lost and scared. I didn't mind. To me he was a closet case and no threat. Rita said they'd never discussed the nature of our relationship, but she assumed that Craig had figured it out. For her, he seemed to be a hobby, someone to fuss over and give advice to now that I'd started school and was around less. I found him to be a playful drinking buddy who relieved the monotony of our life. After all, I drank to have fun and it wasn't much fun any more. Craig spiced things up for us.

153

I don't know why Rita and I went bad. Maybe it was me, sneaking around behind her back that ruined things.

Everything had seemed to start out okay. We'd lived in Rita's flat the first few years, but my duck pond dreams and the buying power of our combined wages often sent us wandering in my Swinger out of Morton River, past the growing suburbs, into the rural areas the developers hadn't yet reached. My school work at Valley U. was steady, but almost for recreation, and my heart had dreaming energy to spare. We always, of course, carried a six-pack on our dreamhouse jaunts.

There was one little place I made it a point to tool past every time we got out that way. One day, mellow on beer, foggy from overtime and studying, or maybe from an all-night standoff with Rita (our fights were already places where we got stuck and spun our emotional wheels till we sunk deeper and deeper, flinging more mud with each turn), we passed the little plot with its camouflaged pond. I'd dreamed us inside, stocked the pond with two ducks, planted a lush garden—by the time we stopped at a gas station on the River half a mile away.

I asked the station owner what he knew about the shack, for that's about all it was then.

He owned it. "I'm working with the town," he said, his blackened mechanic's hands busy with the dipstick, "to divvy up my lot and sell that half acre. I built that ranch house up the hill from it," he finished proudly, wiping his hands with a flourish.

"What are you thinking of asking for it?"

He named a moderate price, explaining that it was only three rooms and while the plumbing worked, the roof sometimes didn't.

Rita and I drove back over there and, with the keys he'd given us, looked the place over.

"It'll need a lot of work," I said, certain I'd grow old right there, whether Rita chose to or not. I didn't see my enthusiasm in her eyes, but sensed an awareness that work on the house promised an out from the mire we'd sunk into. We embraced right there in the stripped, lonesome place which would refocus our waning spirits and lend new energy to our love.

So I closed the deal. In due time I added two rooms, mended the roof, tilled the garden, bought the ducks. Rita had lived in apartments all her life and didn't want to put her savings in property, or to spend her leisure time improving a home. But she was willing to live there and furnish it, and she got into interior design like a born homemaker.

After all that activity, though, three years later we found that we were still left with us. The house, the courses I'd managed to keep taking, the roots I was sending down into my half acre, were strengthening only me. So much so that Rita, the frustrated mother, the fixer, the protectress, was lost without my neediness. She began to collect, one by one, the ragtag people who culminated in Craig. Shari, the drunk who practically lived down at Marcy's; Stephen, the older gay guy whose lover of thirty-one years had just died; Gip, the diminutive butch who'd even moved in with us for a few months when her worker's comp ran out. I blessed them all for giving what they did to Rita—and for leaving me in peace, to my stupor of job/school/work/garden/sixpack.

Sure I slept with Shari when Rita was out and I was drunk. And with some of the others. It was hard not to. There I'd be sitting around feeling good and all of a sudden she's looking at me that way—what was I supposed to do? I didn't know anybody who'd been one hundred percent faithful. It might have gotten awkward with the house guests afterwards, but they knew my position. It was only later, much later, that I started to feel the guilt well up toward Rita, toward these women whose neediness I guess I took advantage of. But

155

damn it, Rosa, I thought it went with the territory, with being gay. I thought I couldn't help myself.

At Mystic, Craig gave us his bedroom with its view of the Atlantic, of bobbing white boats and historical homes. Mystic Seaport is a national monument I'd longed to see for years: old shops spiffed up for tourists, businesses and houses reconstructed and staffed by costumed guides. I'd been high on the thought of our visit since Rita proposed it, weeks before, and I must have acted like an eager kid set loose in a toy village, noticing nothing but magic.

The promise of that day, Rosa! Everything painted white, new grasses sparkling light green, sun on the ocean like a million mirrors winking toward me. We'd driven up the night before, when the Seaport had been sleeping, nature rinsing it for us with a tender rain. I took Craig's warm welcome as a tribute to us both, and to the perfect weekend ahead.

We frolicked all day, on and off the ships, in and out of the shops. Rita and Craig often strolled before me arm in arm, in endless conversation, while I lagged behind, fascinated by the nautical paraphernalia. At lunch we ate chowder and "sea biscuits" (large unleavened wafers of bread) in the tavern, and liked the mugs of ale so much we went back each time one of us got thirsty. One of us was always thirsty. I was glad we had no need to drive and was ignorant of any other dangers might loose.

Craig was a perfect playmate: silly, imaginative, ready to follow the whim of his aunties, as he teasingly called us. For dinner Rita wanted to treat him, to return his hospitality she said, at Mystic's most elegant inn. We drank cocktails before dinner, played at being monied merchants from the clipper ship era. We drank wine till we got so loud and giggly the other diners looked disapproving.

A glaze had come over Rita's eyes which I couldn't recognize, but I was befuddled enough to ignore it. She seemed very uninterested, once we returned to Craig's place, in coming to bed, and poured me wine from the stock in our cooler. I couldn't get my high back from that afternoon, but I kept trying.

Craig had grown quiet, and I supposed he wanted us to go to bed so he could open up the couch Rita and I were sitting on. I was about to tell him goodnight and leave Rita to follow. Instead, she thrust herself into my arms, and kissed me in front of Craig.

"What the fuck—" I protested, pulling dizzily back from her, the liquor and shock unbalancing me.

Quietly, Craig said, "I'll leave if you want."

"No, don't go," said Rita, too quickly, the words slurred.

I looked at her. We had a lot of problems, but one of them had never been Rita pushing herself on me.

She wouldn't meet my eyes. Instead, she leaned against my shoulder, one hand seductively outlining my breasts. "I've been kind of wondering for a long time now, what it would be like," she said, then smiled drunkenly up at me.

To me, her smile looked like a leer. I'd certainly seen her this drunk before. Had she gone crazy? "What *what* would be like?" I demanded.

"You know."

"No, I *don't* know." Did she want him in the room? I felt like I was back in San Diego, in that little dive, about to hit the butch-pimp. My mouth tasted sour, all the liquor had begun to churn in my stomach. The river I carried inside me began to rise, set a whirlpool spinning, grabbed me and carried me toward the surface.

"With a man," Rita was explaining. "What it would be like."

She even *looked* like the pimp's girl. I tried with all my drunken mind to recall the femme's name. Jeanine, that was it. I'd refused her once, now here she was again. "*You* want to—"

"I want us to. So it'd be like doing it together."

157

I pushed her off me and stood, murderous words poised to gush from my mouth. But it was my stomach which spoke, and I wheeled and stumbled to the bathroom, heartsick, seasick, sick, sick, sick.

I don't know how long I knelt there, my forehead grateful for the cool of the toilet seat, my body cramping over and over to rid itself of nourishment turned poison.

"It's all right," I heard Rita say after a while. She ran a soothing wet cloth across the back of my neck, my cheeks, my wrists.

"I'm gay," I told her hoarsely. "I've always *been* gay. I'll always *be* gay. I only want my *girl* to be gay."

"It's all right," Rita repeated. "It's all right."

But it wasn't all right. It hadn't been all right for a long time and it would never be all right again. I saw then that what turned her on was enough neediness to make her feel powerful. That I was trapped in a love whose light, if there ever had been light in it, had dimmed and finally gone out. When I looked at her, it was as if water did separate us. Her edges were all blurred, her motions looked slow, we moved in a world tinged green. Jeeze, I'd cheated on her, but at least it had been with women.

Rita and Craig continued to see each other. I, used to the dark, saw nothing I didn't want to. I threw myself into completing school. Then, an associate degree in English and Business in hand, I turned Marcy's Bar into my home port, where I could ship out of my world at will. But no matter what I drank, or how much or how little, it was over for me, my romance with liquor. All it gave me was the old fuzziness that kept the sharp edges off pain—and sleepless nights, terrifying nightmares, physical illness.

CHAPTER TWENTY

Hernando, Jake, and Dusty sat on pillows and crates near the window of an otherwise barren, unfinished attic across from the Queen of Hearts. Grace, a lantern next to her the only light in the room, strummed her banjo well away from the window; Seeker slept at her feet. This was the midnight to 2:00 AM shift. Nothing had happened on Elly's 10:00 to 12:00 PM, or on Rosa's 8:00 to 10:00. Grace touched her watch. Twelve-forty. The diner had closed at 11:30.

Hernando was talking. "No one would even interview me, just new to the States."

"You were in the right place at the right time," Dusty replied. "I wanted a good worker and I got one." She wiggled around on her pillow. To Grace, they all seemed restless.

"I should have thought this out better," Jake said with a sigh. "A jug of wine and some cheese and crackers would have whiled away the hours much more pleasantly."

"I'd go for the jug just about now," Dusty said. Grace started to strum *"Bottle of Wine,"* but stopped herself. Elly had been right when she'd told Grace about Dusty and the beer can at the Halloween party that drinking, and thinking about drinking, were a habit to Dusty. She didn't see the harm in flirting with the idea, but Grace could.

"What did you do in Puerto Rico?" asked Jake.

"I went to school," said Hernando. "I was studying to go into the building trades, but when I graduated there were no jobs. Then I came here to be a construction worker—I couldn't get in a union! So I'm a dishwasher."

"A dishwasher who's bugging me to teach him to cook," Dusty added.

"Ambitious?" asked Jake.

"When I was growing up," Hernando confessed, "I wanted to be a priest. But there were too many like this Father Grimes. I think they make up all their rules because they're scared of life. But we don't live by rules, people. We live mostly I think by love."

Grace liked this kid. Liked his dreams, his stick-to-it-iveness. Liked that he had volunteered, after working all day, to help guard on Halloween night. And here he was, in a roomful of gays. She stopped playing long enough to give Seeker some affection.

"I wanted to do good, too," Jake said softly. "I thought I could be a doctor. But I had such a hard time coming out, accepting myself, staying out of trouble when I did, that I couldn't maintain decent enough grades. Pharmacy school seemed hard enough by the time I got to it. I don't know why everything feels harder when you're gay. Maybe it's because I had to spend so much time hiding who I was, or work so hard to find my own kind."

160

"Yeah," agreed Dusty. "How many straight diner owners have to stand guard at night?"

"Shhh!" said Hernando.

Grace jumped. Seeker sat up, mouth open.

"What is it?" Dusty whispered.

"Something moved out there, behind the diner."

Grace heard the slow scrape of binoculars against the boards. Her stomach knotted in suspense. Would it take them forever to report?

"A dog," said Hernando.

Grace exhaled and began a lullabye. A clock downstairs struck one, sounding very far away and lonely. A car, probably from the bar down the street, hummed along Railroad Avenue; a hot rodder charged the other way. She felt a tiny pinch on her back and a crawling sensation. "Do spiders bit?" she asked.

"Not hard, hon," answered Jake, laughing.

"Thanks," she grumbled, trying to reach the itchy spot.

Dusty laughed too, but came to her. "You okay over here?"

"I'm fine. Except for hundreds of gentle spider bites."

Dusty scratched her back and cleaned out the area behind her.

"Look!" said Jake, his voice urgent.

Dusty darted back to the window. Grace grabbed Seeker's neck ruff and massaged it more to calm herself than him.

"What are they doing?" Jake asked.

"Just walking," Hernando said.

She could feel tension in the attic like a kind of menacing fog, heard he companions' shallow breathing; but long ago she had trained herself not to ask over and over what she couldn't witness, even if it felt like life and death to her. What could she do, for the most part, but accept whatever it was?

Finally, Dusty turned to whisper, "Two kids walking down the tracks in costumes. Balancing."

"Singing!" said Hernando.

"Singing?"

"Listen." He raised the window slightly and Grace could hear two young voices bellowing what, with a melody, might have been a song. She could hear the River surge behind them, bringing trouble, bearing it away.

"They're drunk," said Dusty.

Jake concluded, "If they planned to pull anything at the diner, they wouldn't wake the neighborhood first." He stood to yawn and stretch. "I hate to say it, but I'm a little disappointed. I thought sure we'd see some action on this shift."

"There's time," Hernando reminded him.

"Did you ever think of going to pharmacy school, Her?" Jake asked.

"Sure," said Hernando. "Four years of college at night? I'd be a dishwasher for twenty years. Then I'd be too old to get hired."

"The technical college has a shorter pharmacy-assistant course. I'll need one of those when I open my drugstore."

"Yeah?" asked Hernando. Grace began *To Dream the Impossible Dream*. "You'd really hire me?"

"*If* I get my store."

"You'll get your store," said Dusty. "You've been planning and saving for years. That's not the problem. It's whether people decide you're putting fairy powder in your capsules to spread homosexualitis to their children."

"It might not help," Hernando said, "For you to have a Puerto Rican working for you."

"It might keep their minds off Jake."

"Oh, man," said Hernando. "You're gay, I'm Puerto Rican, Grace is blind—everybody's different, Dusty. Do you really think one different is worse than another?"

"That's not up to me—hold it!" Dusty commanded. Her voice seemed to fill the attic. "Three guys in costumes."

162

Jake said, "Not costumes. Stockings over their heads, dark clothes. What are they carrying?"

Grace's heart beat faster. A chill, as if straight off the River, swept over her. This felt like the real thing.

"Call the police," she whispered. If the floor wasn't full of gaping holes, and if the slanting walls were more than insulation between boards, she'd find her own way downstairs to the phone.

"Olive oil cans?" Jake was saying. "Why would they be carrying olive oil? To break into the diner and make salads?"

"Don't be an ass," Dusty said. "They're cans of gasoline."

Someone rose and stumbled toward the stairs.

"Call the Fire Department too!" Dusty said in a loud whisper.

"Don't let them pour it," Grace pleaded aloud, her voice tight and dry. "*Please, please.*"

"They're walking around the diner now with the cans. Looking for a place to start."

"They can't really want to burn the Queen of Hearts down just because you and Elly love each other, can they?" Hernando asked, horror in his voice.

Grace hunched over her banjo. "Hurry, hurry," urged her strings.

"I'd better go down and get rid of them," Dusty said. "The hell with witnesses." She got up.

"No!" Grace cried. "We've got to stop them for good, not just for tonight." Elly had warned her that Dusty might be reckless when faced with physical danger.

"I want my Queen whole," Dusty replied stubbornly.

"You'll only have her whole another week, a month, if you go down there." Grace could feel Dusty's anger and tension and fear all bunched up and ready to strike.

Jake burst in. "The cops are coming. They'll be right here!"

She heard Dusty's steps, pacing back and forth.

"There they go," said Dusty. "To the back with the cans. I've got to go down there."

"No! Give the police another couple of minutes," Jake said.

"If that was your drugstore you wouldn't be so ready to wait for the cops. Who knows if they'll even come? What do they care? They'll dance in the rubble with the priest."

Grace felt helpless. She might well have run down there by now if she were Dusty. "I hear vibrations," she said, just catching the feel of them, not even the sound yet. "Like trucks."

"The Fire Department."

"There goes a match."

Grace turned icy.

"Wait," Hernando said. "They let it die. You can hear the sirens now."

"Come *on* you beautiful firemen," Jake crooned.

The attic's cramped space filled with their excitement. Grace heard the trucks glide to a stop outside.

"Hot damn!" cried Dusty. "I love those flashing red lights!"

"Look at those punks run!"

"They left the gas cans behind. At least someone will know we're really in danger!"

"And there's the cops! Let's tell them where to look," Dusty said. She stopped briefly before Grace. "Thanks for holding me back, lady. You were right." Then she was gone.

Grace stood, fearful of making her way across the boards with just Seeker.

She was startled by Hernando's voice. "Don't forget your banjo."

She could hear him pull the lamp chain on and blow out the lantern. "Thank you for staying," she said. She took his arm. Seeker followed as they carefully made their way down the stairs and into the noisy world of safety outside.

CHAPTER TWENTY-ONE

Elly sat moodily on a stool at the rear of the Queen of Hearts, smoking, and drinking another cup of coffee, listening to a radio talk show discussion of the need to get POWS out of Vietnam. A few workers on their dinner break ate at the other end of the counter.

She was aware of the priest in his booth as she would be of a yellow jacket buzzing dangerously nearby. He watched her, as always. It was the first time she'd seen him order food, and she imagined him unreasonably angry at her because his parish was too poor to allow him to dine at Rossi's Amorbello Restaurant out on Main Street. It was there that the parishioners from the more well-to-do churches held receptions for weddings and the bankers held their business lunches.

Elly was about to get her period and she felt as ornery as the priest looked. Now and then she studied his hunched posture, trying to judge when to offer dessert. He was a glowerer, the kind of customer who expected her to guess his needs without being told.

Normally she'd be flirting and joking with the other customers to while away the evening, but she was new to night shift and didn't know the customers yet. After the torching attempt business had fallen off, as if the customers wanted to avoid the Queen's troubles, or as if there was a campaign to drive them away. When the night waitress had quit yesterday without even the courtesy of calling in, Dusty had stayed on days with Rosa. She was doing the ordering and Elly, working the even quieter nights, was to keep up the books at work instead of at home on her time off.

She stared through her curling smoke, past the thick white coffee cups they'd chosen for their red stripe. Hadn't Rosa left her anything to do? The ketchup, bright orange, looked ready to burst from its sparkling bottle as if the darn thing had been filled and polished at every use. Next to it the packed sugar bowl waited in ambush for some sweet-tooth. The mustard squeeze jar, lean and gold, wore a pointed clownish hat—and was spanking clean. All the little things she loved reproached her now, each a reminder that every swipe of Rosa's rag meant another customer who'd stayed away.

She stubbed out her cigarette and went exploring behind the counter. She filled the straw box again, but the squat napkin dispensers were already stuffed. Even the dark and light pairs of salt and pepper shakers, silver-capped, stood like soldiers ready to march the counter toward inspection. She felt like screaming, accustomed as she was to quick movements, attentiveness, working past exhaustion, and a lot of laughs. When a diner got this slow, the staff began to fall apart, feel

166

ill, think of unemployment benefits, fear the volume that had been second nature to them. Waitresses without customers were empty-nesters of a sort.

The priest pushed his plate away, wiped his mouth daintily and looked toward her. It was hard to hide her repulsion, to walk toward him all brisk and friendly, like he was just another guy.

"Can I get you something else, Father?"

"More coffee and a piece of pie. Is the apple baked fresh?"

His voice was the only priestly thing about him, she thought. It was low-pitched, seductive like a good radio announcer's. She tried to at least keep her voice expressionless. "We haven't been able to do any baking with the staff cuts. Table Talk's delivering all our pies."

He sat with hands folded, looking at his fingernails. "Not doing as well as you'd hoped in our little neighborhood?"

In her hand, the mess on his plate teetered dangerously toward his lap. "It takes time, Father," she said instead, turning away from him. "And we have all the time in the world." she lied.

The workers were lining up at the register, suddenly in a hurry. A group of young women needed menus, and watched her every move curiously, giggling. She could hear the whispered word "queer" and willed herself not to steam inside.

"And what about you, Father," she said as she returned, drawing the title out to suggest insult rather than respect, "what would you do without the diner?" She wanted to add, and all your free coffee.

He accepted the food without thanks. "There's always someone in here trying to scrape together a living," he said matter-of-factly, as if failure came with the attempt. "I understand our Mr. Rossi's been thinking of making an offer. Now there's a businessman." He used a gold toothpick. "Gave me this as a gift, a token of respect," he said, holding up the toothpick. "You girls would be smarter to stay home and make husbands fat instead of me." He gave his smile like a benevolent and rare blessing.

Elly swiftly turned her back on him and put all her surprise and rage into her walk, rudely swishing her bottom on her way to a waiting booth. So Rossi the real estate rat, the slumlord and empire-builder, wanted the Queen. Why?

The women's orders were complex, with a lot of changes of mind and more giggling and demure looks up from under their lashes, but she laughed back, and teased, to show them they had nothing to fear from her. As she pinned their order up she heard the inevitable whisper, "She don't *look* queer." Sometimes she wished Dusty had chosen a place other than the Valley to get born in.

She brought Father Grimes his check.

When he passed the register a few minutes later he asked, "What's this?"

Elly looked at him. "Did I add wrong?"

"The regular night girl knows it's good business to keep the check to herself," he said, his voice rough, his eyes angry. He speared the receipt onto the check spindle. "Common courtesy to the clergy!"

Elly just stared at him. He stood with hands on hips, breathing heavily.

"She was *not* authorized to do that." She gulped air, trying to stay calm. "I'm sorry, Father, but you'll need to pay for your suppers like anyone else. And I don't know where you got the idea that coffee is free. It's *not* any longer. We can't even stake our friends!"

"Common courtesy!" he huffed again. He stalked through the door.

Customers continued sparse through the night. She told the tale of the priest to Earleen who now doubled as dishwasher after 8:00 PM.

168

"I don't know why they keep that spiteful thing in business over there," said Earleen. "He's already driven away most of his church. Don't you worry about him, you hear?"

Elly hugged her. "Thanks," she said, but went back to work on the books in a desultory way, hating to face their proof of decreasing sales. By the time she left she was exhausted more from boredom and discouragement than from actual work. She had the period blues all right.

"Looks sort of sad," said Earleen as they left. She was eyeing the neon sign. The gang had played target practice on it till it read: DUSTY'S QUEE— —— HEAR—— DINER.

"Like a fighter with some teeth knocked out," agreed Elly. From the shape the books were in there wouldn't be money again this week to repair the sign.

Elly waited until the cook was in her car, motor running, door locked. She waved that she was safe too. Any of them would be afraid to be alone outside the diner now. Elly drove off, hating to abandon the Queen and its ragged rosy glow, but she'd have to rise in a few hours to ride in with Dusty, then take the car home, hoping Dusty could get a ride when she got off work.

She snapped her gum viciously at the memory of who had been driving her lover home lately. Just the thought of Rita made her blood feel like iced tea. *Just friends*, she thought with scorn.

"We're just friends now, Elly," Rita had whispered at the door of the Queen of Hearts, Dusty in tow. "She's perfectly safe with me!"

That musical lilt to her tinny voice. How could Dusty have stood her all those years? She laughed to herself. By drinking, how else?

She shifted down to cruise Main Street. Even at this time of night there was traffic here, johns without time to drive into Upton looking over the sparse Valley hooker population. The bars were still open, their own neon glows making this ride almost exciting. Her favorite was the Pelican Lounge sign, complete with flashy green pelican, so out of place on sooty cold northern streets. Her depression abated a bit.

As she passed the smaller dingier shops, Rita returned to her thoughts. The Swinger penetrated the main factory district and plunged across the clanging metal bridge over the River, so small next to her own Mississippi, yet so enormous in this Valley and in her new life. A few factories were fully lit tonight, heaving great stacks of smoke against the night, white cloudy stuff that thinned as it rose toward the moonless, star-bright sky.

"Dusty wouldn't mess around with that teeny Yankee bitch," she told the Swinger as her foot pressed the accelerator. Tenements rushed by, old and wooden, interrupted by cinderblock projects and vacant lots. Her hands were icy, despite the car's strong heater. She felt the seat beside her for her gloves and pulled them on, futile protection against such a chilly mood. Her insides were trembly, but she willed herself to believe in Dusty. The first of her cramps began. Her insides felt rotted out, crumbling.

"You're the only girl for me," Dusty had said over and over. Then why was she seeing Rita? It was hard, now that the Queen of Hearts was floundering, not to wonder if it wouldn't cast a shadow darker than either of them could fight. She feared becoming the symbol of Dusty's failure. Would this crashing dream unhinge Dusty more and more? If so, Rita had arrived just in time to rescue Dusty once again.

Trees became more frequent on the streets. Duplexes and two-family homes with converted attics huddled under them as if for comfort. Would Dusty be home tonight? She seldom spent a whole evening alone now, and sometimes stayed out until she knew Elly would be there, as if afraid to be by herself. Then Dusty would be restless with stimulation, unable to sleep. "Want to come?" Elly would ask, hoping for assent, knowing it would help Dusty relax. "Not tonight," Dusty would say. Then Elly would hear her turning beside her, over and over, till the alarm went off and Dusty, raspy-voiced, would say, "I *can't* get up. I haven't slept yet."

Mama had suffered from insomnia like that. She'd drink to put herself to sleep, but until she passed out she'd come in and out of Elly's room, a dark shadow in her doorway, her bourbon smell reaching the bed before she did. "Hold Mama, pretty darlin'," she'd croon, then rock Elly, crying sometimes, babbling out her hurt and loneliness. "Mama don't," Elly had learned to say soothingly, over and over, scared, scared, scared. Like Dusty scared her now.

Why had Dusty gone and fired John? He was about as mean as a striped snake, and that wasn't mean at all. Grace had told her how Dusty could have blown everything Halloween night by trying to play vigilante. Dusty did such stupid unthinking things. Couldn't even *see* that Rita wanted her back or that she needed to stay about three miles away from the nearest liquor. Damn, she should be more responsible. So close to success one day, so reckless the next.

Elly couldn't forget the picture in her mind of Dusty and the beer can at the Halloween party. Look where that had led. A month later, when they'd gone to the Thanksgiving dinner at Marcy's Bar, Dusty had sipped Grace's drink. Sure, she'd made a face and said she didn't know why she ever indulged at all. But the next minute she was swapping drinking stories with Rita, swearing by her favorite whiskey. Every night since then Elly had feared that the house, on her arrival, would reek of whiskey. That she'd have to roll away in bed to avoid breathing Dusty's tainted breath. But so far there had been no liquor smell. Just evenings out and the tossing and turning. Sometimes in the night she thought she could hear Dusty's troubles eating big holes inside her lover, eating away at her college education, her high principles, her big dreams, till Elly feared waking one morning beside a shell whose insides actually had rotted and been washed away in the night.

171

This unsteady, self-consuming Dusty was the one she'd first met at Marcy's. Dusty had acted so much the part of the drunken sailor that it had been weeks before Elly had seen a glimmer of the real woman who was to become her lover. She'd had no idea Dusty arrived at the bar only after classes, that she owned her own home, had been with one lover so long. Dusty had never said a word about putting herself through college. Yet when they'd started talking a warmth grew hotter and hotter between them as Dusty went on about a poet named Edna St. Vincent Millay in one breath, and explained how to set up books, how to buy real estate, with the next. Elly had burst out, "You're *just* who I've been lookin' for!"

"Who's that?" Dusty had asked, as if uncertain who was inside to be found.

Tonight Elly wondered who also—who she'd find at home—the charming, well-spoken lover she'd helped disentangle from a long and torturous breakup—or the drunken sailor again, moody, full of self-doubts and discarded yearnings. She'd have to know before she told her about Rossi closing in, like a vulture smelling death.

The Swinger turned into Puddle Street, almost by itself. There were no cars outside the house. The dark, silent, lifeless-looking house. Was Dusty even there? As if in a dream she walked for what seemed like hours toward the front door.

CHAPTER TWENTY-TWO
Dusty's Tales

It was the most beautiful of warm clear spring days when I declared myself to Elly—or tried to. I wanted this to be different, Rosa, not something quick and dirty. Not out of feeling lost and needing an anchor. Not out of inebriated high spirits. I didn't ever want to be ashamed of myself again, to feel shame about how I'd cheated, how I'd treated every woman I'd been with. I didn't care any more if that was the only way it could be for all other gay people. If only one queer in the world broke the pattern, it was going to be me.

I don't think I'd ever seen Elly in daylight before, with sunrays catching in her hair, getting all tangled like red ribbons, with her eyes as blue as little ponds. This one's no kid, I told myself, but she's more than just adult. She's a real live grown woman, surely too rich for my blood, too certain of herself to let me turn her head. I wanted to deserve her.

It was Saturday and I'd invited her to share what I called my weekly run. I couldn't stand being home when Rita cleaned house, I cleared out of there when her Saturday morning hungover angry mood invaded like a surly storm cloud. Maybe she saved up all her resentments till Saturday, maybe she was so angry at me for nothing, for everything, that by that time she couldn't entirely hide it though we were trying to coexist. I hadn't gotten any worse as a housekeeper, but she got mad at me every week all the same: I hadn't done this, or I'd done that all wrong. I'd end up feeling like an inept idiot, so after months of it I started jumping in my Swinger and running away, all by myself, coasting up and down the Valley hills till dinnertime, when I knew a couple of evening cocktails would have mellowed her. I knew it was past time for her to move out, but I couldn't ask her to go. I needed something to happen to make it easier.

Elly was still living in Upton with Rudy and George from the bar. I picked her up at Morton River Station. She stepped off the train in a purply soft turtleneck, light slacks and those funny little shoes she wore, always at least a tiny bit high-heeled. I took the canvas bag she carried. "A snack," she explained. It was so heavy I peeked inside: a long French loaf, cheeses, fruit, a bottle of wine.

What a perfect day. I'd put Rita, grumbling back at the house, out of my mind. And I put Elly, her bag between us, in my life, on the front seat of my car, looking like she'd been there all along. She started talking—could it be nervously I wondered?—her laugh coy and soft one minute, loud and delighted the next. Familiar, but different from any woman I'd

174

ever loved before. Like someone who would have worked with my mom at the Uptown Diner. Someone I would have snuggled against in the waitress' booth, soft and cuddly and smelling like Five-and-Dime perfume.

"Cachet," Elly answered when I asked her what she was wearing. "Like it?"

Like it, I thought to myself. If the Swinger was propelled by gasoline, I was jet-propelled by that scent. I felt so grateful that I had this chance to start all over, that a woman like Elly might—well, I didn't know for sure if she might, even though she'd told me I was just what she was looking for. Who knew if she was just high when she said it? I said all kinds of things high.

Off I went with Elly to the edge of town, to the first place where I could spot the River on my run each Saturday: the dam. It seemed larger than life, creating its own wind by forcing all that water over the huge concrete wall. I always stopped to look at it, maybe to remind myself there was something larger in the world than me and my troubles. Elly and I sat with a mist spraying through the open window, cool under the already warm sun.

"We had dams like this back home," Elly said. "They always reminded me there was somethin' bigger in this world than poor ol' me and my troubles."

It was all I could do not to reach for Elly's hands right there and then. How many nights had I watched this little lady dance and flirt and sometimes cry across the smoky bar? I'd even fast-danced with her a couple of times, sat at the table she shared with her crowd—that cab driver, and the gym teacher in the three-piece suits, and Turkey, who was always clowning. Many a time I'd wondered if she was sleeping with any of them or all of them or if she was lonely too. She had a slinky sexiness in the way she moved that reeled me in like a hooked fish.

We began to climb the hills in the Swinger. I found myself telling Elly about my days—the plant, college. But soon I stopped. She'd begun to notice what was around her.

For all the Morton River Valley's faults, the attitudes, the depression, the economic insecurity, one look at the houses told you it was a special place. No two were alike. Each owner had a different solution to living on hills, on riverbanks, jammed in close to the next house.

When these homes were built there was very little space. Without cars, everyone wanted to live near work. Sheer rock took up a lot of the nearby space, and those who grabbed the precious lots looked out on factories, grey and bleak, yards full of equipment, trucks, supplies and goods. Then there had been the smoke which settled everywhere, sometimes across the sun itself, further darkening the Valley's days. These hill dwellers, many recently from their old countries, combated the visual blight with brightly colored homes or they repainted in white every year. They fought the dreariness with ornate stone or concrete walls, with ironwork or severely trimmed hedges, with elaborate woodworking, with highly organized flower gardens which were feasts to the eyes, with densely packed vegetable gardens, exploding greens in spring, bursting reds and oranges at harvesting.

"Look at those azaleas!" Elly cried. "The colors—they must have planted every variety there is!"

A little later she said, "Stop! Do you mind? How in the world did they do that with the stones?" She was pointing at an archway and wall around a miniature palace.

And, "Oh, Dusty! I've never seen anything like it!" A Victorian house, turreted, painted in shades of salmon and brick red, its trim carefully detailed and highlighted.

I wanted some sights left for her to come back for, so I turned, climbed one last hill and coasted down, under the new-made light green leaves of the same thick old trees that had inspired me about roots. They'd been right about the roots, but I'd gone into staking those roots all wrong. I drove out through the farmlands, lured by the promise of the roads just as I'd been all the weeks before.

It wasn't until we got to Stephen's Falls that I realized we hadn't touched either bottle of wine.

Leaf shadows made patterns across Elly's face. Sunrays put sparks in her eyes and her earrings swung and glittered as she talked. There was more than spring in the air—that breath-held excitement, the feeling of wings beating, seeking the thrust to lift from the ground, the sense that love like a bud on a tree was about to burst from its winter casings into naked and tender curled leaves. I knew I'd found what I needed to cut the last threads of relationship with Rita. All I wanted in the world was to touch with my lips this sweet-smelling Southerner with the womanly ways, kiss her and keep her in my life forever.

A few families were using the picnic tables, but no one was down near the falls except for occasional hikers. As we talked and ate and drank the wine—sparingly, to wash down the food—the sunshine warmed and played on us, and I felt some of the light from my hopeful dreamy Navy days touch me. But Elly asked questions about the life I was living now, and I couldn't find a bright spot to tell her about other than Duke and Duchess, Angelica and Helen of Troy, work, school. And Marcy's, the after-hours place where I'd join the other diehards who had no reason to go home, and who, like me, traveled with a cooler. It was as bleak a picture as Morton Valley without its hillside gardens. I was ashamed I hadn't planted flowers in my own life.

I grabbed Elly's hands, held them in my own that first sweet time, those light, thin, nervous hands. The blue in her pond-eyes darkened. "Maybe this is crazy of me, El," I said. "Maybe you don't want to hear it, especially from someone so tangled up in what's gone wrong I'm tripping on it trying to get out."

While I paused to gather courage I saw that her eyes had widened, were bright with light. She returned the pressure of my hands. "Oh, you silly, old-fashioned, formal darlin'," she said, smiling with tremulous lips. Without another word from me she said, "I love you too." Then, for another first time, I pulled her toward me. Deep in the woods, above the cascading waters, I felt the frailness of her narrow shoulders, the strength of her back, the firmness of her hands on me, the softness of her feathery hair. When I opened my eyes she was really in my arms, telling me how long, how hard she'd been wanting me. Me!

I swore to myself I'd tell her everything, every last dirty detail of my life. I wished I were a guy so we could marry and have a better shot at staying together. I hoped being honest would work as well. What I didn't know was how much I needed to learn about honesty, and that the lessons would start with telling myself the truth.

But at that moment, I felt too much joy for my courage to fail me. I looked beyond her, down to the falls, and couldn't think of a thing then except the water. All that water below on its own promising road, leaping to rejoin its stream, hurrying to be part of something much bigger than itself.

CHAPTER TWENTY-THREE

It had been an hour since Elly had entered the cold silent house. Even the cats weren't home. She'd looked for a note from Dusty, for any sign she'd even been home after work.

The clock chimed a lonely midnight. Was Dusty dead on the road? Drowned in the River by a plotting Rita? Killed by her own despondent hand? Or worse—sleeping with another woman, with Rita? She remembered the night Dusty had gone to Rita to tell her it was over. She'd waited in the car and wondered if it would ever happen to her. Was it her turn now? She should have known she couldn't keep a prize like Dusty.

"What will I do without you?" she whispered into the night sky. It was a deep blue-black, impassive, a blank wall

179

beyond the living room drapes. She'd been like that sky, hiding her fears; tonight they were all rushing out to combine into panic.

A car drove into Puddle Street and her heart leapt with hope. But it was one of the young Corrigans coming in from a date. The car's motor purred interminably, so it had to be the girl, making out with her boyfriend as if nothing of note was happening on Puddle Street. As if Dusty Reilly wasn't missing.

Elly groaned in pain, but not from her cramps. She was aware that she was carrying on, perhaps needlessly, but it felt right to her. She clutched a handful of drape, tempted to tear it from the ceiling to satisfy this need to act out what she felt.

Should she call Grace for comfort? Only if she wanted to listen to the voice of reason. She'd been reasonable long enough.

Another car approached, but didn't turn onto Puddle. A few lights were on across the River—was Dusty in one of those illuminated buildings? One of those bars?

The chill of her fear warmed slowly at first, then faster. Dusty was just looking for trouble in those bars. Even if she wasn't drinking she was acting drunk, not calling like this. Or was tonight the night she gave in and got drunk again, seduced into it by her fear of losing the Queen of Hearts? My weak-willed hero, she thought. She must be with Rita or with some other home wrecker. Dusty was a hot property.

Jealousy flamed her anger and in turn fed her fear. Someone else was getting Dusty tonight. Was touching those places, looking into the eyes Dusty had pledged to her, Elly Hunnicutt, forever.

"The fucker!" she cried, hurling the drapes against the window. She turned her back on the Valley lights and stormed over to Dusty's pennywhistle collection. "How could you!" she shouted, and scattered them along the shelf.

She collapsed on the couch, sobbed, rose again and paced, then returned to the window. She glanced at the clock. Only fifteen minutes had passed. She fled to the kitchen for a cup of tea. If she couldn't face reason, at least she could seek outward calm. But when the front door opened some moments later she was too wound up to react.

The sigh that finally came was a controlled exhalation that did nothing for her nerves. She stood at the sink, fiddling with some dishes. She glanced over her shoulder at Dusty, then back to the sink.

"Sorry I'm so late." Dusty leaned in the kitchen doorway, hands in her pockets, chin sunk low over her navy turtleneck, a distracted, but not distressed, look on her face. "I got tied up." She paused as if waiting for a response. "Coming to bed soon?" she asked.

How—could—she—ask—such—a—thing? With gritted teeth, back still turned, she replied, "No." She was picturing Dusty tied up in the arms of Rita.

"El?" asked Dusty from the doorway.

Her voice had turned uncertain. But Elly was used to hearing that tone these days. She grew angrier. Where was the big strong butch she'd fallen for? What a front Dusty had shown her. What a lousy cheating charade.

"Hey, lady, are you mad?"

She whirled around then, seeking words with which to strike. "*Mad? Mad?* Of course I'm mad. Mad with worry, mad with fear, mad with confusion. Why didn't you at least *call* me?"

Dusty still wore the shirt she'd cooked in, and her spattered white pants.

So she hadn't returned home at all, thought Elly, and added that fact to her fire.

"I tried to get you, El, but you'd already left the diner. And then we were talking in the car and there wasn't a phone." Dusty looked pained, even disappointed. "Why are you so upset?"

Reasonable, be reasonable, Elly told herself. She pictured Grace in her rose garden, cross-legged, serene. But the hot wave of anger washed over her again.

"Upset?" she shrieked, hating the sound of her voice, the ugliness that must be transforming her face, and even angrier at Dusty's self-centered denseness for forcing her to act like this. "You go off with your ex who'd like nothing better than to sink her claws into you again, you stay out till all hours and come in here all cool and collected and you want to know why I'm upset?"

She looked through the red shade that had fallen between herself and the world, watched her own shaky, frantic, jerky motions. She picked up her cup and saucer and hurled them into a corner.

SMASH! went the cup. CRASH! and the saucer was also in bits on the floor. They lay there, jagged, as dangerous-looking as she felt. Broken. Unmendable.

She took a breath and the tears began to spill. Leaning against the sink she sobbed and sobbed, ashamed of collapse, frightened that she'd driven Dusty away.

Dusty came closer, but Elly could feel her tenuousness, as if she feared Elly would try to smash her next. "El," she said.

Elly cried on. Dusty tried to pull her near. Elly resisted, but not as vigorously as she might have minutes ago.

"El."

"What," she spat.

"Nothing happened."

She swung her body toward Dusty. *Look at her,* she thought.

Dusty's arms were raised slightly toward Elly, palms up, as if in supplication. Her eyebrows were drawn up, her mouth was slightly open. She looked as if she was pleading.

Elly grated. "No thanks to *you,* I'm sure."

"We were just talking."

"Did you go drinking?"

"I drank Seven-Up all night."

She nodded, feeling disgusted. "Thank goodness. You'd be back in her bed by now if it'd been liquor."

Dusty was silent. Her arms had fallen to her sides, fingers curled into loose fists. "No," Dusty said, but weakly. "No," she repeated as if unsure. "I wouldn't, El."

But it had sounded like a whine with no conviction to it.

"Oh, Dusty. I should have known. You told me yourself it's the only way you know how to feel better—to blank out your problems and run to someone new. I was so wrong to think if I loved you enough you'd never have to do that again."

Dusty took a step toward her. "But I didn't—"

"*This* time," said Elly, stepping back. "You didn't drink this time. You kept your hands off the girl you were with *this* time. But nothin's going to get any easier, Dusty. And some night . . . Why *else* would you put yourself in that situation, sittin' in a bar close to the whiskey, with a woman in reach? Why else would you be there if you weren't wantin' to drown your sorrows? You told me you don't even like Rita anymore."

Dusty collapsed into a chair. Her legs were widespread, her hands hung helpless between them, her head was down, her shoulders heaved in a sigh. "I don't know, El," Dusty said, shaking her head. "I don't know. I guess I was thinking of the good times."

Elly smiled. This rang true. She felt her muscles begin to relax.

Dusty looked up. "I guess I just don't know what else to do for myself. I was thinking Rita's safe because she's over with. But—"

The anger flooded back in. "Did she try something?"

"Not exactly."

"That bitch!"

"No, El."

"Don't you defend her!"

"But it was me. It really was me. Aw shit. Why am I so *weak?* I didn't drink, but I wanted so bad to be in a bar, El. *Why?* I don't want Rita, but I can't say no when she comes by for me. *Why?* I don't know what to *do* with myself nights without you home. I'm jumpy as a butterfly. I can't concentrate on a book. I start having nightmares before I even go to sleep. One night, El, I even brought a bottle of whiskey home. We sat and stared at each other, that bottle and me, till it was time to come get you. I stopped at a trash bin and got rid of it."

"Poor baby." She'd vented her anger. Now all she felt was overwhelming concern for her tormented woman. She took Dusty in her arms.

"No," said Dusty, holding her body stiff. "No poor baby. I'm a creep to treat a good woman like you this way. I can't control myself. Everything Father Grimes says is true. I turn everything good in my life to shit and then run away because I can't face what I've done." She looked into Elly's eyes. "Even us."

Elly stood for a while with her head against Dusty's shoulder, then she took her hand and led her to bed. "We have to get up in the mornin' and we're not going to solve a thing as exhausted as we are."

They undressed and lay side by side, unmoving. Duchess dug a nest between Dusty's legs. Duke inched under the covers between them. The cats purred loudly in the dark. Elly was on her back, not expecting sleep. Something had to give soon, she thought. I can't go through this over and over, no matter how much I love her.

For the first time the thought occurred that they might not be able to work things out. A cold sweat covered her body and she realized that her cramps had finally come full force. She kicked the covers off.

"El? You awake?" whispered Dusty.

"Um-hum." She took Dusty's hand.

"How was it tonight? At the diner."

"Slower than molasses." She twisted a lock of her own pubic hair absently around a finger, then realized how terribly sensitive she was feeling down there. Because of her period? Because of their fight? "But I think I won over a crowd of women who came in ready to scream rape if I dropped a crumb on a lap. They left suspecting I might belong to the human race."

"No wonder I want to drink. Good work, lady."

"I wish that creepy priest would retire and fly South or wherever priests who've lost their usefulness go."

Dusty leaned on an elbow. "I almost forgot to tell you what I learned tonight. Rita—do you mind if I mention her?"

"If you can't avoid it," Elly said sourly.

"Then you-know-who was telling me about him. She was brought up Catholic, remember. She's heard some things about this Father Grimes."

"Like what?" She turned on her side toward Dusty, felt Duke pressed between them.

"He got in big trouble a while back. Remember reading in the paper about cross burnings around here?"

"It was front-page news. He didn't—"

"No, but a youth group he sponsored did. The church claimed he knew nothing about the burnings, but the parents, in court, said their kids had only been trying to please Father Grimes. One of the kids got off because he testified Grimes was always complaining about minorities trying to get into his parish and how they were ruining the area. The court saw him as an authority figure, the kid as a misguided youth. The church censored Grimes and has been watching him ever since. And the kid's name—you won't believe this—was Leon Rossi. Leon the gang leader."

"Rossi the rat's son?"

"None other."

She swallowed hard to keep from saying more. Not tonight, she thought. Then remembered what they'd just been through. Holding back was no way to run a relationship. She told Dusty what the priest had said about Rossi.

But instead of getting upset Dusty became excited. "Maybe it's not just senseless hate, El. Maybe they're using our gayness to get the diner. I wonder why Rossi didn't outbid me in the first place? Why does he want the Queen of Hearts now?"

"I don't know, but I want to hold onto her even tighter."

Neither spoke for a while. Elly could hear the furnace hum below them in the basement. Duke wheezed as he slept. Duchess outright snored. Elly still held Dusty's hand.

Dusty broke the silence. "I wonder if the priest is like an over-the-hill boxer. You keep waiting for his best punch and then find out you've already seen his best, or worst."

"Why, Dusty Reilly. This isn't you seeing a ray of hope, is it?" teased Elly. She pressed closer to Dusty. Duke squeezed out from between them and stomped off the bed. As they lay there, touching from cheek to toes. Elly felt as if she had regained something precious she'd almost lost.

After a while, Dusty slipped one long arm between them. Elly was surprised at her own slickness down there. She moved against Dusty's nearly still hand, the knuckles gently touching her on and off, like a heart beat. Elly's mons lifting, falling, lifting.

Dusty's other arm tightened against her. Elly pushed her breasts against Dusty's. Would she really be able to come from so little movement? There was only the night around them, dark, comforting. Their breaths quickened, bodies heated, needy, tired.

"Ohh," sang Elly, for the sheer joy, after all the pain, of being on the edge of climax. "Ohh," she sang again, but stopped, realizing by their position that if Dusty's knuckles were on her clitoris, then her fingers—her swiftly rotating fingers—must be her own.

"El," said Dusty, as if gasping for air. "El, *come* with me."

She forgot her surprise. The thought of Dusty touching herself, while she touched Elly too. . . .

"Ohhh," she sang once more to Dusty's "Lady, lady, lady," and didn't stop singing, thought she'd never stop, till she was crying in joy, crying in relief, till she lay holding Dusty's sleeping hopeful head against her own heart.

CHAPTER TWENTY-FOUR
Grace

The next day, with a flourish of flailing tree branches reminiscent of the hurricane, the rain began. Grace stepped into the Queen of Hearts hungry for a cold milkshake to drink to the rhythms of the jukebox. Seeker's toenails clicked on the tiles, a customer clanked a cup on a saucer, someone rustled a newspaper, Dusty snapped an order off its clip. Grace arranged herself on a stool and ran her fingers along the vinyl seat mended with plastic tape, then around the cold metal sides beneath the vinyl.

"What can I get you, *amigito?*"

Grace listened to her strawberry milkshake whir in the machine, to the scrape of its rotors when Rosa pulled its metal cup down and poured the stuff, so thick Grace could hear it. Elly had once walked Grace through the magical process when Grace had asked how shakes were made. A chunk of strawberry was stuck at the bottom of her straw and she was struggling to suck it out when she heard someone else come in.

"How's the service in this dive?" Jake stage-whispered to her.

Grace could hear Rosa nearby. "You know these greasy spoons," Grace replied loudly. "Give the waitress thirty percent and she might take the fly out of your soup."

"Maybe make sure the bubble gum's off the bottom of your plate," Jake cracked.

"Maybe bring you the ketchup before your fries go cold."

"And," said Rosa, setting a plate smelling strongly of lemon meringue in front of Jake, "make sure there's enough pie for everyone who doesn't need it." She moved away.

"Well, I never," Jake said.

The friends were gathering these days at change of shift, when there was a chance of catching both Elly and Dusty together.

"Grace!" called Gussie from the doorway. At the counter she said, "Here's Dale, the woman I was telling you about from San Francisco."

"Berkeley," Dale corrected in a laughing voice, as if she'd made the correction before.

"Berkeley, San Francisco, when you're in New England they're all the same. And this is Jake. I want you both to meet my very best friend in the world, Dale."

"I love your Panama," said Jake in a cooing voice.

"Panama?" asked Grace.

"A Panama hat," explained Dale gently, placing the hat in Grace's hands.

Grace smiled in pleased surprise. She examined the hat, feeling Dale's cheerful presence above her. When she handed it back, Dale took her hands, pressed them, lifted them to her face.

"Is this okay?" she asked as Grace explored angles and planes on the smooth, just slightly lined flesh. Dale's hair was a wild mass of curls much longer than her own and had lost its youthful spring. "Grey?"

"Since shortly after my last accident," said Dale. She passed Grace a rough and knobby cane. "I spent three years in a wheel chair, more on Canadian canes—the ones with the elbow braces. Now I'm hobbling around with this."

"Hobbling, my foot," said Gussie. "You're just plain debonair with that walking stick."

"It's real nice," said Grace, in awe of this sensitive stranger with an aura about her of romance and adventure. She wished for more impressive words, for soaring speech that would woo this lovely being, fascinate her, make her long for Grace's company forever.

"Gussie's just never accepted my altered circumstances," Dale said, laughing.

Grace had never heard such a wonderful laugh—like a stream falling on pebbles.

"When I first knew you, Dale, you were fleet as the wind."

"Fleet to crawl into your older woman's bed," Dale said to Grace, "I wanted badly to come out, but once I did I couldn't handle it on my own in that small town. I got a job and bought an old hot rod which I proceeded to demolish accident by accident."

With an unfamiliar shyness, Grace said, "So you gave up full use of your legs to save your life."

"Exactly how I see it," said Dale. "Wow. That's amazing. You understood just like that!" She snapped her fingers.

"I know someone else like that. A cousin down home who drove like the devil to drive the devil out of himself." Grace decided she'd follow the purr of Dale's voice anywhere.

"Come on, kids," Gussie said. "Let's go sit in a booth where an old lady can be comfortable. We seem to have driven off the last customer."

"You're not an old lady," said Dale.

"'She's never accepted my altered circumstances,'" Gussie quoted Dale's earlier barb.

Grace and Seeker followed.

"Am I invited to this party?" called Elly.

"Change of shift already?" Dusty asked, having come out of the kitchen.

"*I'm* having more pie," Jake announced, "if this is a party."

Elly offered to get it. Grace could hear her hang up her coat, could hear her greet Dusty. She wondered what had happened to put such tentativeness in their hello.

"You only go to the gym to work off what you put on in pie here," Rosa accused.

"What gym?" asked Jake. "I *wish* I could work this off there. It's the only gym in town."

"Why can't you use it?" asked Dusty.

"John's pals have taken to hanging around it. The night there was just me and them in the locker room I got out of there so fast I must have broken an Olympic speed record."

"How incredible," said Dale. "It sounds like you haven't even begun to organize Morton River."

"Organize?" said Jake. "We're ready to organize a full-scale retreat."

Dale went on, "It's nineteen seventy-two, you know. There's a big gay liberation movement getting started."

"Yeah," said Jake. "Once a year a bunch of drag queens get themselves on television."

Quietly, Dale said, "It's more than that. Ten percent is a powerful number."

Ten percent?" repeated Elly. "How many people live in the Valley?"

Gussie answered. "Twenty-eight thousand, they say, though it's dwindling with industry. So, Dale, you're saying there's twenty-eight hundred gay people in the Valley?"

"That's the statistic."

"Where are they?" Elly demanded. "That many customers could support the Queen of Hearts."

"Hiding," Dusty said. "Like us." Rain beat steadily against the Queen of Hearts' windows.

"I personally think we are one wise race of people," Jake said. "When you consider what we're up against. Have you heard how Father Grimes has gotten his hooks into Rossi to pressure him to buy the diner?"

"We know he's interested, but not why," Dusty said. "I can't see Rossi doing it just to rid Railroad Avenue of an infestation of queers."

"The rumor around the hospital is that the old factory up the road from here, the one that runs over the tracks and right up to the River's edge, has been sold to some developers."

"What kind of factory would go into that old shell?" Rosa asked. "It's huge, and the big companies are all settling out in the suburbs."

"Not a factory, hon," Jake said. "A shopping mall. Enclosed, with a couple of dozen cutesy shops to pull in the college crowd and the people restoring the Victorian houses around here. It's supposed to be a pilot project. If it takes off here, they'll repeat it all over the country."

"A shopping mall on Railroad Avenue?" exclaimed Gussie. "I remember when hobos camped out along here."

Elly laughed, an arm linked in Grace's. "I'd consider the mall a personal favor. No more driving all the way to Upton."

"I can't wait," said Jake. "To browse on a Saturday afternoon through *Ye Olde Red Brick Sweat Shop Emporium*? Heaven."

Dusty laughed. "I can't take this all in. Next they'll put a restaurant with a view of the River in there. That'll kill us for sure."

"Oh, Dusty," Elly said. "Think of all the new customers the stores would bring. They can't all eat there. Why would Rossi want the Queen of Hearts if he couldn't make a buck?"

"He'd tear her down and put in a parking lot," Dusty complained.

"What a perfect balance you two would be," said Grace, "if the bad didn't weigh so much more than the good."

"Lighten up, Dusty," said Jake. "It'll all work out."

Some customers entered. Elly and Rosa returned to work.

Jake hugged Grace. "I'm off to push drugs at sick people;," he said. "Will it rain for forty days and forty nights, do you think? I mean if it does, I might as well get a perm, my hair's going to kink up anyway."

"Dusty's Ark," suggested Grace. "Don't say it, Dusty—your ark would sink."

Dusty's laugh was weak. "You're probably right. A flood would come along and wash us down the River."

"Will you stop and say hi to Nan up at the hospital, Jake?" asked Gussie.

"The hospital?"

Gussie's voice sounded thin and dry. "I hated to do it, especially with Dale coming, but Nan just wasn't getting well at home. At our age, these lingering illnesses can be dangerous. The doctor felt hospital care would have her up and around in a week or we'll know something more serious is going on."

"Of course I'll check in on her," Jake said. Grace could hear the kiss he gave Gussie. "You come and visit me down in the dispensary later, okay?"

Gussie's sigh broke the silence after Jake left. Dale spoke. "I'm glad I came just now. You need a rest, Gus."

"At least you can visit with her in the hospital. I hoped so much that you'd like each other."

"I do like her. And I'm only a *little* jealous. I'm glad you think Elly's too young for you. Just your type, if I recall."

"Don't you start trouble," Dusty warned with a laugh.

Rosa had returned. "Nothing to cook, Dusty. Just dessert customers." She remained at the booth. "Did you two keep in touch all these years?"

Dale said, "While I was still home she'd write me in care of the garage where I worked on my car."

Grace sighed. "How romantic."

"But one thing led to another," said Gussie. "She found younger women, and I began my pilgrimage back toward my roots."

"Then you really do remember hobo camps along Railroad Avenue," Rosa said.

"Oh, yes, dear. The factories would give them a day's pay during the Depression to feed coal to the furnaces or what have you. It looked like the Valley would go under then, too, but it came back. I'll be glad to see the factories put to good use again. Especially if they help Dusty and Elly."

"I don't know," Dusty grumbled.

Gussie laughed at her. "*You* ought to get on the Chamber of Commerce or whatever committee is going to boost this thing, instead of grumping around worrying about it."

"They wouldn't let me on anything like that."

"Dusty," said Dale in a persuasive tone, "I know this isn't the Bay area, but I've been pretty involved in both gay and disability rights out there. I've learned a thing or two about the ins and outs of city politics, at least enough to demystify it. I also know the politicians want all the power they can get and will often overlook their own prejudices if someone has something to bring them. From what you've said about this Rossi character I'll bet he hasn't endeared himself to the business community. I'd love to spend some time talking to you. I think I could help."

"I don't know, Dale. That's what Elly said, too. Make friends with the other businesses—maybe some of them have problems like ours. I didn't know till this week that all our problems might be a conspiracy. Rossi and son in cahoots with the church is a combination I'm not sure I'm big enough to beat."

"Alone," Elly added, back with coffee refills. "You've got some orders on the clip." Two men from the factories had settled at the counter.

While Dusty cooked, Gussie and Dale talked old times. Grace listened, fascinated. She'd just told them what a blessing it had been not to come out till now and miss tortured adolescence, when Hernando began shouting.

He'd been sweeping, whistling along with the jukebox. "Hey!" he cried suddenly. "Dusty! Come quick! Someone's fooling with your car!"

CHAPTER TWENTY-FIVE

Elly rushed to the window, but Dusty ran straight for the door. Despite her fear, Elly felt a flash of pride to see her big woman charging at full speed, full power. She darted to the door to follow Dusty.

On the steps in the rain Dusty paused for a second to take in the scene. In this dank daylight, the Queen's neon sign signaled its red passion over Dusty, over the sidewalk, over the two kids by the Swinger.

"What the hell are you doing?" Dusty demanded of the kids.

Elly saw one boy pull his knife out of a tire. He'd already punctured another. He stood and glared defiantly at Dusty, then gave a contemptuous grin and raised a middle finger. Elly watched in rage as both boys turned to leave almost non-chalantly, as if they felt they held all the power.

Elly had just decided to call the police when Dusty rushed at the kid who held the knife.

"Dusty!" she screeched. "Stop!" But she knew it was too late. Dusty had been pushed beyond bearing. Nothing could restrain her now. Elly pressed her hands against her thudding heart, horrified.

The kid flipped open his knife again. Dusty hurled toward the cruel shining blade. His friend had stopped smiling, had stepped back. "Come on, man." His voice was timorous.

Easily evading the loosely held knife, Dusty took hold of the slasher to fling him face downward against the Swinger. "You ignorant hooligan!" she roared. She smashed his hand over and over against the roof until the knife dropped into the stream of water in the gutter.

"Stupid fucker!" Dusty shouted, then kneed the kid in the rear, hard, and turned him, a jelly-like pathetic creature, dripping wet, eyes astonished in his pain-twisted face.

"Scum! Ignorant worthless scum!" She kneed him mercilessly in front and he doubled up. "You tell your sick little gang," she bellowed, her voice filling Railroad between the diner and the church, "they're not getting away with another thing! Tell them I've had enough of their crap!" She slapped his head, his ears, his cheeks, as if her fury would never be spent. "Tell them.—" The men who'd been at the counter pulled her away.

There hadn't been a sound in Elly's ears but Dusty's wrath. Now she heard the other kid, sneakers slapping against puddles, careening across the street toward the church. A siren grew closer. Dusty was still struggling with the men and cursing at the slasher who leaned, half-collapsed, against the poor lopsided Swinger. Elly, with no memory of having moved, found herself at Dusty's side. Now that she'd let her lover go into peril with only her own strength and Elly's angry

197

wishes for weapons, Elly was acutely aware of the love that tied them to each other. More than romance, as strong as danger, it felt like a good stout rope between them.

"Fucking queer!" the boy was whining at Dusty. "You ruined me for life."

"Better your ruin than mine, boy," Dusty shouted, straining against Elly and the men as they tried to lead her inside. Elly smiled proudly. Dusty had found her battleground and defended it well.

A police car pulled up. Elly quickly explained to the officer what had happened. Fortunately, he was a customer and well aware of the harassment to which Leon Rossi's gang had been subjecting them. The cop went to frisk the knifer, promising to come in the diner for a full report.

Earleen had arrived for her shift and stood on the top step with Grace, Rosa, Hernando and a regular customer whom Elly recognized by his cigar. All four applauded and cheered as Dusty passed. Earleen said, "You showed the little shits!"

Hernando slapped Dusty on the back. "Boy, are you strong for a girl!"

"About time," said the cigar man, whose white hair ringed a wrinkled bald pate. "About time somebody put those hoodlums in their place. Always whispering to me when I go by: *'Don't go in there, old man, those witches will poison you.'* "

Hearing this, Dusty, bedraggled, hair streaming with rain, tore away from the group at the door. "You leave our customers alone, you creeps! I'll sleep here with a gun if you come near the place again! *Get out of my life!*"

Once inside, though, she crumpled, and slumped at the counter, crying like a little girl. Elly couldn't have cared less about hiding how she felt just then. She smoothed Dusty's hair back and handed her a napkin.

The workers were stamping their feet dry on the mat.

"*Look* at that boy try to get inside the church before the cop spots him, will you?" said one of them, a stocky man with a deep voice.

The other laughed. "I suppose Father Grimes will try to fix this too."

"That poor excuse for a holy man won't get away with his trouble-making this time," the stocky man replied.

Dusty looked up. "Thanks for helping, guys." She sniffed.

"Hey, anything for the old Queen of Hearts," the stocky man said, helping himself to a toothpick and pulling out his wallet to pay for lunch.

"On the house, guys, you earned it."

"Thanks, ma'am."

"Call me Dusty."

"I've been wanting to ask you," the stocky man said, "if you're the Dusty that was Ned Reilly's little girl."

"That's me."

"What do you know! I worked with your dad on the railroad, then quit to come work over here. How's he doing?"

Elly watched them talk about Ned Reilly. Dusty's pleasure was evident. "What a morning," she said to Grace.

"I hope you've been doing your deep breathing," Grace jested.

"I about had all I could do to draw one breath after another, sweetie, never mind deep breathing."

Dale and Gussie had left for the hospital as soon as Dusty was safe. Grace sighed. "Dale was surely impressed."

Elly looked at her friend. "If you ask me, I think you're the one who's impressed. With Dale."

Grace grinned foolishly.

"We're going to get canned," said the other worker, looking at his watch.

"He's right. We'll be back, though, Dusty. You're just like Ned. He was a scrapper too when somebody got his goat."

Tears ran down Dusty's cheeks again as she looked back to Elly when the men had left. "Does that mean," she asked Elly, "that he's on our side?"

"A lot of people are," said Rosa, giving Dusty's shoulder a squeeze. "They're just scared to say so."

Dusty blew her nose and laughed softly.

"What's so funny?" Elly asked. She felt exhausted, and her shift hadn't even started yet.

"Me, I guess. I keep meeting people who are on our side, one here, one there. I wonder how many will crawl out the woodwork now that *I'm* on our side."

Elly stood, and tied on her apron. She might be tired, but Dusty's smile was exhilarating. As she went to make fresh coffee the rain began to beat even harder on the metal roof. When, she wondered, would it all end?

CHAPTER TWENTY-SIX

The stainless steel clock read 5:00 AM. It was an ungodly hour, thought Dusty, but hers, all hers until Rosa got in at six. She loved being the first one up on Puddle Street, the only car on the road. It gave her a feeling of worth to be one of those behind-the-scenes people who got the world going each day in her streamlined little restaurant.

It had rained all day, every day, for a week. Nan was still in the hospital, Grace had been spending all her time with Dale and Gussie. The gang hadn't come near the Queen of Hearts or sent any letters, sprayed any graffiti. Dusty expected they were plotting.

She'd gotten used to the rain, to the sight of the pond rising daily, her ducks stamping their feet in soggy delight; to the swelling River and the dam invisible under all that water; to the sound of the rain beating on the tin roof as she set up the Queen of Hearts for the day. When she had a minute, she'd stand at the open back door to watch the glistening steel tracks under the barrage of the downpour. Customers were saying it hadn't rained this much since the dam broke back in 1955. Dusty slammed around for a while at the thought of that new riverview fancypants restaurant trying to ladle out hot soup to the workers if there was a flood now, in 1972. Hah! It'd be good old Dusty Reilly they'd look to for help, queer or not.

Down at the ice cream parlor Dusty had seen pictures of the diner from the 1955 flood. She'd been headquarters, practically, for the sandbaggers. There were pictures, too, of the devastation the flood had caused when the dam broke. The water entered the factories and ruined whole machines. Tore down smokestacks. Some of the businesses never fully recovered and let go more and more workers until they folded. Railroad Avenue had been impassable for cars, with water right up to the diner's second step. It had crested just below the top of the cement foundation. Dusty remembered huge trees ripped from the River's banks, the collapses along the cliffs that followed, homes teetering over space. Between drowning, downed electrical lines and falling trees, twelve people had died.

The dam just above the Queen of Hearts was shored up after that flood, but not rebuilt. The federal government had not wanted to spend the money then and over the years the tax base had diminished so much that Morton River could never afford it either.

Rosa came in the back door. "Do I ever have news for you, *hombre*." She shook her umbrella out the door.

Dusty was beating pancake batter. "I'm all ears."

"Only it has to wait. I'm running late and not ready for the morning grumps yet. They'll be here any minute."

Dusty could hear her out there, flying from coffee pot to the front door to bring in the hard rolls and doughnuts, and then to the counter. She didn't see her again to talk to until after nine when she flew into the kitchen like a bright red hummingbird in her cardigan and hugged Dusty's arm. Dusty was taking a tea break; Hernando had just come in and was washing dishes.

"Whew," said Rosa. "If this keeps up we'll have to get Elly back on days."

"Keep dreaming," Dusty said.

Rosa gave her her best evil eye. "You moody creature. And here I'm bringing you good news."

"Better late than never."

"There's a proposal to build a new church in the neighborhood," she said.

Dusty was sharpening knives. "Am I supposed to cheer? I have enough troubles with the old one."

"I don't know why Elly puts up with you. To *replace* the old one."

"Where are they putting it, across the street?"

"Not if I can help it." She had a triumphant expression, a look of conspiracy on her face. "Guess who's funding most of it."

"The Klan."

"Worse."

"Is there something worse?"

"Rossi."

Dusty groaned. "There is something worse."

"The story Jake brought home is that Rossi couldn't elbow his way into the downtown church politics. He'd made too many enemies in business, just like Dale said." She peered over the swinging doors and returned. "Father Grimes does need him. Grimes thinks it'll bring back his parishioners, Rossi plans to own the land it makes valuable and get into heaven at the same time."

"This lot gets more valuable every day."

"Whether Rossi kept the business or razed the diner and put in a parking lot, he couldn't lose. And neither can you, Dusty. Whether they build a church or not, you're sitting on a gold mine."

"I wonder if those old cross-burnings Grimes and Rossi's kid were involved in have anything to do with this new alliance. Funding a church might be a back door to respectability for Rossi, but he won't do anything unless it'll make him richer. I'll bet the Queen of Hearts is key to doing just that. A going business would keep raking the cash in for him. Then, if the priest can drive us out he's got a moral victory plus he gets credit for enhancing Rossi's investment. Neat."

Rosa nodded, stripping the foil from a stick of gum. Dusty could smell spearmint.

"This neighborhood," Rosa said, "doesn't need a new church. The Father doesn't have more than ten or fifteen people a mass in there. *I* think people are going to be upset."

"It sounds like the holy terror is getting more powerful, not less."

"I have a feeling," said Rosa with a pop of her gum, "this is his last stand. He couldn't even get the charges reduced for your tire-slashers. And word has spread around the neighborhood that he tried. No one approves. All the decent people who wanted to respect him, who refused to look at his bad side, will be hit on the head when this business with Rossi gets known. Instead of feeling sorry for him they're going to say, we want a new priest."

A throat was loudly cleared out front and Rosa was gone in a flash. Dusty didn't know what to think of her news. What more could Rossi or Grimes do to force them out?

Rosa came back. "He's here," she hissed.

"Rossi?"

204

"No. He never does his dirty work in person. It's Mr. Popularity, the priest, so puffed up-looking I'm surprised his Roman collar doesn't split open."

She went off again and Dusty got too busy to be concerned. It wasn't till the worst of the lunch rush was over that Rosa stormed into the kitchen.

"The pressure must be on," she announced. "Now it's not the gang harassing people on the street, it's this . . . this *pathetic* excuse for a holy man giving out lectures. He ought to have that collar stripped right off him!"

She looked as if she would cry. "He pulled me down next to him—at my busiest no less!—and warned me I'd burn in eternal hell for consorting with sinners. You, *mi cocinera*, have been touched by the devil himself and he called Elly a painted whore. Elly who gave him free coffee for so long!"

"Damn!" Dusty spat. But when she got through the swinging doors he'd left; she could see him sloshing across the rainy street in floppy black galoshes to his parish house, looking as mean as the weather.

Back in the kitchen, Rosa pretended she hadn't been crying. She had, after all, been brought up to believe what priests said. Hernando just shook his head.

"What's this about free coffee?" Dusty asked.

Rosa shrugged. "I'm always talking too much." She explained about Elly and the coffee. "She was trying to keep the peace. But when she found out that the night waitress hadn't been charging him for dinner Elly put her foot down. No free anything. It's war to him now.

"I feel like a heel. Poor Elly, squeezed between Grimes and me, scared of us both. I sure know how to mess things up. Why in hell does she stick with me?"

A wicked look came into Rosa's eyes. "I think she's hot for your body."

"Rosa!" Dusty cried at the waitress' retreating figure.

At change of shift, Rosa reappeared and leaned wearily against the back door jamb. "You think it'll ever stop raining?" she asked.

The rain beyond her was so heavy Dusty was having trouble making out the details of Nan's little house. She supposed Gussie and Dale were at the hospital. Nan had gotten better, then worse, then better again. Grace was playing hooky from the diner every day now. Everyone suspected that she and Dale were lovers, but no one could get close enough to ask.

"You know the Valley," Dusty answered Rosa, who'd lived there most of her life. "The rain stops when it's ready and not before."

"I'm worried about the River. Everyone is. The weather forecasters are giving hourly reports. Listen to how loud it is. If it floods we'll lose so many businesses, my cousins will get laid off and want to move in with me again!"

They all laughed, ever cousin Hernando, but Dusty was worried too. The factories and many of the houses weren't in as good a position as the Queen of Hearts. If enough of this section of town were wiped out by a flood, the Queen might as well fall right into the River.

Dusty was opening cans of peeled potatoes for the boiled dinner special when, like a separate burst of rain, she heard a volley of small hard objects against the diner's side.

Rosa yelled in Spanish out the back door. When Dusty came up behind her she saw several little boys scattering across the tracks. But one slowly, reluctantly, approached. It was Luis, Rosa's own little hornet.

"Uh-oh," Dusty said.

The boy stood under his mother's hand, shoulders hunched, tears silently falling, Rosa's face more punishment than any spanking. "Did you stone this restaurant?" Rosa demanded.

He shook his head, looking much too defenseless to have committed such an act. Dusty would have apologized and let him go right then. Or maybe that was how she'd keep the truth from herself.

"Luis," prompted his mother.

"They made me! They made me!"

Dusty felt her heart sink, despondency filling her so completely and quickly she couldn't think of anything that would stop it. Fear followed. Was hate a power so strong it could hurl stones from an innocent child's hand? How could she hope to win against it?

"Oh, *mi precioso*, no one can make you do something you don't want to do." Rosa's voice was heavy with disappointment.

"They said I was a queer unless I showed them I didn't like no queers."

Poor little boy. Dusty quartered her potatoes to keep from crying, to keep from thinking: poor little Dusty. She remembered how it felt to have the pack suddenly turn on her, picking and picking relentlessly till she would run, run, run to her mom's diner. Now where could she run? It was all her fault. If she wasn't gay none of this would be happening. Shit, she felt like throwing in the towel and parking herself down at Marcy's Bar for the rest of the afternoon, for the rest of her life. When Rosa looked up with pain-filled sadness in her eyes Dusty said, "Maybe I ought to sell if Rossi makes a decent offer."

"And teach Luis stone-throwing is the answer? Are you crazy?"

"I just thought—"

"You want to hide from this fight, go ahead, but don't use my *niño* as an excuse." She turned away from Dusty. Hernando signaled that he was watching the front.

"What's a queer, Luis?" Rosa asked.

Dusty winced.

Luis blinked up at her under his red baseball cap. He was a small-boned boy, undersized compared to the grandsons of earlier immigrants. "A bad lady."

"Do we know any bad ladies?"

Luis glanced shyly, nervously, toward Dusty. He shook his head.

"Did the other boys tell you Dusty is bad?"

He nodded, eyes to the floor. Dusty would have done anything at that moment to avoid this scene: sell, drink, hide any way she could.

"Are they right?"

Luis raised his eyes as far as Dusty's waist. He seemed to take in the stains on her uniform, the hands busy with dinner. Then he looked at Hernando, and all around the shining, warm kitchen. By the time he was ready to look Dusty in the eye he was standing taller. "*I* don't think so," he said.

Dusty felt so ashamed of her fear compared to this little guy's bravery that she got off her stool and bent to Luis, arms out. He came to her without hesitation, as he'd always done. Dusty looked up over his head as she hugged him, at the back door. And saw Rita.

"What a pretty scene," she said sarcastically. Dusty made a face at her to shut her up. What did she want, anyway? Dusty had thought they could be friends, but she was beginning to think Elly was right: Rita wanted more.

"I *told* them, Dusty. I told them and told them." Luis was crying again. "But they wouldn't listen. Then they said Mama's bad like you, Mama's going to marry you. I got mixed up."

"I would too, kid."

"Congratulations, Rosa," said Rita. "Maybe you'll have more luck than the rest of us."

Rosa ignored Rita and came over to Dusty. Dusty turned Luis to face her, but kept one arm around him. "How can I explain this, Luis?" she asked, straightening his jacket. "Dusty is different, but not bad. Like we're different because we speak Spanish. You know they call us names too."

"Why?"

"Yeah," Dusty asked, smiling. "Why?" It was something she hadn't thought to ask Dale when they talked about changing the world a week ago. Why did people hate difference so much? She was glad Dale hadn't been in today to see old faint-hearted, chicken-shit Dusty. But no one had ever suggested that the enemy might appear in a little boy.

Rita laughed with a humorless sound. "Why? Because we're such winners, right, Dusty?"

"That's enough, Rita," Dusty said, angry.

"*Precioso*, if I could answer that question I could end all the wars, feed all the hungry—"

"Make sure everyone got a job!" called Hernando.

"Luis, *¿donde esta mi hijita?* She's supposed to keep you out of trouble."

He seemed to hesitate. "She went home. Her nose was still bleeding. But only a little."

"*What?*"

"She hit a kid that said Dusty was queer. He hit her back. She's okay, though. It only bled a little."

Rosa looked at Dusty with a smile, shaking her head.

Luis went home. Rosa went to finish her shift.

"What'd they do, Dusty?" asked Rita. "Threaten to kidnap the kid if you don't sell?"

Dusty resented telling her the details, but she explained.

"Sounds like you need a long, tall Seven-Up. Want to ride down to Marcy's with me? I had a heck of a day. They're talking layoffs. I may have to go on graveyard shift."

Dusty looked at her. She wore a green rainjacket over darker green pants. Her makeup was blurred from the damp. She'd never been less attractive to her, but Dusty still felt a pull. Marcy's. Warm. Dim. Dry. Music and clinking ice cubes.

She could taste the cold calming whiskey and soda. "No," she said. "No."

"Need a ride home then?"

"Rita, I need not to see you for a while."

"Elly won't let you out to play any more?"

She'd always talked baby talk. It rankled Dusty now. "Our friendship started out okay, Rita, but something's gone sour. I need to think about it."

"Suit yourself," she said. "I thought we ought to keep up ties where we have them. I know how you always felt about roots."

Rita and roots, she thought. Roots can strangle too. Can suck all the nourishment away from other growing things.

"Maybe I'm just not ready," she said.

Rita's face turned furious. "Don't call *me* when you are!" she said and slammed the back door behind her.

Dusty's hands, arms, legs shook as she finished up the potatoes. She tried to keep herself from crying, about Rita, about Luis, about how hard everything was right now, but then she thought, Why? It had felt so good to cry lately, like she'd been saving up tears since she was Luis' age.

She was dry-eyed by the time Elly and Earleen came in shortly afterward. Hernando was whistling over by the sink. Everything was back to normal. They'd even had quite a few customers when Dusty checked the tapes on her way out. Maybe the rain was driving them in, or maybe the neighborhood wasn't listening to Father Grimes and the gang any more.

She went for a long walk by the River in that pounding rain, feeling as if it was herself, not Luis, Rosa had been talking to. Feeling as if she needed this rain to pound Rosa's simple lessons of pride and courage into her heart, into every pore of her being until they were part of her.

CHAPTER TWENTY-SEVEN

"Bloated, I feel utterly bloated," said Jake, his pale face showing the recent stress of events in faint lines. "I feel like something that's been in the River too long. I am so *damn* sick and tired of rain, rain, rain. Grey skies, wet roads, all this rubber rain gear hanging off my body. I'm not even into rubber! Why oh why did I ever pick Morton River? Why am I drinking wet orange juice? We must be *breathing* in more moisture than we can absorb right now."

The wild Morton River had raised the Valley's collective adrenalin. Nowhere was this more obvious than at Dusty's Queen of Hearts Diner. Elly was too busy to linger long, too frazzled to tease him at length, but she couldn't resist watch-

211

ing Jake's face while she shared the tidbit of news she'd been saving. "Have you been listening to the radio today, sweetie?"

"I've developed a phobia for weather forecasters. I think this is a plot. *They're* into rubber."

"The National Guard is on standby."

"Oh, girlfriend," said Jake, a light rekindled in his eyes. "And me without a thing to wear. I wonder if Bloomingdale's carries classy rain clothes. Let's see, when can I get to New York? I'm working so many hours at the hospital because of the bugs this rain encourages I'll never be able to go. El, this could be a disaster."

She reached to straighten his collar. "Funny, that's just what the radio said." Jake was helping her cranky mood. Even down, he talked like he was up.

It was late in the lunch hour, she was back on days, gratefully colliding with Rosa behind the counter, meeting her in the aisle to do a high-stepping cha-cha while a smattering of customers applauded. The city had put all of its maintenance workers and even some white collar people on the dam. The town was on alert, volunteers were streaming into Flood Headquarters to sign up for the call if they were needed. Headquarters had been set up in a narrow little house between Nan's and the dam. Dusty's Queen of Hearts Diner was the closest restaurant and everyone wanted coffee and pie.

When Elly returned from cleaning a booth, Jake said, "You look wiped out, El. But happy as a queen in ladies' lingerie. I don't know about you girls—the whole town is about to be swept to sea, and you're higher than the day the Queen of Hearts opened."

Elly kept one eye on Dusty and two men who had asked to speak with her. She hoped they weren't trouble. "I'm too tired to feel high. Business is way up, but enough is enough. We don't have staff yet to handle it and we extended our hours. If I'm high," she said irritably, "it's because this town lit my fuse and I'm bound and determined to show them what

I'm made of." She rushed to a booth, took an order, served coffee at the counter and returned to Jake. "Look who's talking anyway. You'd think a whole platoon of National Guardsmen just strutted into the men's room the way you're all of a sudden sittin' up straight, preening that jungle of hair under your nose."

"Entertaining the troops is important to morale."

"So's feeding them! But why am I defendin' myself for being happier than I was when we were sinking? I've waited all my life for the breaks we're getting now. I can't stop the River and I can't change the way we've had to prove ourselves here, but if everything had to happen the way it did, you're damn straight I'm going to enjoy any spoils that come our way." She went to another booth, joked with four men who'd been given time off by their factories to sign up as sandbaggers.

"El!" called Dusty. She'd hired an on-call cook and had left her in charge of the kitchen. Motioning Elly to where she stood, Dusty looked tall and equal to anything, even the men with her.

"Elly Hunnicutt, this is Marty Holland and John Brockett from Flood Headquarters. They're trying to work out a way to feed the volunteers."

"I know Dusty told you how much we'd like to help," Elly said, shaking hands with them.

Dusty said, "We'll be making soup and sandwiches. The workers will have IDs and each meal gets charged to flood relief. Coffee, tea, hot chocolate, they're all thrown in free."

"Boil that coffee by the bucket, then, Dusty," said Brockett, a tall man with a bushy red moustache. "If I'd known how good your coffee was I'd have switched from the donut shop long ago!"

Martin Holland was more formal and older. "You'll get a city commendation for your service, ladies."

She saw Dusty blush to the roots of her wavy hair. "All we want are customers, guys. Just come on back when we get this thing licked."

In the kitchen, after the men had left, Dusty tugged her red turtleneck collar away from her neck. "Negotiating's hotter work than cooking any day," she said.

"Did you hear what that man said, Dusty?" Elly exclaimed as the assistant cook scurried around the kitchen. "He just didn't know how good we are. That was all that was keeping him away, not—"

Dusty smiled her sideways smile, looking sheepish. "I know. I've been hearing that from dozens of people. I was too scared to hear it before." She shook her head. "It looks like I was in the minority, thinking being queer guaranteed failure."

Elly took care of a line at the register, then returned to Jake at the counter. He was still discussing the National Guard.

"*I* wouldn't have called in the Guard, of course," he said. "This is a flood emergency. *I* would have called in the Marines."

"I think it's a good thing they know enough not to ask your advice. Want some pie today?"

"Oh, talk about depression. Will you look at this waistline? Poor Jake can't even have a bite of anything sweet now."

She left to deliver some sandwiches. At her return she lit a cigarette. "I haven't finished one of these things in so long I might as well give them up." She inhaled luxuriously. "Speaking of sweet things, John's gang has been in here umpteen times a day. For once they're making themselves useful, picking up coffee for Flood Headquarters, twisting people's arms to volunteer."

"Not literally, I hope," Jake replied. "I suppose they don't have any more time to get to the gym than I do. Everyone in town's down with flood flu, or damp-aggravated arthritis. I'm certain Nan and most of the rest of the people up at Morton Memorial will get well the minute the sun comes out. Maybe I should go across the street and drop a wooden nickel in the coin box to light a candle and pray for a drought."

"Shh," said Elly. "The priest just walked in. He's just about living here these days. I don't know whether he's keeping an eye on us or the weather's got to him. He's a bundle of nerves, picking at his fingers, his face, his clothes all the time. Now his mouth has started to twitch, like it wants to scream. Or, heaven forbid, smile. He's even paying for everything without a peep. I wonder if Rossi's putting some kind of pressure on him that's making him crack?"

"Or if you are. You seem to be winning."

She gave Jake his blue plate special.

"Ah! Your Southern Fried Mustard Chicken with yams! This will cheer me up."

For the next twenty minutes Elly went on automatic, a survival tactic no waitress could do without. She couldn't have said afterwards who or what she'd served. Her mind was back in Tennessee, remembering her mama taking her down to the Mississippi after a long rainy period. The sight of its force had frightened her. She'd been wearing a navy blue coat and little white gloves and she could recall those white hands clinging to Mama for dear life. "Is that where Papa went?" she'd asked. He'd run off to be a Merchant Marine.

The next summer she'd screamed bloody murder when Mama had taken her on an outing in a rowboat. "Hold onto Candy Marie's hand," Mama had urged her. They were sharing a boat with her first cousin and aunt. While she terrified herself with visions of the River taking Mama to join her father, of taking her away from Mama, Candy Marie held her hand. This cousin was older, a tall girl who'd been allowed to wear a sailor hat for the occasion. Candy Marie had held little Elly. Held her close, calmed her, giggled with her, till Elly had wanted nothing more than to stay in that little boat forever with this big girl who could take her fears away. She'd forgotten all about Candy Marie who was probably a grandma by now, while Elly was with her own grown up sailor girl—

Elly reached Jake again.

"If I had the capital," he said, "I'd build myself a pharmacy right next door to the diner." He was looking at the frantic activity around him.

It seemed to Elly as if the minute Martin Holland and John Brockett had left the flood crews had doubled in size. They had to get more help out on the floor. At least everyone was served at the moment.

"What would you call it," she asked, *"The Queens' Drugs?"*

"Be serious. After what you two have been through I wouldn't ask for trouble. But look what's happening to this neighborhood. Look at this crowd! There's *us,"* he whispered with heavy emphasis. "There are people speaking Spanish, people with brown skins. There are all the young professionals who get off the train at Upton now and come home to their Victorians. And then there's the old school finally waking up to Grimes. No wonder Rossi wants to gain a hold on the neighborhood."

She took a long swallow of Coke. "When I was working with Sam the other day he told me Rossi had been pumping him, trying to get an idea of what Dusty would take for the Queen of Hearts."

Jake laughed. "Did Sam run Rossi out?"

"No. He told the man we'd really built up the business, that we wouldn't sell for the world, and on and on. Finally, sweetie, he told Rossi not to make an offer under a quarter million."

"What?" exclaimed Jake, his eyebrows arched in disbelief.

Elly went off to a booth, enjoying Sam's audaciousness again, and Jake's reaction. That figure was four times what Dusty had paid for this tiny business on the wrong side of the tracks. She wished she could share Jake's astonishment with Dusty, but there wouldn't be a minute, the way things were going today, until after three.

Every piece of good news seemed to change Dusty, to straighten her back, help her face up to what life demanded of her. A few nights ago Dusty had even apologized for being so intimidating about the struggle with the priest. She had praised Elly for the way she'd handled the free coffee and meals. And yesterday she'd asked Sam to stay over from his midnight shift while she went downtown to join the Chamber of Commerce. And Rita—she wasn't coming around any more, though Dusty hadn't said why. Elly felt she was well on her way to rebuilding her trust and respect for Dusty. It felt wonderful, but she realized the irony of the timing: now that things were back on track with her love life, she was too tired to enjoy it. She simply had to get more help quickly.

Grace stepped through the door with Dale and Seeker. Dale shook the water off her hat. They had to wait for seats, but soon settled to either side of Jake. Elly stole moments to be with them.

"I always thought," Grace said, "that life after forty would be an even flow running its course."

"Then," Jake interrupted, "Dale arrived in her dashing Panama hat."

Grace swept the curls off her face, her hand coming away wet with rain. "Even before that. Coming out, I never expected the *flood* of emotions and desires and activity. Never imagined a whole week would go by before I'd get down here to tell you about—us!"

"So it's official!" Jake cried.

Elly squeezed Grace's hand, then Dale's. "You know I think it's fantastic, sweeties." She wanted to set them up with free Cokes to celebrate, but was drawn back to the floor where muddy footprints were replaced immediately by more, where kids let out of school because of the danger giggled

217

with excitement, where housewives bunched in booths to talk about their men down on the dam, where, it seemed, the whole town was congregating in sopping rain gear. The steamy smell of warmth filled her haven from the chilly wet world.

The thundering River seemed to push them all inside. And this funny long room, such a fragile shelter, took them all in. Decorated only by mirrors, windows, stainless steel and neon, it held all these people who were struggling for a living, for a decent life, for life itself right now. She felt tears well up as she looked around the magic room of light, felt the measure of caring she, and Dusty, and the whole crew, had created in such a hard world where victories must be won—when they could be won at all—with wise deliberate dreams.

She fought her way back to the counter and to the continuously grinning Grace.

"I hope you're stayin' around for a while, Dale," she said. "This girl's happier than I've ever seen her. That's plain as a hand before my face." She saw from their expressions that she had blundered into a problem.

Dale said gravely, "Except for Grace, my whole life is in California. I've built up a reputation for my work there, and I just got word that the grant proposal I wrote for a disabled elders' outreach program will be funded."

"She wants me to go out there with her, El." Grace's face looked frightened. "To California."

"Why, Grace," she said. She could hear the plaintive note, the what-should-I-do similar to her own when she'd considered a life without Dusty. "I have never heard the adventurous Ms. Gladstone so flustered up before." She touched Grace's hand. "Breathe," she reminded her. "I'd miss you real bad, sweetie, but I'd love to have someone to visit in San Francisco."

"Berkeley," said Dale, with a resigned smile.

218

"Help!"

It was Rosa, with a tray of dirty dishes in her hands. "El, we need more help out here. I swear, these customers are running my poor dogs to death. I'll need new shoes before the rain stops!"

Elly moved quickly from the counter. "It wouldn't hurt if I were doin' my part," she commented.

"It's going to take more than even the two of us, *mi amigita.*"

"I used to waitress," Dale said, standing, cane on her arm. "I can stay in Morton River a few weeks longer if I can earn some money. If you put me behind the counter I wouldn't need this," she added, proffering the cane. "But I would have to sit down periodically."

Of course! thought Elly as she filled three dishes with ice cream. Steam from the deep cardboard containers rose around her arms. Dale would be perfect for counter work. And Grace—it might buy her the time she needed. She didn't blame the woman for being scared. Moving to a strange hilly city she didn't know, after learning Morton River so well, would double her blindness. And by coming so irrevocably into the gay world, by taking this lover, she was moving in yet another way, blinding herself even further with the unknown. Oh, Grace, she thought, brave Grace shouldn't falter now. She'd been right, though, a flood was sweeping her along. Elly resolved to help Grace build the strength to go with it.

She pushed a heart-shaped apron at Dale, looked more closely at her, and took it back. "Why don't you grab one of Dusty's aprons from the kitchen, girl. More your style. Then would you get that order, please?"

She dashed to a booth to deliver the ice cream and to another to set the table.

Jake caught her arm. "Grace has a suggestion."

"I know you need me around here like a hole in the head, El," Grace said, talking in a whispery voice, as if muted by fear. "But I can't stand being across town from Dale any more than across the continent. I know how to wash dishes. Dry. Stack. Unload."

"I should have thought of you sooner! It would free up Hernando to do some busing. But the kitchen's Dusty's realm. Hang on a minute."

Dusty was spicing the minestrone. "Sure," she said. "Let's try her out. I'd love to have someone in here I can shoot the bull with."

Racing to the front, she told Grace, "You can tell Hernando to teach you. Let him know exactly what you want to try and what might be too dangerous for you. Seeker can stay on the back stoop. It's covered."

"You mean you *want* my help?"

"I'd always rather hire family, girl." From the look on Grace's face she suspected this job would help give her more confidence about Dale and the move West than a hundred lectures.

Through the kitchen window came the sound of Dusty's loud laugh. Elly hadn't heard it so spirited in months and it seemed to give her energy again.

"I see we've got a new waitress, too," Dusty was saying through the window. "What's this, 'two eggs over real juicy!' West Coast lingo?"

Just then a gang member ran in, looking like a drowned rat. His boldness shocked her. That the gang would *dare* to come in here now.

"Anybody seen Leon?" shouted the punk. He stood in the doorway to the vestibule, obviously reluctant to step all the way onto this alien turf. But his excitement propelled him forward. He caught sight of the priest.

"Hey, Father," he called. "We're going into high gear! Spread the word—*we need everybody on the dam right now*! You can help too!"

Elly watched the kid run out and past the window. Men all over the diner were standing and throwing money on tables, on the counter, Jake among them. But he was making his way to the priest. What was he up to?

"Going down to bless the boys, Father?" Jake asked, his tone decidedly snippy.

The priest sat up and blustered some answer.

Jake stood, one hand on a hip, and in his bitchiest manner said, "I would have thought you'd be in the thick of it long ago, leading your flock."

The priest stood and glared at Jake, but Jake swung around and left for the hospital.

Elly wanted to applaud his pot shot, to thank him for striking a blow for the Queen of Hearts. The priest's power had diminished right before her eyes. She wondered if the flood would turn out to be Morton River Valley's gay liberation movement.

CHAPTER TWENTY-EIGHT

Fourteen hours later, the River crested. It was early morning and Elly watched from the front steps as the exhausted, filthy emergency crews collapsed into cars and the backs of trucks to be driven home. Huge patches of blue mottled the sky. Though the rainfall had ruined the fall colors, now that it had stopped she smelled a tang in the air that announced autumn. Morton River Valley had survived; its people had held onto what they'd built once again. She turned to go inside feeling a measure of pride that she was a survivor in a survivor's town: she was home.

The Queen of Hearts almost echoed with emptiness. Today would decide the Queen's fate. She might stay empty now that the imminent peril had ended, or she might fill up later in the day, once people had dried and rested. If the town came to the diner to celebrate, she thought, all the promise of the last several days would be realized.

Dusty had sent the extra cooks home for a few hours. Grace and Dale, looking made for each other, were whispering at the kitchen door.

In the kitchen Dusty's forearms were white with flour. Elly brushed some from the tip of her lover's nose. Hernando sang boisterously in Spanish down under the sink where he was unclogging a drain. He'd received word just the day before that he'd been awarded a grant to enroll in the Valley U. Pharmacy Assistant Program. Elly could hear Rosa humming as she served the few customers out front.

That sideways smile of Dusty's was in place. "What are you makin'?" Elly asked.

"Pie, pie and more pie. Apple pies and Southern nut pies. When this place gets hit later, I want to give the whole damn town a treat?"

"And what if they don't beat down the doors?"

Dusty laughed at her. "Now you sound like me!" Her smile faded, though. "I guess I just assumed they'd come. Maybe I'm being overconfident."

"Stop it, Dusty!" Elly said as she had so many times before. She never wanted to see that look of panic in Dusty's eyes again, and here she'd brought it on herself. "I'm just teasin' you, girl. There's no *way* this town's going to turn its back on us now. People might think they can't stomach gays, but give 'em a couple of live ones just like themselves and they plain forget to hate us."

Dusty blew air out her cheeks. "Doesn't take much to get me going, does it? But I know everything's turning around, El. And everyone."

"Did I blink my eyes and miss somethin'?"

"Didn't Sam tell you before he went home? John's going to be off the streets of Morton River for a good long while."

"John the dishwasher? Was he busted?"

"Enlisted. In the Navy. He signed on to be a cook."

Their eyes met, but for a moment neither said a word.

"Well, well, what do you know," said Elly in wonder. Of course, if she was a youngster she might follow in Dusty's footsteps—but John?

At lunch time Father Grimes took his usual booth. Nothing had come of Jake's taunts except that the priest had slunk out of the diner yesterday and hadn't been seen since.

"Hey, Padre!" she heard. It was Leon Rossi, enroute to the priest's booth. When she delivered a slice of chocolate layer cake there, they both ignored her.

"Where you been, Padre?" Leon's voice was full of the authority of his newly productive days as he towered over the priest in his muddied boots, his layers of dirty sweatshirts, his tangled coal black hair. Elly had heard that he'd been kept on as part of the flood clean-up crew.

"In prayer, my son. Interceding with the heavens for the salvation of the Valley."

"Oh, I get it," said Leon, a sarcastic sneer twisting his lips. "You're the one got the rain to stop. Must be hard work." He glanced down to the cake. "Really whips up an appetite."

Elly had moved away, but when she heard the gang leader's tone she stopped and busied herself within earshot at the register. She was enjoying this loud challenge to the priest's complacency.

"We could have used you down at the River, Padre," Leon continued. "We needed every man we could get. I couldn't believe you never showed up. The guys are saying you like your soft life too much to get wet."

Father Grimes looked up sharply from his plate. A muffled guffaw came from the booth behind them. Elly could see him fill his chest with air and indignation. He protested, "My every thought was for those boys. I plan to visit the flood victims today."

224

Leon folded his arms. "Come off it, Father. There *are* no flood victims because we broke our necks holding the water back. You don't even know what's going on!"

The priest spread his arms, raising the palms of his hands skyward. "An old man like me—"

"Could have held lights at night, could have directed traffic, could have worked on the radio—could have just cracked jokes to keep the guys' spirits up!"

Standing, Father Grimes said, "Who are *you*, young man, to dictate how a priest will minister? How dare you—"

Leon was not to be intimidated. Elly had to answer the calls of customers, but heard as she turned away, "I really used to look up to you, Father."

In the nearby booths Elly saw people nodding their heads and craning their necks to see the priest's reaction. Leon moved swiftly away, his face dark. Elly wondered, was this the end of their evil union?

The stocky man who'd witnessed the tire-slashing was sitting with two women.

"Can you imagine?" she heard one woman say to him. "A priest wanting to tear down our homes that we've sweated and scrimped for, to build a fancy church. I say let him fill his own first."

Elly cleaned their booth and gave them place settings.

"I was baptized in that church," said the stocky man. "And christened and made my first communion there. We were married by old Father Limonge," he finished, placing a worn hand on his wife's. "I think we should keep it, dress it up, be proud of what it's seen us through, not scrap it so the rich can get richer and the lazy be rewarded."

"What was all that about?" asked Rosa.

"I'm not sure," Elly said. "But I think the tide is turning."

Rosa nodded her satisfaction.

Elly poured herself some warm Coke. "Why would Leon push the priest?"

225

"Because the priest is all of a sudden pushable?"

Elly served a customer, then came back to sip her Coke. The pies smelled spicy and rich.

"But why," she continued, "is he all of a sudden pushable?"

"Maybe Leon knows something from his father."

"And maybe Rossi finally noticed what's happening with this neighborhood." Elly felt a wicked grin spread over her face. "Maybe he sees that it's too late, that he lost out and he's blaming it on Father Grimes."

Little by little, the diner filled up that afternoon. By the time the high school kids swarmed in, every booth was filled. It felt like day one again, Elly thought, but she knew that what had been ahead of them last Valentine's Day would never come again. She swung from one booth to another, danced with Rosa in the aisles, taught Dale the language of diner work, moved to the beat of *Galveston* on the jukebox.

Jake appeared, Gussie on his arm.

"Blessings on the Queen of Hearts for serenading me with the Wichita Yenta," Jake said. He couldn't stand the singer. They both asked Dale for one apple, one nut pie apiece.

"Two *each*?" Elly exclaimed. "But your blood pressure, Gussie!"

Gussie stamped a foot. "To heck with it, sweetheart! I'm celebrating!"

"Nan?"

"As soon as this flood nonsense is cleaned up she's coming home! She's finally on the mend!"

Elly left the two of them to gorge themselves.

The afternoon wore on, endless, exhausting, exhilarating.

"Look who's here again," Dale said later.

"The priest, damn him," said Elly. "And it's not even mealtime. I hope he's not going to expect free coffee without an ID. If *he's* joined the flood workers now, *I'm* voting for

George Wallace!" She patted down her bobby pins, her bracelets jangling with resentment.

"You don't recognize who that is with him, do you?" Rosa asked, slicing into another pie. "Rossi Senior."

"I've got to tell Dusty."

The kitchen was as hectic as it had been at the height of the flood, but the last of the pies was in the oven. Elly stood still, enjoying the sheer happiness she felt. Dusty came to her.

"Rossi? The good Father must want to show him how much moola he's going to rake in once he gets his henchmen back to work on us." Dusty dried her hands thoroughly. The sideways smile was gone. She looked at the clock and dusted off her pants.

"Dusty?" asked Elly. "What are you plannin'?" She felt the return of fear. Would Dusty be reckless and lose all their recent gains?

She got a wink in response. "You're on your own for a few minutes, Katie," she told the other cook.

Dusty strolled over to the men. Her sleeves were rolled up and her arms looked powerful. Her glasses were tilted forward on her nose from sweat. She wore a white jacket today, not her apron. Elly, eying Rossi's booth while she served her other customers, couldn't recall a moment when she'd been more in love with Dusty. She looked so confident and purposeful and competent that Elly's fears vanished. Dusty leaned on the heels of her hands over the men in their booth.

"It's an honor to have you gentlemen visit," she said with a straight face.

"Dusty's at the top of her form today!" Elly whispered to Rosa.

Dark was beginning to come outside the windows. It would be the first nightfall without rain. The clean-up crews staggered in for soup, brandishing their badges. Quickly, the afternoon character of the diner shifted. Gone were the women and kids. Male voices, boastful, swearing, flirting,

227

filled the diner. Out of the corner of her eye she saw Jake take in the scene.

It had been almost ten minutes since Dusty had left the kitchen. What was she doing still talking to those men? But just then, Dusty rose, brushed her hands against each other as if cleaning loose dirt from them. She looked smug as she returned to the kitchen.

The priest, stooped, beaten-looking, went to the register to pay. Rossi stood at the door, collar up, eyes down as if to disguise himself. He looked away when Elly caught his eyes. The priest glared at her and she swung her hips as she walked in the best imitation she could manage of the painted whore he thought her. She was still too busy to get to the kitchen, and as she rushed about, her mind wandered to the previous night.

Dusty had been so graceful, so gently forceful. As tired as she was, Elly had pampered herself, taken a long bath, shaved, put on her Cachet and Dusty's favorite nightgown.

Dusty had been reading in bed. She'd set down her book and lay there, nothing on but her glasses, watching Elly approach—with interest.

For the first time in a long while, Dusty's fingers were like magnets drawing down the skinny straps from Elly's shoulders, pulling the silken stuff up along Elly's thighs.

She'd never gotten the gown off Elly, just plunged down under it, her lips and tongue fast and hungry. Elly had cried out again and again.

Today Dusty had moved with that same masterful manner. Whatever she'd said to Rossi and Father Grimes, she couldn't have failed.

At four o'clock, night crew in place, Elly swung open the kitchen doors. "Are you going to tell me what happened Dusty Reilly, or do I have to shake it out of you?" Dale and Rosa had followed her as far as the swinging doors. Grace and Hernando were still hanging around the kitchen.

Dusty grinned her sideways grin, cocked her chef's hat over one eye. "He offered me a quarter of a million," she said calmly.

Too stunned to respond, all Elly could do was watch Dusty laugh. Earleen stopped stirring a pot of soup. Rosa and Dale swung the kitchen door slowly open, both silently staring. Hernando reached over to turn off the dishwasher. The only sounds were the waves of voices out front and the River crashing by all too near.

"The Queen of Hearts didn't cost a fourth of that!" Elly breathed.

Dusty spoke again. "Between the new church that guy thinks he's going to build, and the shopping mall which is a definite, the new dam that's almost approved—we've got a quarter of a million dollar business, lady!"

"I can't believe it, Dusty," Elly uttered.

Dusty held a hand out to her.

She advanced and took it, shook on their amazing luck. But looking into Dusty's eyes, she knew the triumph she saw there had little to do with money. And that the Queen of Hearts, in all her red-streaked glory, had a different value. She'd been aptly named: a Queen in a crazy Valley of steep crooked streets lined with homes as hard won as the Queen herself had been. It was the people of Morton River Valley who'd finally named a price for the diner, and her measure could be taken in nothing less than love.

As their friends crowded around, shaking their hands, hugging them, a small, familiar-looking man pushed through the swinging doors—the owner of the Sundae Shop. He carried a framed picture pressed to his chest.

"Hi!" said Elly. "Welcome to *our* sweet shop!" She was hugging Dusty's arm to herself and wouldn't have dropped it if Father Grimes himself had appeared.

The man seemed taken aback by the emotional gathering, but stammered, "My sons were on the flood crew. They've been telling me about what you did for them, about your long hours, everything you've been giving away, how good you made the boys feel. I couldn't help much myself, but I wanted this to hang where it belongs."

He turned the picture around. It was the Queen of Hearts, on her first opening day almost thirty years before. She was shining, splendid, a wise deliberate dream.

A few of the publications of
THE NAIAD PRESS, INC.
P.O. Box 10543 • Tallahassee, Florida 32302
Phone (904) 539-9322
Mail orders welcome. Please include 15% postage.

SEARCHING FOR SPRING by Patricia A. Murphy. 224 pp.
Novel about the recovery of love.   ISBN 0-941483-00-2 $8.95

DUSTY'S QUEEN OF HEARTS DINER by Lee Lynch. 240
pp. Romantic blue-collar novel.   ISBN 0-941483-01-0   8.95

PARENTS MATTER by Ann Muller. 240 pp. Parents'
relationships with lesbian daughters and gay sons.
ISBN 0-930044-91-6   9.95

THE PEARLS by Shelley Smith. 176 pp. Passion and fun in
the Caribbean sun.   ISBN 0-930044-93-2   7.95

MAGDALENA by Sarah Aldridge. 352 pp. Epic Lesbian novel
set on three continents.   ISBN 0-930044-99-1   8.95

THE BLACK AND WHITE OF IT by Ann Allen Shockley.
144 pp. Short stories.   ISBN 0-930044-96-7 $7.95

SAY JESUS AND COME TO ME by Ann Allen Shockley. 288
pp. Contemporary romance.   ISBN 0-930044-98-3   8.95

LOVING HER by Ann Allen Shockley. 192 pp. Romantic love
story.   ISBN 0-930044-97-5   7.95

MURDER AT THE NIGHTWOOD BAR by Katherine V.
Forrest. 240 pp. A Kate Delafield mystery. Second in a series.
ISBN 0-930044-92-4   8.95

ZOE'S BOOK by Gail Pass. 224 pp. Passionate, obsessive love
story.   ISBN 0-930044-95-9   7.95

WINGED DANCER by Camarin Grae. 228 pp. Erotic Lesbian
adventure story.   ISBN 0-930044-88-6   8.95

PAZ by Camarin Grae. 336 pp. Romantic Lesbian adventurer
with the power to change the world.   ISBN 0-930044-89-4   8.95

SOUL SNATCHER by Camarin Grae. 224 pp. A puzzle, an
adventure, a mystery—Lesbian romance.
ISBN 0-930044-90-8   8.95

THE LOVE OF GOOD WOMEN by Isabel Miller. 224 pp.
Long-awaited new novel by the author of the beloved *Patience
and Sarah*.   ISBN 0-930044-81-9   8.95

THE HOUSE AT PELHAM FALLS by Brenda Weathers. 240
pp. Suspenseful Lesbian ghost story.   ISBN 0-930044-79-7   7.95

HOME IN YOUR HANDS by Lee Lynch. 240 pp. More stories
from the author of *Old Dyke Tales*.   ISBN 0-930044-80-0   7.95

EACH HAND A MAP by Anita Skeen. 112 pp. Real-life poems
that touch us all.   ISBN 0-930044-82-7   6.95

SURPLUS by Sylvia Stevenson. 342 pp. A classic early Lesbian novel. ISBN 0-930044-78-9 7.95

PEMBROKE PARK by Michelle Martin. 256 pp. Derring-do and daring romance in Regency England. ISBN 0-930044-77-0 7.95

THE LONG TRAIL by Penny Hayes. 248 pp. Vivid adventures of two women in love in the old west. ISBN 0-930044-76-2 8.95

HORIZON OF THE HEART by Shelley Smith. 192 pp. Hot romance in summertime New England. ISBN 0-930044-75-4 7.95

AN EMERGENCE OF GREEN by Katherine V. Forrest. 288 pp. Powerful novel of sexual discovery. ISBN 0-930044-69-X 8.95

THE LESBIAN PERIODICALS INDEX edited by Claire Potter. 432 pp. Author & subject index. ISBN 0-930044-74-6 29.95

DESERT OF THE HEART by Jane Rule. 224 pp. A classic; basis for the movie *Desert Hearts*. ISBN 0-930044-73-8 7.95

SPRING FORWARD/FALL BACK by Sheila Ortiz Taylor. 288 pp. Literary novel of timeless love. ISBN 0-930044-70-3 7.95

FOR KEEPS by Elisabeth Nonas. 144 pp. Contemporary novel about losing and finding love. ISBN 0-930044-71-1 7.95

TORCHLIGHT TO VALHALLA by Gale Wilhelm. 128 pp. Classic novel by a great Lesbian writer. ISBN 0-930044-68-1 7.95

LESBIAN NUNS: BREAKING SILENCE edited by Rosemary Curb and Nancy Manahan. 432 pp. Unprecedented autobiographies of religious life. ISBN 0-930044-62-2 9.95

THE SWASHBUCKLER by Lee Lynch. 288 pp. Colorful novel set in Greenwich Village in the sixties. ISBN 0-930044-66-5 7.95

MISFORTUNE'S FRIEND by Sarah Aldridge. 320 pp. Historical Lesbian novel set on two continents. ISBN 0-930044-67-3 7.95

A STUDIO OF ONE'S OWN by Ann Stokes. Edited by Dolores Klaich. 128 pp. Autobiography. ISBN 0-930044-64-9 7.95

SEX VARIANT WOMEN IN LITERATURE by Jeannette Howard Foster. 448 pp. Literary history. ISBN 0-930044-65-7 8.95

A HOT-EYED MODERATE by Jane Rule. 252 pp. Hard-hitting essays on gay life; writing; art. ISBN 0-930044-57-6 7.95

INLAND PASSAGE AND OTHER STORIES by Jane Rule. 288 pp. Wide-ranging new collection. ISBN 0-930044-56-8 7.95

WE TOO ARE DRIFTING by Gale Wilhelm. 128 pp. Timeless Lesbian novel, a masterpiece. ISBN 0-930044-61-4 6.95

AMATEUR CITY by Katherine V. Forrest. 224 pp. A Kate Delafield mystery. First in a series. ISBN 0-930044-55-X 7.95

THE SOPHIE HOROWITZ STORY by Sarah Schulman. 176 pp. Engaging novel of madcap intrigue. ISBN 0-930044-54-1 7.95

THE BURNTON WIDOWS by Vicki P. McConnell. 272 pp. A Nyla Wade mystery, second in the series. ISBN 0-930044-52-5 7.95

OLD DYKE TALES by Lee Lynch. 224 pp. Extraordinary stories of our diverse Lesbian lives. ISBN 0-930044-51-7 7.95

DAUGHTERS OF A CORAL DAWN by Katherine V. Forrest. 240 pp. Novel set in a Lesbian new world. ISBN 0-930044-50-9   7.95

THE PRICE OF SALT by Claire Morgan. 288 pp. A milestone novel, a beloved classic.   ISBN 0-930044-49-5   8.95

AGAINST THE SEASON by Jane Rule. 224 pp. Luminous, complex novel of interrelationships.   ISBN 0-930044-48-7   7.95

LOVERS IN THE PRESENT AFTERNOON by Kathleen Fleming. 288 pp. A novel about recovery and growth.   ISBN 0-930044-46-0   8.50

TOOTHPICK HOUSE by Lee Lynch. 264 pp. Love between two Lesbians of different classes.   ISBN 0-930044-45-2   7.95

MADAME AURORA by Sarah Aldridge. 256 pp. Historical novel featuring a charismatic "seer."   ISBN 0-930044-44-4   7.95

CURIOUS WINE by Katherine V. Forrest. 176 pp. Passionate Lesbian love story, a best-seller.   ISBN 0-930044-43-6   7.95

BLACK LESBIAN IN WHITE AMERICA by Anita Cornwell. 141 pp. Stories, essays, autobiography.   ISBN 0-930044-41-X   7.50

CONTRACT WITH THE WORLD by Jane Rule. 340 pp. Powerful, panoramic novel of gay life.   ISBN 0-930044-28-2   7.95

YANTRAS OF WOMANLOVE by Tee A. Corinne. 64 pp. Photos by noted Lesbian photographer.   ISBN 0-930044-30-4   6.95

MRS. PORTER'S LETTER by Vicki P. McConnell. 224 pp. The first Nyla Wade mystery.   ISBN 0-930044-29-0   7.95

TO THE CLEVELAND STATION by Carol Anne Douglas. 192 pp. Interracial Lesbian love story.   ISBN 0-930044-27-4   6.95

THE NESTING PLACE by Sarah Aldridge. 224 pp. A three-woman triangle—love conquers all! ISBN 0-930044-26-6   7.95

THIS IS NOT FOR YOU by Jane Rule. 284 pp. A letter to a beloved is also an intricate novel.   ISBN 0-930044-25-8   7.95

FAULTLINE by Sheila Ortiz Taylor. 140 pp. Warm, funny, literate story of a startling family.   ISBN 0-930044-24-X   6.95

THE LESBIAN IN LITERATURE by Barbara Grier. 3d ed. Foreword by Maida Tilchen. 240 pp. Comprehensive bibliography. Literary ratings; rare photos.   ISBN 0-930044-23-1   7.95

ANNA'S COUNTRY by Elizabeth Lang. 208 pp. A woman finds her Lesbian identity.   ISBN 0-930044-19-3   6.95

PRISM by Valerie Taylor. 158 pp. A love affair between two women in their sixties.   ISBN 0-930044-18-5   6.95

BLACK LESBIANS: AN ANNOTATED BIBLIOGRAPHY compiled by J.R. Roberts. Foreword by Barbara Smith. 112 pp. Award winning bibliography.   ISBN 0-930044-21-5   5.95

THE MARQUISE AND THE NOVICE by Victoria Ramstetter. 108 pp. A Lesbian Gothic novel.   ISBN 0-930044-16-9   4.95

OUTLANDER by Jane Rule. 207 pp. Short stories and essays by one of our finest writers.   ISBN 0-930044-17-7   6.95

SAPPHISTRY: THE BOOK OF LESBIAN SEXUALITY by
Pat Califia. 2d edition, revised. 195 pp.   ISBN 0-930044-47-9   7.95

ALL TRUE LOVERS by Sarah Aldridge. 292 pp. Romantic
novel set in the 1930s and 1940s.   ISBN 0-930044-10-X   7.95

A WOMAN APPEARED TO ME by Renee Vivien. 65 pp. A
classic; translated by Jeannette H. Foster. ISBN 0-930044-06-1   5.00

CYTHEREA'S BREATH by Sarah Aldridge. 240 pp. Romantic
novel about women's entrance into medicine.   0-930044-02-9   6.95

TOTTIE by Sarah Aldridge. 181 pp. Lesbian romance in the
turmoil of the sixties.   ISBN 0-930044-01-0   6.95

THE LATECOMER by Sarah Aldridge. 107 pp. A delicate love
story.   ISBN 0-930044-00-2   5.00

ODD GIRL OUT by Ann Bannon   ISBN 0-930044-83-5   5.95
I AM A WOMAN by Ann Bannon.   ISBN 0-930044-84-3   5.95
WOMEN IN THE SHADOWS by Ann Bannon.
                                    ISBN 0-930044-85-1   5.95
JOURNEY TO A WOMAN by Ann Bannon.
                                    ISBN 0-930044-86-X   5.95
BEEBO BRINKER by Ann Bannon   ISBN 0-930044-87-8   5.95

Legendary novels written in the fifties and sixties,
set in the gay mecca of Greenwich Village.

VOLUTE BOOKS

JOURNEY TO FULFILLMENT   Early classics by Valerie   3.95
A WORLD WITHOUT MEN   Taylor: The Erika Frohmann   3.95
RETURN TO LESBOS   series.   3.95

These are just a few of the many Naiad Press titles—we are the oldest
and largest lesbian/feminist publishing company in the world. Please
request a complete catalog. We offer personal service; we encourage and
welcome direct mail orders from individuals who have limited access to
bookstores carrying our publications.